twincerely yours

FRANKLIN U BOOK 8

EDEN FINLEY

emmett

BOWSER LEANS IN CLOSE, whispering in my ear. He's been doing that more and more lately: invading my personal space. I have no idea why or what has changed, but dude, calm down. We may be seat buddies, but we're not friends.

I'm not allowed friends.

Not here, anyway.

Not when I'm known as—

"Benny, are you following anything this professor is saying?"

—Benny. My twin brother.

To answer his question, yes, I'm following every single word that falls out of Professor McHottie's mouth. Maybe if my English professors at San Diego State were this hot, I wouldn't have made Benny take any writing-heavy classes for me. Maybe I wouldn't have so easily accepted my expulsion from the school. Maybe I'd be more interested in learning.

Numbers I can understand. English? Sentence structure? Hell, even spelling, none of it sounds like, well, English.

Benny and I definitely shot ourselves in the foot by deciding to swap places all those years ago. In theory, it was a perfect plan. Ben does my English classes, I do his math classes, and that way, we'll ace our way into college.

The issue with that now is I can't tell the difference between a comma and an apostrophe, and Benny can't do basic multiplication.

We used to joke that being identical twins, we're two halves of the one brain. Together, we make one smart human being. Separately ... we're kind of hopeless.

I've always had the need to fix Benny's life. To make his life easier. I'm the fixer. The one who makes everything better. But it's gotten to a point where it's getting difficult to step back and separate myself from Ben. It's getting difficult to keep his mannerisms and attitude separate from who I am. It's impossible to just stop and be me because I don't know who that is without my other half.

I don't want to know.

Eventually, we're going to be a package deal to whoever we end up with.

I hope whoever is my person, they'll look like Professor Brooks. The more he talks, the more I stare at him.

He has this whole founder of a start-up vibe. A bit nerdy but in a sexy way. He's young, mid to late twenties, and his closet only consists of sneakers, jeans, T-shirts, and blazers.

His caramelly-brown hair is neat, smooth, and styled. Unlike the mess of blond curls I have tied up in a bun that sits through the small hole in the back of my cap.

It's Brooks's first year here as a professor. Supposedly, he did his undergrad and master's here, but I've never seen him on campus before. Not hard when I was only here for a few classes a week the last couple of years.

He talks a mile a minute, locks the doors so you can't be late to class, and I get the impression he's trying to be authoritative and scary.

It's cute, honestly.

"I'm not following," Bowser says.

I reluctantly pull my gaze away from Professor Brooks and show Bowser how to do the formula and replicate it with different numbers attached.

"You're so good at this. Maybe you should be teaching statistics."

I let out a loud "Pfft" noise, catching the attention of a small group around us. I slink further down in my chair.

Benny is dating some Harrison guy in this class. Someone who I cannot let see me here and let him think I'm Ben. We swap places often but never with partners or boyfriends. It's a rule.

The less attention we have on us while pretending to be the other one is best.

"Seriously. You make it easier to understand."

"Math is easy when you have the formulas." Which is why I decided to study engineering. There was a lot of math.

But just because I can do math doesn't mean I enjoy it. I actually despise it. Well, despise is a strong word. I don't *care* for it.

There's really only one thing I've ever been passionate about, and even though the culture can be toxic, the pressure is severe, and Benny and I decided to quit for a reason, I can't help missing it anyway. Hockey was our life for so long. It's in our blood, it's in our family, and I thought I was ready to let it go, but I was wrong.

So fucking wrong.

emmett

THERE'S NO BETTER sound than blades hitting the ice. No better feeling than gliding over the smooth surface. And nothing quite hits like home than a freezing, temperature-controlled rink.

Three days a week isn't enough. Maybe it would be different if I were actually playing hockey, but this is almost as good.

"Coach Dalton." My boss, Fletcher, waves me over from across the ice.

He's standing by the side boards with ... *oh, fuck.*

Professor Brooks. From last semester's statistics class.

When Bowser, aka Harrison, aka Benny's boyfriend—the reason Bowser had suddenly gotten so friendly with me—found out Benny and I had been switching places for classes since middle school, Benny vowed to stop, and he dropped the class. He'll have to make it up eventually, but until he can get the learning resources he needs, there's no way someone with his level of dyscalculia could pass a college statistics class.

When Ben said he wanted to be tested, he asked if I wanted to as well. It would make sense if I had dyslexia, but the thing is, I have absolutely no plans to go back to college and get my degree after leaving San Diego State. And by leaving, I mean getting kicked out.

Fires are a big deal to them, apparently. Oops?

I have no idea what I am going to do with my life, but I know it's not going to be in some engineering firm being bored to death.

Fletcher cocks his head at me, probably because I'm only staring at them and haven't changed directions, but I don't know how to handle this.

I can't be recognized as Ben because I'm known as Emmett here. But if Ben's professor sees Ben on campus and mentions seeing "him" here, I'll be in just as much trouble.

Because as much as Ben likes to think we don't have secrets from each other, I've been keeping this one massive thing from him. How do I tell him I have a job as a hockey coach?

When he decided for us to quit hockey, I didn't protest. I agreed with him on his reasoning. That the pressure of being Dalton legacies was too much. The expectation for us to be the greatest players of our generation thanks to our pedigree made us crumble. To the world, our big brothers are NHL royalty; to us, they're the guys who stepped up when our parents passed away. West quit the NHL, and Asher put his career on hold.

Ben hated seeing how the media treated West and Asher. Reporters pitted them against each other, compared Asher's stats to West's all the time, even when Asher won a Stanley Cup his rookie year and smashed all of West's rookie records. He's still compared to him years after West has retired. Ben hates the industry for that, so he decided to become a sports reporter to write real stories instead of the toxic shit our brothers had to put up with. I hate the industry for how they treated West and Asher too ... but ... it turns out I love the game more.

So yeah, Benny doesn't know I'm here, and his professor doesn't know I exist.

"Dalton." Fletcher waves me over again.

I pull my Buffalo cap with Asher's number down further on my head and slowly skate over to them.

"Coach Dalton, this is Jonah Brooks and his nephew, Cullen. Cullen will be joining your class today."

"How old is he?" I ask with maybe too much judgment in my tone. He's short and completely swimming in his hockey gear.

Sure, the classes I teach are intro to skating and hockey, and most of my students average between seven to ten, but my youngest student is five.

"He's six." Professor Brooks pats his nephew's helmet. Six is a good age. And he *is* adorable in his oversized jersey and helmet.

"Momma says I haven't hit my growth spurt yet," Cullen says. He's articulate and has a confidence about him.

I smile down at him. "Well, the good news is you don't have to be tall to be a hockey player. The skates will make you taller, and the smaller you are, the faster you'll skate."

"And the harder he'll get hit," Professor Brooks mumbles.

I make the mistake of lifting my head and locking eyes with his rich brown gaze. My throat feels thick as something like recognition crosses his face.

I avert my attention back to his nephew but talk to Professor Brooks while avoiding eye contact. "We don't play contact at this level. We teach the kids how to skate, shoot, some puck-handling skills, but most importantly, we show them how to fall safely."

"Fall ... safely?" Brooks asks. "Bit of an oxymoron, isn't it?"

Fletcher steps in for me. "You're welcome to watch his first lesson if it will make you feel any better."

Noooo. That doesn't help, Fletcher. Jeez.

Brooks's smile catches my eye. "I think I'll like that."

"Great," Fletcher says. "I'll show you to the stands." He turns to me. "You got Cullen from here?"

"Of course." I hold out my hand for Cullen to take, and I'm about to let out a breath of relief when Brooks and Fletcher go to walk off, but then the professor pauses.

"Have we met before?"

I swallow hard. "Nope. I just have one of those faces." Technically, not a lie. He has seen my face around. On *Ben*. Or me pretending to be Ben.

Choosing between blowing my cover with Professor Brooks or telling my brother I'm coaching hockey because I miss the sport we both vowed to hate, I'd choose option C. Whatever that may be. A skate to the face, a broken wrist, ankle, whole-body cast. In my brother Asher's favorite words, I'd rather eat shit and die before doing either of those options.

I watch Fletcher and Professor Brooks as they walk around the rink to the other side where the stands are and am caught off guard when Brooks turns to look at me.

We lock eyes again, and I know this is bad. He might not have recognized me from class, but it won't be long before he pinpoints exactly where he knows my face from.

And then?

Well, nothing might happen. People have twins. There's no logical reason for Professor Brooks to jump to the conclusion that I was taking some of Ben's classes for him.

But with my secrets piling on top of secrets, thanks to taking Professor Brooks's class, I know statistically, one of them is bound to get out. And if one gets out, they all will.

Like the accidental fire at San Diego State that had me kicked out of college. I'm keeping that little tidbit from my older brothers.

Taking Ben's math classes that I'm keeping from the entire campus other than Benny's boyfriend, Harrison.

And my day job from the one person I promised to never lie to or keep secrets from.

We were always known as the chaos twins, the Dalton Duo,

but at twenty-one years old, I'm starting to think there is such a thing as too much chaos.

I'm losing myself more and more each day, and the only time I get that sense of self again is when I'm here on the ice.

I refuse to let anyone take that away from me.

Ben isn't in Jonah Brooks's class anymore, so they have no reason to speak if they run into each other. Ben probably doesn't want to face his statistics professor after dropping the class and getting an incomplete in fear Professor Brooks would figure out Benny wasn't the one in his class.

Ben can't know what I do with my spare time, and Professor Brooks can't find out there are two Bens.

I just have to hope Professor Brooks and my brother never cross paths again.

CHAPTER THREE

CULLEN WON'T SHUT up about Coach Dalton all the way home, and I get it. It would be difficult not to be enamored by him. But I still can't put my finger on why he's so familiar.

It's possible he's a student in one of my classes—he looks young enough to still be in college—but I think I'd remember a face like his.

He has plump lips and these amazingly bright eyes. His hair was wild and barely contained in a manbun under his cap. But it wasn't only his looks that caught my eye. His competence on the ice was hypnotic. Yet, the whole time I was watching, something kept telling me I knew him from somewhere.

It's like watching a movie with an actor I'm sure I've seen in something before but can't remember what. Only, with Coach Dalton, there's no simple internet search to find out. I know because I might have spent half the night searching variations of "hockey" and "coach" and "Dalton," but the only results I could find were about some ex-NHL player turned college coach in Vermont. That dude has an amazing resume, but it wasn't the Coach Dalton I was searching for, obviously. Even narrowing it down to California didn't bring up anything.

Either way, I'm glad Cullen is happy. I've taken him to football, lacrosse, soccer, and even surfing lessons. None of them have stuck, and I have no doubt this new hockey obsession will be over after one season too. I thought we'd turned him away from contact sports when he gave up football, but no. Hockey is the new thing that he's determined to use to give his mother and me early heart attacks.

But like Coach Dalton said, they're not doing contact at this level, and I have faith Cullen will be over it before he gets to that point. Though, he's already obsessed with his coach.

He was so patient with the kids. Nurturing.

There's something about seeing a man in a caring role that's so damn attractive.

An email alert goes off on my phone early the next morning, which is probably a good thing because it distracts me from thinking about the attractive hockey coach who's familiar but not and is also most likely straight.

The email is from one of my students in my morning statistics class, and I internally cringe.

This is my first year as a professor, and my master's degree didn't prepare me for actual students or the constant drama in their lives.

I'm only twenty-five, but it feels so far away from the eighteen- to twenty-two-year-olds I teach.

And as expected, even the subject line makes me groan.

Still durkn.

I'm guessing she means drunk. The body of the email isn't much better.

> *hi professor brookies,*
>
> *so i'm still drunk from wknd. how impromptu imports ugh do i needs to class today?*
>
> *Kristeen*

I want to feel sorry for her, but she's so drunk she can't even spell her own name, so my sympathy is low.

I reply with:

Kristine,

I'm glad you had fun on the weekend, but weekdays are for classes. I can only assume you're asking how important today's lecture will be, and that all depends on the answer to this question: How important is your degree?

If you do decide to come to class, I want to remind you that doors are locked at nine sharp to prevent interruptions.

Regards,

Professor Brooks.

I hit Send and then hold my breath because I'm waiting for a follow-up. There usually is.

When a few moments go by, I relax and go to get ready for work. Kristine will either show up or not, and other than worrying about my attendance record being low and comparing the number of students passing my class against those who fail, I don't care if I lose a student here or there.

These are adults I'm teaching. If they're too drunk to come to class, it's on them when they fail out because they don't understand the material.

I get everything I need together but don't have time to make coffee, so I'll stop by one of the many Bean Necessities coffee carts on campus.

I have a tiny one-bedroom apartment that I moved into as a grad student, and while it's nothing amazing to look at, it's cheap and right near campus. A lot of students live there as an alternative to on-campus housing or the share housing options like Liberty Court. I did the dorms thing during undergrad, only lasted one semester in share housing before my roommates drove me crazy, and that's when I started looking for alternative living spaces in the area.

I could have moved in with my sister, Lauren. It would be easier when schlepping Cullen to all his sporting activities, but considering I don't live well with others and I know what my sister was like growing up, I decided it would be smart to live apart and still love her than ruin our whole sibling relationship by sharing a space constantly.

It does feel weird, being a professor here and still living in a building that's majority students, but it's really convenient.

I get to campus with only minutes to spare, and thankfully, the coffee cart line isn't too long. I can't help looking at the few students around me though, trying to see if any of them are Coach Dalton. I also begin to question whether Dalton is his first name or last name. The professor who retired, the one who recommended me to be his replacement, always called students by their last names, and aren't sports ball people like that too? So it really could be either.

"Jonah," the barista calls.

Ah. Interrupted obsessing again.

The coffee took longer than anticipated, so now I'm going to be late to class. Not super late, but as ol' Professor Notting used to say, if you're early, you're on time. If you're on time, you're late.

And when I get to the large lecture hall and enter, everyone is in their seats, and their murmurs are loud.

The doors should already be locked.

I hurry through the doors. "Sorry I'm late."

When I turn, there's a set of eyes glaring at me. Kristine did make it, evidently. Without brushing her hair or changing out of her pajamas. While here I am, walking in late.

My predecessor also loved the phrase "do as I say, not as I do."

I get my bag, coffee, and remainder of my crap on the desk

by the opposite wall to the entrance and turn to the class. "Let's get stuck into where we left off."

Suddenly, everyone's straightening up and paying attention.

I didn't mean to fall into teaching the way I did. Being a professor wasn't part of my five-year plan, but to be fair, I didn't have much of a plan at all.

For someone who got bullied in school for being obviously gay, standing in front of a room full of two hundred college students isn't my idea of a good time. But as long as I don't make eye contact with any of them while I talk, I'm good.

I already made the mistake of looking at Kristine this morning, but it was hard not to. The daggers she was sending were unmistakable.

What I like to do, and it's something I liked as a student, is to write the formulas on the whiteboard and then get the class to work through the example calculations on their own. I learn by doing, and I know not everyone is the same, but by doing it this way, I'm not slowing down the entire class for that handful of students who don't understand. Those struggling can come to me personally to ask for help.

The most daunting part is having to turn my back on them so I can get the numbers written down. No one has thrown anything at me yet this year, but hey, old scars are still wounds. It's always a relief when I can go to my desk in the corner and watch everyone as they work.

"As always, if you have any questions, don't hesitate to come down to ask me."

The morning moves quickly, and while some students bite the bullet and make their way down to see me, I'm thankful they all don't rush me at once.

In between classes, I head out for more coffee, but as I get in line at the coffee cart, I notice a lock of curly blond hair out of the corner of my eye. By the time I turn to look properly, the curly hair is gone, and I don't get a chance to see if it was Dalton.

Does he go to this school? Is that where I've seen him before?

Stop. Thinking. About. Dalton.

But it's driving me crazy not knowing where I've seen his face before.

I'll have to ask him next time I take Cullen to hockey practice and insist we've crossed paths somewhere. I won't stop until I figure it out.

I head back to my lecture hall as it begins to fill with students again.

I wasn't sure how I'd like being a professor, but it's easy, and it puts my master's degree to use. Do I love it? I haven't decided yet.

But I know I don't hate it. So that's something.

emmett

ONE THING about no longer taking Benny's classes is I have a lot of time on my hands. I'm only at the rink three times a week officially, but I find myself going there and skating to fill in the hours. Or going to the beach.

Some days when Benny has a full day of classes, I'll hang around the DIK house and pretend to be him so I can hang out with real humans and not get lost in my thoughts.

Considering I've lived in this house for six months and no one has noticed there are two Bens says a lot about the intellect of frat boys.

The whole frat thing wasn't something I had any desire to be a part of, which is why when I was at San Diego State, I did the dorm college experience. My roommate was an okay guy, but it wasn't like we were friends.

I wasn't friends with many people at all other than a small group from my dorm block. I think my expectations were too high going to a separate school from my brother. Benny and I have been inseparable since we were born, to the point that when we made the decision to go to two different colleges, our older siblings thought we'd had a fight, were sick, or were having a collective breakdown. Our family being dramatic? We were used to it.

We didn't want to go to separate schools, but considering how hard it was to take each other's classes in high school—wardrobe changes, remembering who we were supposed to be and when—we figured going to schools close by would be easier for switching purposes.

And it was in that sense, but I'd never lived without Benny before, so not seeing him every day was weird. It was as if I was missing a limb. An extension of myself.

I thought the kind of friendship we had was what all best friends had. I was under the delusion that our twinly bond wasn't a twin thing but a best friend thing.

I was wrong.

No one comes close to Benny.

Speaking of which, he barges into our room with a massive growth on his face.

"Uh, bro? You might need to see a doctor to remove that Harrison from your mouth."

Benny and Harrison pull away from each other.

"Told you we should've gone back to mine," Harrison says.

"I thought he'd be out," Benny complains and then turns to me. "Why aren't you out?"

"I missed you all day too, Benny Wenny."

"Get out." He points to the window.

I sigh and roll off the bed. "Fine. Text me when you're done." I grab my phone and backpack and slip out the window.

Honestly, I could probably go through the house, and no one would think twice about seeing Ben pass while making out with his boyfriend and then, thirty seconds later, walking back out boyfriendless.

But even though it's tempting to see how far we could push it, I don't. Because if anyone figures out Ben has been two people this whole time, not only will they ask why, but they'll kick me out of the frat house, and I'll be homeless. My only option would be to go home to Vermont and explain why I'm not in school anymore.

I have nowhere to go while Benny and Harrison fuck, so I end up making my way down to the beach.

Halfway there, my phone vibrates in my pocket, and I'm hopeful that either Benny or Harrison were too quick on the trigger and it's already over, but no. It's our oldest brother, West, who has been trying to get a hold of me for months.

Every time he's called, I've answered and told him I'm too busy to talk, but I think it's time I give him something. Anything.

Just not the whole getting kicked out of school thing.

I hit Answer. "It's about time you called me. What, did you forget I exist? You never call, you never write ..."

"Do I really need to call bullshit on that, or do you want me to?"

I don't open that can of worms. "What's up?"

"What's up? You can't ignore my calls and then casually ask what's up. Why don't you tell me what's up?"

"The sky. Your blood pressure ... presumably ..."

"Emmy. You're hiding something, and I want to know what it is."

"I'm hiding a lot of things. Like the time I walked in on you and Jasper having sex when I was a very impressionable teenager. It might be your fault that I'm, like, ninety-five percent gay, but I kept that a secret."

"No, you didn't. You told everyone in the house."

I laugh. "If we want to get technical, I told Ben, and Ben told everyone, but you thought he was me."

"Still don't believe you on that one. I got really good at telling you apart for a while there."

"Sure you did. Or ... did you?"

"Fuck," he mutters under his breath. "Tell me what's going on with you. How are classes?"

I swallow around the lump in my throat because I'm sick of lying. I'm sick of hiding. "Fine. I'll tell you. But you have to promise not to tell Benny what's going on."

"Benny doesn't even know? I need to be sitting down for this, don't I? You got arrested, didn't you? No, you killed a man. Married an alien from outer space, and now you're pregnant with an alien baby. You—"

If I don't stop him, he won't stop at all. "I took a coaching job because I miss hockey."

Complete silence comes down the line.

"West?" I croak.

"I'm here. Just processing. Did I make a mistake letting you quit? I thought you were adamant you hated hockey, hated the pressure, hated the press—"

"It's true I hated the pressure, and I agree with Benny when he says the press is toxic, but ..."

"But you didn't actually want to give it up? Em, I had no idea. You know, it's not too late to get back in the game. You could come back to Vermont and transfer to CU. I hear the head coach is a bit of an asshole, but he could get you a spot on the team." He snickers because he *is* the head coach at CU. He's not an official dad but is full of dad jokes.

"I've gone years without conditioning or playing properly."

"Reconditioning would be easy at your age."

"I ..."

"You don't want to leave Benny."

"If I had to choose between hockey and Ben, you know I'd always choose him. I haven't told him I'm doing the coaching because, well, you know how he feels about hockey."

"I think he'll understand," West says softly. "After all, isn't he the one going into sports journalism to fix the toxic standard of the sport? Coaching is in your blood."

I roll my eyes. "You're only my half brother. I don't think DNA works like that or that coaching ability is genetic."

"Whatever. You get all your best features from me. I practically raised you."

Not practically. He did raise us. I remember him more than I do our dad, so to me, West is my father. And I hate keeping secrets from him, but it's impossible to dig my way out of this one. He wouldn't approve, he'd be disappointed about the fire, even though it wasn't …

I shake my head.

"Again, that's not how DNA and genes work, but I'll let you have it. I'm awesome because of you." If I don't snark, I'll crack.

West lets out a humorless laugh. "Actually, you're awesome because you're so damn loyal. You know, when you and Benny were younger, I always wished Asher and I could have a relationship like yours."

"Asher? Mr. Eat Shit and Die Asher?"

"Crazy, I know. I'm not going to get all parental on you and tell you what you can and cannot do, but I do think you should tell Benny what you're doing after classes." There's a pause. "It is after classes, right? You're not skipping out on lectures and your degree to do these coaching sessions?"

Ugh. My options here are to lie some more or avoid it completely. "What was that? You're breaking up. Can't … hear … what? Oh, no, gotta go. Byyyyyyye."

I don't think he bought it.

An hour passes, and I still don't have a text from Benny saying it's safe to come back. It probably is. Surely, they're done by now. Then again, Harrison seems like a snuggly type. I should give them post-sex cuddle time.

It's not so bad where I am, sitting on the sand, listening to the waves gently crash against the shore, the nice breeze on my face. It's not as cold as I'd like it to be, but it's calming. The moon is bright tonight, the beach a picturesque landscape, but all I can think is how this night would look back home. The snow, the frozen-over lake, the air so cold it hurts my nose and I can see my breath.

I know Benny loves the beach, but for me, I prefer ice.

"Coach Dalton?"

I'm snapped out of my trance and glance up to see Professor Brooks standing above me. "U-uh, umm—"

"Jonah," he says as if not being able to remember his name is the reason I'm a stuttering moron.

"Jonah Brooks. I remember." I stand and shake his hand.

"Do you go to Franklin? Maybe that's why you're so familiar."

My mouth opens to say something, probably a lie. That I'm Ben. That I was in his class. Instead, I take a risk and go for the truth. "My brother does."

"Ah. That must explain it. Do you look alike?"

My lips twitch. "A little bit." I laugh, but he misses the joke. I go to clarify when he cuts me off.

"Maybe he's in one of my classes."

I shrug like I don't know.

"What are you doing out here? It's freezing."

I cock my head at him.

"Oh, right. You're a hockey coach. You probably think this is hot." He pulls his jacket tighter around him.

"Something like that. What are you doing out here if it's too cold for you? Let me guess, Cali boy born and raised?"

"Yup, and to answer, I'm on my way home and thought it was such a nice night out that I'd walk home along the beach. I regret all my life choices."

"I'm out here because my brother brought his boyfriend

home, and they told me to get out so they could have sex. I regret all my brother's life choices."

Professor Brooks frowns. "They couldn't go into a bedroom?"

"Ah, that's where it's kind of my fault. We share a bedroom because I got kicked out of San Diego State, and—"

"You got kicked out? How?"

I wear a small smile. "Probably shouldn't have said that to a professor."

"You know I'm a professor here?"

Oh, fuck. Shit. Cock. *Balls*. "Didn't you say that? You said something about my brother being in your class."

"How do you know I'm not a student?"

"Because my brother's a junior, and you're—"

"If you say I'm too old ..."

I snort. "No. You seem a lot more together than a junior." I wave my hand down my body. "Exhibit A. Or, you know ... I *was* a junior. Before I got kicked out."

"I'm tempted to tough it out in this wind to hear exactly how that happened, but I don't think I have enough body fat to keep me warm." He's probably right about that. He's tall and slim. He has wide shoulders, but I can't see if he has any muscle underneath his loose-fitted shirt. "You could come back to my place and tell me."

My immediate reaction is to say no. No way. But someone to talk to who isn't related to me or having sex with someone related to me? I do kinda need that. Doing it with Professor Brooks? Worst idea ever.

But I mean ... if he knows me as Emmett, as me first, there's no reason why this would get messy. Ben's no longer in his class.

I'm no longer pretending to be Ben.

I'm rationalizing this because I'm realizing I really want to say yes.

"Okay, so you're just blinking at me and probably think I'm a creep. I get it." Professor Brooks goes to back away, but I reach for his arm to stop him.

"You're not a creep. That's actually ... yeah. I mean, yes."

"Are you sure? If it helps, I wasn't hitting on you, merely offering you a warm place to hang while your brother and his boyfriend go to bone town."

Maybe I misread his tone. "You're not gay?"

"Oh, I am. But I'm not assuming you are because your brother is. Statistically—"

"I have six siblings. Five out of the seven of us are queer."

"I take it back. Let's go to my place to discuss *that* and not the school thing." He pauses. "Actually, no, I want to hear about the school thing too."

Someone wanting to get to know me? As me? I haven't had that since I left San Diego State. Six months isn't a long time, but it has felt like an eternity.

"Lead the way."

jonah

"OKAY, so let's see if I've got this straight. West is the oldest, and he's bi. Asher is labelless, the next two middle children are straight, lesbian sister Hazel, and then gay brother Ben. And you're ..."

Dalton smiles, and with his bright eyes and wispy curls that have escaped his hair tie, he's breathtaking. "I joke that I'm ninety-five percent gay, but only to people who know I'm not being biphobic. I'm a five on the Kinsey scale, so I guess you could call me fluid? Pan? I'm under the bisexual umbrella, skew toward men, but have dated some girls in the past."

I take a sip of beer, even though I'm not a huge fan of it. I only had it in the fridge because I had a friend over a million years ago and he left them here, but I thought it would be rude not to offer Dalton anything and then sit here and watch him drink alone. I swallow and try not to get excited over what he's just said. He bats for my team, and he's hot.

"Sometimes I think labels do nothing but box people in." Look at me being all philosophical.

"That's why Asher refuses to be labeled anything. I'm not

against labels. For some people, they like to know where they belong. But for me, a label feels too permanent."

"It's not like you have to get it tattooed on you."

"I know. It probably doesn't make sense."

We're on the same couch, but there's a good foot between us. I want to reach out to comfort him, but I hold firm.

"It doesn't have to make sense," I say. "We are who we are, and we like what we like."

"Exactly." Fire burns in his eyes, and there's that temptation to inch closer to move in and kiss him.

He looks like he wants that too, but before either of us makes a move, Dalton turns his head away and lifts his beer to his lips.

I slink back, shuffling down so my head rests against the couch cushions. "Now that's out of the way. How did you get kicked out of San Diego State?"

He picks at the label on the beer bottle. "Are you sure you don't want to keep talking about families? What's yours like?"

I make a mental note that he totally deflected there, but it's only fair to talk about myself. "I wish I could say my family is as interesting as you and your siblings, but we're pretty boring. Well, other than my little sister getting pregnant at sixteen. That was peak Brooks family drama."

"I think when Hazel came out, West and Asher high-fived and said, 'Yes, no teen pregnancy!' Zoe was already twenty by then."

"Yeah, my parents didn't take it so well. They didn't kick her out exactly, but they did make it obvious she and the baby weren't welcome. When Cullen was born, she moved in with Cullen's dad and his family, but Cullen was about two when the dipshit told my sister he wanted nothing to do with her or Cullen. He was going to go to college to actually have a life. A life he couldn't have if he was tied down with a girlfriend and baby."

"What the fuck?"

"Yeah, that was my reaction. Mom and Dad took her back in, and as much as they were against Lauren having Cullen, they love that boy almost as much as his uncle does."

"Is that why you take him to hockey practice?"

"It started out of necessity because my sister couldn't afford the cost of childcare and needed to work two jobs to support them, but now that she's in a more stable position with work and money, I do it because I love being a part of Cullen's life. Along with hockey, I've taken him to every other extracurricular you could think of and everything in between. I'm sorry to tell you this, but even if you're the best coach in the world, Cullen will probably give up after this one season."

"Eh, hockey isn't the right fit for everyone. It takes hard work and dedication. A lot of kids get sick of falling, which is a huge part of the sport, so I won't hold it against Cullen if he decides to stop. He does have a lot of natural skating talent though."

"Ugh. Don't say that. Hockey is the one sport I wish he wasn't interested in."

A loud gasp comes from beside me. "I ... I'm sorry ... what? How ... I am offended."

At first, I think I really have crossed some kind of line, but then he breaks into a laugh.

"I'm messing with you. Like I said, hockey isn't for everyone."

"It's fun to watch, but it's so rough. I don't want Cullen getting hurt. He's short for his age, and—"

"Well, at his age, there's very little contact."

"Yeah, you said, but ... what if this is the one sport he takes to?"

"Don't go to games so you don't have to watch him take hits?"

"And make him think I don't accept his life choices? I could never."

Where I thought I saw heat behind his eyes before, now I see something softer. "That's a really great and supportive attitude to have. Cullen's lucky to have you."

"Are your family not so supportive? You'd think with that many queer kids, your parents would be used to it?" It's only after the words are out of my mouth that I realize Dalton hadn't mentioned his parents in the whole conversation about his family.

He bites his bottom lip. "We, uh, don't have any."

"Any parents?"

"Obviously, we did at one point. The seven of us weren't born out of thin air, but West and Asher's mom died when Asher was only a baby. Then Dad married Mom and had the other five of us. So when they went out one night and didn't make it home ... West ended up raising us." He lowers his head.

"That's heavy." I don't even know what to say to that. I haven't experienced a big loss in my whole life. My grandparents are still alive, my parents, my aunts and uncles, everyone.

"It is, but I was eight when it happened, so my big brother is really all I've ever known as a parent. He struggled in the beginning. I remember a lot of burned dinners and—" He abruptly cuts himself off.

"And?"

"How did we get back on the topic of me when we were talking about you?"

I smile. "Because I'm very good at diverting attention away from me?"

"Why would you want to do that?"

"Eh. Same old story. Only gay kid in school—"

"I call bullshit on that one. Statistically—"

"Sorry, I'll rephrase. The only kid in school who was so flamboyant he had no choice but to be out. Therefore was the first kid to be bullied for it, making all the other queer kids hide who they were until college. You have no idea how many people have messaged me since graduating high school."

"I could see that. I'm sorry it was difficult for you. We didn't have any of that back home. It probably helps my older siblings are queer, so it wasn't shocking that Benny and I were too. Weirdly, Hazel was the one who got teased for being a lesbian before she even knew she was a lesbian."

I turn my head toward him. "That time, it was you who brought it back to talking about you. Maybe I'm not the issue here."

Dalton looks as if he's about to protest, but he doesn't. "Huh. That really was my fault that time."

"See. I'm completely innocent. But speaking of not being innocent, going to spill the beans on San Diego State yet?"

"Nope. Going to tell me why you don't like attention being on you, even though you're a total—" He cuts himself off again. He's done that a few times, and I want to know what he doesn't want himself saying.

"I'm a what?"

The corner of his lips turns up. "I was going to say a total ten." He stares at me, his chest puffed out and holding still like he's not breathing.

I'm far from a ten. I'm like a seven. Maybe a 7.5 on a good day. And that's on a generic scale. On a gay scale, I don't even want to know. I'm not muscular. I don't work out. I'm average height, average build—

"You don't believe me?" The challenge in his eyes turns me on something fierce, but I'm not going to let myself read into it.

"Kind of hard to when no one has ever said that about me before."

His mouth drops. "You're lying."

"I'm not the one who's lying in this room."

Dalton's eyes widen.

"It's okay. I know I'm not a ten."

He groans and bites his knuckles.

"What?"

"The fact you don't know you're a ten makes you an eleven."

Even if he is lying, I don't care. He makes me feel attractive. Wanted.

I want him too. But there's something obviously holding him back.

He stands. "I should go."

See?

It's impossible to find words because it's not like keeping him here against his will is legal. "I-if you have to," I manage to get out. "Is your brother finished hooking up?"

Dalton checks his phone. "No text yet."

I stand too. "Then stay."

He runs a hand over his hair, but it's tied back, so he can't get a grip of it. I imagine him having the habit of wrapping his fist in his long hair, and then I have to tell myself not to picture it because it would be superhot. Even hotter if I was the one doing it.

Now I really need to stop.

"I shouldn't," he says.

Damn. "Oh. Okay. No problem."

"I want to. But ..."

"You shouldn't."

He nods, but then he says, "Hypothetically—"

"I love hypotheticals," I blurt.

He smiles. "If I were to stay ... like, could it be a onetime, forget tomorrow type thing?"

At this point, if he asked me to murder someone so he could spend the night, I'd agree to it. If all he can handle is a one-night stand, then that's all we'll have. "Anything you need. I don't care. Just ... stay."

"Okay. I'll stay."

emmett

BENNY and I have made a lot of mistakes in the past. So many I can't even count them on two hands. So many that when Benny called our brother Asher for some money so he could get tested for dyscalculia but didn't want to tell him what it was really for, Asher assumed it was for bail money and wired it across. No questions asked.

But this? This has the potential to be the biggest mistake yet.

Because even though Benny is no longer taking statistics, if Professor Brooks was to ever put two and two together, we'd be screwed, and I wouldn't be the only Dalton twin who got kicked out of college.

Not that there should be a way to find out academically, but I've almost outed myself so many times tonight already. Like when I said he was a professor before he'd told me. I think I played it off, but who can be sure?

I shouldn't want to stay. Protecting my brother has always been my number one priority, but since meeting Harrison and getting diagnosed with dyscalculia, Benny hasn't exactly needed me. Other than to keep hidden so no one finds out there are two of us. This jeopardizes that, but at the same time, when is the last moment I got to have for myself? As me.

"Dalton?" Professor Brooks brings me out of my internalizing.

I smirk. "Brooks?"

My brain screams at me to leave while my body begs me to sit back on the couch. Or lie on it. With Ben's statistics teacher on top of me.

"Want another beer?" he asks.

I didn't finish the first one. "I don't want to drink."

"What do you want to do?"

Kiss him. Suck him. Be fucked by him.

I spent so long in his class trying to concentrate on the numbers and not how hot he is, but I can't deny how many times my mind went there. Now's my chance to make those fantasies a reality.

Before I can find the words, before I truly decide what I could do with him if I only have this one shot, my phone vibrates in my pocket.

I slump and pull it out to check it.

It's Benny.

> Clothes are back on, and the place doesn't even smell like sex because we swallow. You're welcome.

"Your brother?" Professor Brooks asks.

"Yep." I pocket my phone. "Coast is clear to go home."

"Ah. So you no longer need me, then."

I can't tell if he's joking or not.

"I don't." I hesitate to get this next part out. "But I still want you."

His sheepish smile is fucking adorable. "You do?"

"Like I said, you're a ten. An eleven when you're all bashful and oblivious to how hot you are."

"Then why are you still standing all the way over there?"

Because I know I shouldn't do this. I don't say that though. "Because I can still only give you one night."

"I don't care about that."

"Are you sure? I'm not going to wake up one day with you outside my window crying my name, am I?"

"Has that happened before, or are you building a highly unobtainable expectation for sex that I'll be disappointed afterward and not want to do that?"

Goddamn, he makes me smile. "Who says we're talking about sex? Maybe I want to stay for a cup of tea." I like this game.

He steps closer to me, his five-o'clock shadow making him appear older than he is. If he's fresh from his master's and it's his first year teaching, he's twenty-fiveish give or take a year or two. He's also taller than me, so when he steps into my space, he towers above me, and a shiver runs down my spine.

His lips quirk. "Were you talking about tea when you said you could only give me one night? Does tea have a limit on how often it can be sipped between friends?"

My gaze narrows. "Are we friends?" I ask teasingly. "I coach your nephew. You're ..."

"I'm what?" He moves even closer now.

I can't walk out of here. Not when he's within reach. "You're my latest mistake in a whole slew of mistakes." This time, I'm the one who takes a step forward.

As soon as I do, Professor Brooks's hands go to my hips.

"I'm going to get that story out of you, you know. How you got kicked out of school." His voice has taken on a raspy tone that I could melt into. Suddenly, I know what I want from Professor Brooks.

"Do you want to talk about that, or do you want to fuck me?"

"Don't suppose you'll tell me while I'm fucking you?"

I laugh. "You could try to drag it out of me, but I don't like your chances. I'm not much of a talker during sex." I slip my hand under his T-shirt and up his stomach. "I'm more of a moaner."

Professor Brooks sucks in a shuddery breath.

"You think you can make me moan?" I taunt.

"I sure as hell am going to try." No longer holding back, he surges forward, bringing his lips against mine, his rough stubble scraping my skin in delicious ways.

His tongue pushes into my mouth, and as much as I try to hold it back, he already makes me moan.

He pulls back. "That's one."

This time, he doesn't hesitate like before. He goes back to kissing me even harder.

He steals the breath from my lungs and drowns out the voice in the back of my head telling me this is risky. This is wrong. But considering the high I get from it, maybe there's a reason my brother and I are known as the chaos twins.

We both thrive on it.

Even if I want to be a good person. Even if I'm the "sweet one" between Benny and me. It's only because in comparison to him, I am. That doesn't make me sweet.

In fact, this is pretty damn selfish of me.

But with his tongue in my mouth, his hands clawing at my clothes, I don't care if this is wrong.

"Where are you going to fuck me, *Professor Brooks*?"

He growls, and it's all dommy and hot. "Bedroom. Now."

He grips my wrist hard and pulls me through to his bedroom. There's one of those storage ottomans at the base of his bed, and he pushes me down so I'm sitting on it.

His rich brown eyes bore into me, alight with desire and something else I can't quite pinpoint. Or can I?

"Do you like that fantasy? Want me to call you Professor Brooks while you fuck me?"

His eyes flutter closed.

"Want me to suck your cock and then beg for that A?"

"Damn," he hisses. "That shouldn't turn me on, and there's a whole lot of conflicted feelings happening in my head, but—"

"I'm not really a student. You're not my professor." Technically true, but I'm not going to think about that. "Live in the fantasy with me."

"Get naked," he orders.

Mm, bossy professor is hot. I almost want to resist so I can see how bossy he can get, but I'm too desperate for him to touch me. Kiss me. Turn me inside out.

I'm too desperate for *him*.

Because I've been relegated to pretending to be Ben for the last six months full-time, I haven't been able to hook up. Sure, I could've gone somewhere far from campus to get off, but I haven't had the motivation.

Maybe I should have forced myself to because it's unhealthy how much I want this. Like, if he were to change his mind in this second, I would legit cry.

And so would my dick.

We both rush to get rid of our clothes, me wriggling out of mine where I sit while he strips in front of me.

He's tall and lean with a smattering of chest hair on an otherwise smooth body. And it's a fucking sexy body. He might be skinny, one of those people who are straight up and down except for his wide shoulders, but there's something about a lanky person who's more arms and legs than torso that seems to be my type.

Maybe it's because of years in locker rooms with hockey players that I don't see the appeal in the muscular "typically attractive" body.

Besides, I refuse to be with anyone who has a better butt than mine. Hockey butt for the win. If it weren't for Benny deciding to quit hockey, I'd probably work hard to make my ass as bubbly as possible.

Now that I'm back on the ice, my body is no doubt going to tone up, and I'll have to tell Benny something about that. Maybe I'll drag him to the gym and tell him that's how I've been filling my hours.

Or I could do what West said and tell Ben what I'm doing.

"Hey." Professor Brooks cups my face, gently forcing my gaze to his. "You still okay to do this? You disappeared for a second."

"More than okay. I spaced out from how hot you are." I run my hand down his chest, and he stands straighter, putting his long and thin cock that matches the rest of him in front of me.

He smiles down at me. "I love the way you compliment me, but you really don't have to. I'm a sure thing."

Being humble and oblivious to his attractiveness is one thing, but not believing it is a whole other issue. One I know I won't be able to solve with one night.

But I'm going to try.

"I'll show you exactly how irresistible I find you." I lick my lips and lean forward, my fingers wrapping around his cock the exact same moment my mouth does.

His hand grips the back of my hair, holding on to the manbun that's barely holding together, and his hips thrust forward.

He tastes salty as a drop of precum hits my tongue, and I make it my mission to draw more out from him to flood my mouth with his flavor.

I bob my head and stroke him in tandem, and even though I'm bringing him pleasure, I can't help the stir of neediness in my gut. Of my own personal satisfaction when his legs tremble and his knees threaten to buckle.

Even blowing him draws out another moan from me, but

the second the sound comes from the back of my throat, Professor Brooks pulls out of my mouth.

"That's two." He pushes me down so I'm lying on my back, but I'm still half on the ottoman, my legs hanging off the edge and the top half of me on the mattress.

Professor Brooks sinks to his knees and lifts my legs so they rest over his shoulders. He licks his fingers. "Let's see if I can make it three."

He doesn't even need to try that hard. All it takes is for him to swallow my cock and press a wet finger against my hole.

He lifts his head and lets out a small chuckle, his breath still close enough to ghost along my aching shaft.

"I can't help it," I say.

"I'm not complaining. You really know how to give a guy an ego boost."

"Maybe I really want that A." I wink.

Professor Brooks pushes a single digit inside my hole. "You going to let me in here and show me how much you want it?"

God damn, if the real thing isn't even better than I imagined while sitting in his class doing Benny's work.

"I don't want it. I *need* it," I breathe.

"I'll be right back."

I whimper as he stands.

"Don't move." He goes to his bedside table, taking out supplies.

And after the eternity that is five whole seconds, he's back to where he was, only this time, his fingers are lubed up properly, and he's not in the mood for teasing.

With his mouth on my cock and his fingers working their way inside my ass, I'm so close to coming it's not even funny. But I'm not ready to come yet. I don't want to unleash until his cock is inside me, pounding my prostate.

I think about unhappy things. Unexciting things. Like how much trouble I'll be in when my older brothers find out not only have I been kicked out of college but that I have absolutely no plan on going back. I think about telling Benny that I want to coach hockey or play hockey or have a career in the sport he hates.

He's becoming a sports journalist to fix the industry. I want back in as it is. Toxicity and all. Sure, I could do without all that, but for me, my love for the game outweighs all the bullshit that surrounds it.

Benny will be okay with it eventually, but maybe the real problem I'm ignoring when it comes to telling him is coaches travel. AHL players get paid next to nothing and are never home. We would have to live apart.

That's the real reason I don't want to tell Benny what I want to do with my life. That's why I'm avoiding it all, including telling the truth about that fire at San Diego State.

I never set it.

My roommate did.

But he was on scholarship, he actually liked school, and while we weren't close, I took it as my opportunity to get out of a situation I didn't like. I took the fall so I had an excuse to quit.

Now that I've managed to depress myself so much that my hard-on begins to flag, I lift my head and stare down at Professor Brooks, his head between my legs, his soft lips around my cock, and all my problems are instantly forgotten.

His fingers brush over my prostate, and I let out another moan. This time, he doesn't stop to add it to his count, just starts moving his fingers in and out faster while sucking on my cock like a lollipop.

"Fuck," I let out on a stilted breath. "If you keep going, I'm going to come."

He pulls off my cock but keeps his fingers inside me. "You ready for it?"

"Yes. Give it to me."

"Roll over."

I go to get on my hands and knees, but he pushes me down on my stomach.

"Just like that," he whispers.

My hands ball into fists on top of his comforter, my head turned to the side. Out of the corner of my eye, I see him dealing with the condom.

"You going to come hands-free for me?"

I smile. "You're determined to make me moan again, aren't you?"

He lowers his body onto mine. With the way the ottoman is a smidge lower than the mattress and my legs spread apart a tiny bit, his cock rests along my crack.

He lowers his mouth to my ear. "I'm going to count every ..." He kisses my neck. "Single." Kisses my shoulder blade. "Sound."

"Hope you're good at math," I taunt.

"You have no idea."

Actually, I kinda do.

CHAPTER SEVEN

I LOSE COUNT SOMEWHERE around the fifteen mark. Dalton's so vocal as I move in and out of him, but he's right about not being a talker. It's not words but downright sinful sounds.

He feels so good, his ass so tight, but I don't focus on me. I only focus on what makes him moan. Slow but hard thrusts, short and shallow ones, what he'd do if I grip his ass cheek so hard it'll leave bruises in the form of my fingertips. All of it draws out specific noises, not only moans. His grunts are addictive, his harsh breaths give me a high, and when he fists the comforter and begs for me to put him out of his misery, I stop exploring his different sounds and focus on getting us both off.

I push him harder against the mattress, holding him down by the middle of his back with one hand while the other clings to his manbun at the base of his neck.

"This going to get you there?" I thrust deep inside him.

Another moan. "Yes. Keep going." He cries out. "Don't stop."

I need him to come soon because there is no way I can keep this up without coming.

Sweat drips down my body, the rhythmic sound of our

bodies slapping together fills the room, and just as I think I can't take any more, Dalton stiffens and cries out once more.

It only takes two more thrusts for me to follow him over the edge, unloading inside him. His ass contracts around my cock, milking everything I have.

When I still inside him, he lets out a small laugh. I try not to be offended, but then he says, "It's been a really long time for me, so there's a lot of, umm ... yeah, I might have ruined your comforter. I would be sorry, but I'm really, really not."

I laugh with him this time. "Eh, cum stains are easy to get rid of. It helps that my bedding is white."

"Smart."

I'm still inside him, unwilling to pull out yet, but if I don't soon, my body will give out, and then he'll be trapped under me all night. I wouldn't complain, but he probably would.

Reluctantly, I force myself to stand on wobbly legs and duck into my bathroom to get rid of the condom. When I come back into the room, Dalton's sitting up on the edge of the ottoman, still naked and looking wrecked.

He smiles over at me. "I really needed that."

"Same." When I think about how frantic this year has been, I realize I haven't even had a date since before school started. I've been too worried about being a good professor and impressing my new bosses that I haven't even been to a bar or looked at an app.

Dalton stands. "I guess I should—"

I run my finger down his impressive bicep, landing on an intricate tattoo inside his elbow on his forearm. Two triangles, tangled together. "Do you have to go?"

"Isn't that what we agreed? One night?"

"The night's not over yet."

He pouts. "You mean, I still haven't earned that A?"

"Ugh. I hate what that does to me. You know I'd never cross

those kinds of lines with actual students, right? I'm sick just thinking about it, but with you ..."

He grips my shoulders. "I'm not a student. It's like ... watching porn. I have a thing for stepdaddy porn, but would I actually ever have sex with West's husband? God no. Eww. Gross. But porn gives me the fantasy of it in a safe way. If that makes sense."

"I guess." It does, but I can't wrap my head around Dalton being young enough to be a junior in one of my classes yet not acting like any of the ones who email me stupid shit.

"We didn't do anything wrong," he says, trying to persuade me.

"I know."

"But it can't happen again."

That's the suckiest part, honestly, but it was the deal. "I know that too."

"I really should go before Ben wonders where I am." Dalton collects his clothes from the ground, so I do the same with mine.

"I'll walk you out." I only get my underwear on.

"You don't need to do that. Crash. It's what I'm going to do as soon as I get home. I think we both earned it after that." He steps close to me and brings his lips to mine for a soft kiss.

"Guess I'll see you at hockey practice tomorrow."

Dalton nods. "Where we will never speak of this again."

"Agreed." Even if I'd bring it up every chance I had if I were allowed.

That was explosive. Amazing.

Best sex I've ever had.

Yet all I can do is watch him leave my apartment and close the door behind him.

Professor Brooks,

I won't make it into class today. I have a mad case of pink eye.
Photo attached.

Regards,
Malcolm Reids.

Mr. Reids,

I am sorry to hear about your pink eye, but for future reference, photo evidence is not necessary or wanted. Thank you for saving me money on breakfast this morning as I can no longer stomach it. Also, you should really get a doctor to look at that.

Professor Brooks.

I thought I was going to wake up refreshed and happy before that email came through and gave me a dose of reality.

I'm still sated. Still boneless from orgasmic bliss, but the real world is knocking.

From the outside, I shouldn't have been so turned on by someone who doesn't take his college education seriously—you don't get kicked out of school for doing nothing—but I get the impression that whatever he did wasn't his fault. Or, if it was, that it was an accident. Throwing away two years of college would be a waste of his and the school's time and money.

But he never did end up telling me what it was. That doesn't mean I'll let it go.

He said we're not allowed to speak of sleeping together ever again, but that doesn't mean we won't be seeing each other.

This afternoon, I'm dropping Cullen off at practice again, and maybe I'll stick around so I can see his coach. No sex. Just friends.

Or maybe he'll see that similar to tracking him down and banging on his window, and no one wants to be that guy.

Ooh, maybe that's why he left San Diego. Maybe he had a stalker. No, wait, then why would he get kicked out and not the stalker? Hmm ... He could've been the stalker. Maybe I shouldn't have invited him back to my place last night.

Or maybe I could be reading into this way too much.

I'll go, I'll say hi, I'll act friendly, but I'll let him lead the interaction. If he's standoffish, I'll back off, but I do hope we can be friends.

I'd love to break down his walls, find out what makes him tick, because even though we covered the topic of families last night, we didn't really talk about much else.

As an academic, I'm intrigued by his nonchalance over school. How did he become a coach of hockey for kids? Was hockey his first dream? Was he trying to make it to the NHL?

I also still haven't worked out if Dalton is his first name or last. There's so much I want to know about him, and I have to hope I get the chance.

Everything about him that I already know shouldn't interest me to know more, but for some reason, he has a hold on me. I have fallen victim to his charisma, exactly the same way Cullen has.

And there's still that nagging familiar feeling I can't shake but have resigned myself to believing it's because I've probably seen him or his brother around campus. Or maybe on my way home from work the same as last night, but I didn't know who he was then.

I'm sure that's it, but it still doesn't stop the niggly feeling.

Either way, I'm excited to see him this afternoon. So much so that time moves agonizingly slowly. It's like Christmas Eve as a kid. I swear that was always the longest day ever.

I move through my classes on autopilot, and when it's time for my last class, I dismiss them all early and head for my car.

Usually, I walk to and from campus—save the environment and all that crap—but on days I have Cullen, I take my car so I can head straight to his school to pick him up.

I swear he's the slowest dawdler on the planet and is last

out of his school every time. "Come on. You've got hockey practice."

His brown, floppy hair falls in his eyes, and the backpack he's carrying bounces up and down, with his legs moving as fast as they can.

Before Cullen came along, I never pictured having kids. I was only nineteen when he was born, so I hadn't thought about it too deeply. It wasn't until I was holding my nephew in my arms that I started thinking about my own future and what it would look like.

At twenty-five, things aren't any clearer, but I do know I'd like to be a dad someday.

Cullen finally reaches me and gives me a big hug.

"How was school?" I ask.

"Good."

"What did you learn?"

"Nothing."

"As long as you had fun. That's the main thing." I think. Eh, it's first grade. He can focus on school later.

When we pull up to the rink, we're both eager to get inside. He jumps up and down by the trunk of my car when I grab his gear bag for him, and as much as I want to tell him to calm down, I'm practically buzzing out of my skin myself.

I'm suddenly nervous Dalton's going to blow me off and pretend he doesn't even know me.

When we walk inside, I lead Cullen to the locker rooms so he can get changed into his gear, but my head swivels around, hoping to lay sight on the dude I totally didn't have sex with last night.

Nope.

Not even a little bit.

Dalton's coming out of the staff locker rooms in his skates at the same time Cullen's done changing and runs out, forgetting his helmet. I chase after him and almost bowl into the back of Dalton.

He's in jeans, a black sweatshirt, and his blue hockey cap. Don't ask me what team it is. It's the blue team. Obviously.

He turns at the commotion, and when his eyes meet mine, they widen slightly before they relax, and his lips turn up. "Professor Brooks."

I glance around the practically empty skating rink. "You should probably call me Jonah if we're going to pretend you didn't use my name highly inappropriately last night."

He tsks me. "Already breaking the rules. I wouldn't have taken you for a rule breaker."

"I'm not. Usually. I guess the guy who did something so bad he got kicked out of college is a bad influence on me."

"You really should get better friends. Here, I'll take that." He holds out his hand for Cullen's helmet. When he goes to walk off, he pauses. With his skates on, he's my height, and he says, "You can still call me Coach Dalton."

I laugh.

It's a shame there won't be a next time because I'd totally be down for some "coaching."

emmett

JONAH STAYS for the practice again, watching from the stands, but I don't think he got the memo that he should be watching his nephew and not me.

Not that I mind. The heat of his stare is somehow empowering. When I was in his class, I was in a sea full of two hundred people, and as much as I couldn't have his focus on me, I wanted it. Now, it's all on me. Only me.

Though, again, he really should be paying attention to Cullen. Cullen's taken to skating like a duck to water, and as much as his uncle hates the idea of hockey, I think he's going to have to get used to it.

Cullen is a natural. He's at a good age where kids pick up everything easily, and if he keeps with it, there's no telling where he'll be when he's a teenager.

But I'm getting ahead of myself. It's exciting, sharing my love of hockey with others, encouraging the kids to chase that high from being on the ice, from scoring a goal, and taking home a win.

I understand not everyone will feel the way about hockey as

I do, but I see the fire in Cullen's eyes. The excitement. He loves gliding on the ice. Just like I always have.

Jonah says he'll be supportive no matter what, but my bet is he's still hoping Cullen tires of hockey and quits before some older kid flattens him. I understand it from a protective stand-point, especially with the injuries and even deaths that have occurred in pro hockey, but there's a long way to go before that stage.

I hope Jonah changes his mind about the sport and encourages Cullen to chase it. Or figure skating.

There's something about the kid that screams potential to me. I know hockey. I've grown up with it, and maybe West was onto something that coaching is in my blood. Or it could be that I'm trying to think of any excuse to need to talk to Jonah. It really could be either.

I shouldn't need an excuse, considering I had the man's tongue in my mouth last night and his cock in my ass, but I'm hesitating to go say hey and have small talk?

I think my logic behind it is if I have a reason to talk to him, I'm not crossing lines I shouldn't cross.

Having sex with Ben's professor would be bad in itself. Having sex with the professor where we cheated in his class? Recipe for disaster.

Wanting to find excuses to see him and keep talking to him? I'm a hazard to myself. And Benny.

This isn't like me. If anything, Ben is the risk-taker. The one who does shit in the hopes he gets caught. Any attention is still attention. But he's never dragged me into any of that. Sure, I've volunteered and been right alongside him while he did it, but if it were to get out that one of us was kicked out of school for setting a fire, all five of our other siblings would assume it was Ben.

Which is why I'm surprising even myself by going after Jonah. By sleeping with him. By wanting to talk to him.

Yet, I can't stop myself from doing it.

After practice and back in my regular shoes, I personally hand deliver Cullen to his uncle, who's sitting in the small food area where most of the parents wait if they don't drop the kids and flee.

There's coffee and stale cakes for sale, fried food, and even a game arcade that has a whopping three whole video games to play.

"Why don't you go play with the other kids for a bit?" I say to Cullen. "I want to have a word with your uncle."

He doesn't question anything and runs off.

"Now who's bringing up last night?" Jonah taunts.

I sit across from him at the small table. "You. I'm here to talk about Cullen." Yup. Still sticking to that story.

A frown line appears in Jonah's brow line. "What happened? Is he okay?"

"Yes, pappa bear, calm down."

He does. Marginally.

"I don't know if you were watching him out there—"

"I was. Until he fell that first time. I jumped up to see if he was okay, but he literally got back to his feet and skated off. I couldn't watch after that. I was worried he might start to think he's supposed to act concerned like me whenever he falls."

"Kids are resilient, and he's really advanced for his age."

"As in, he's smart?" He cocks his head. "Really?"

I snort. "As in hockey. I can't speak to his academics."

"I asked him what he learned at school today, and he said nothing, so I can't speak to it either."

"I know you want to support Cullen in whatever he does, and I bet you're hoping I tell you he has no hope of ever taking up hockey seriously, but he's amazing on the ice. Like some kind of skating prodigy. He's already skating circles around kids who have been doing this a lot longer than he has."

Jonah hangs his head. "Damn it."

"I know you're worried because he's smallish, but all their helmets have cages, the padding is thick, and they have every shin guard, neck guard, every guard out there."

"Why are you telling me this?"

"You said you'd be willing to be supportive, but there's a big difference between being supportive and being encouraging. Supportive is when your kid comes out and you say, 'I don't agree with it, but I'm behind you.' Encouraging is embracing every aspect of him. Even the aspect that loves hockey."

Jonah's eyes narrow. "Are we still talking about hockey or being queer?"

I wave him off. "I might have mixed analogies there, but it's the same result either way."

"Encourage him. Got it."

I stand. "Who knows, after a few more lessons, Cullen might get over it anyway, and all your hopes and dreams will be fulfilled."

Jonah smirks. "That wouldn't be *all* my hopes and dreams fulfilled. There's another one I desperately want, but apparently, it can't happen again."

I try to hide my smile. I swear I do. "It was good to see you, Jonah."

He licks his lips. "You too, Coach Dalton."

Damn, if it isn't the sexiest thing hearing him call me that.

Jonah Brooks has the potential to ruin me. Not only me but also my brother. This professor might be my downfall, but instead of running away, all I want to do is chase after him.

I text Benny on my way home to make sure I'm not going to be walking in on him and Harrison having sex. I don't get why they can't go to his house and let me take over frat boy Ben's persona all the time. My own room, my own bed, and not having to sleep on a mattress on the floor? Sign me up.

But then I think about having to be Ben whenever I'm home, and it would be full-time, so no. I'll stick to my current plan of trying to save enough money to get my own place.

I'm not hopeful though. I can't get any of the discounted student housing because I'm not a student, and I can't apply for it as Ben without Ben getting kicked out of the DIK house. Benny and I had talked about getting an apartment together once upon a time but realized our cover would be harder to keep if we couldn't bring hookups back to the house.

Enough time has passed between Ben dropping statistics for him to introduce his twin brother to everyone, but maybe he's still keeping me a secret in case he needs to call on me again.

What if he can't complete that subject at another school? He can't tell Franklin that he has dyscalculia when I was acing his math classes for him.

The other thing is me not technically being allowed to stay at DIK house. I'm not a DIK. I'm not even enrolled here.

Maybe I'm wrong and we can't let everyone know I exist.

Which means I'm back at square one: crawling inside Benny's window. He texted saying he won't be home until later, so I have the room to myself for once.

The annoying thing is if we were to ask one of our brothers for the money to get our own place, they'd probably give it to us. They'd want to know why now and what's changed, and even though I'm hating the secrets, hating lying to them, I'm still not ready to face them. Not without a long-term plan.

I want to be in the hockey world, but unless I move home and get into a strict training regime, pro hockey is out. Even at an ECHL or AHL level. I'm loving coaching so far, but at three days a week, I'm not even earning enough for rent in a share house in California.

I could enroll at Franklin for a coaching degree, if those are even a thing, but I doubt I'd be able to fake my way through my classes where I'd need to know how to spell basic words.

I don't want to leave Benny, but I'm not sure my future is here.

Benny eventually comes home, but it's after I've crashed for the night. Overthinking is tiring. Do not recommend.

I lie awake on my small mattress on the floor, not wanting to disturb Benny so early in the morning, but my overtired, overthinky brain wakes him anyway.

"Ugh. Why are you thinking so hard over there? It's so loud." He puts his pillow over his head like that will fix the issue when we both know it won't.

We have one of those twin hyper senses situations going on. We know when one of us is sick, upset, even hungover.

"Sorry. Can't help it."

"I thought you'd be all sex happy still."

Apparently, we can also tell when each other is ... happy. "I think you're mistaking me with you. You're the one with the steady boyfriend."

"Don't lie. You had sex two nights go. Who was he? She? They?"

"A random guy."

"Get his number?"

"Nope."

"Socials? Any way of contacting him?"

The small hesitation is enough to send Benny into a frenzy. "You should stalk him. Like, in the 'I want to see you again' way. Not problematic stalking."

"Any stalking is problematic. It's why it's called *stalking*."

"You know what I mean."

"What do you care if I'm getting any or not? Boundaries, Benny. Learn them."

"We've never had boundaries, and ... well ..."

I already know what's coming.

"You've been mopey ever since getting kicked out of State, and I finally saw a sliver of my Emmy back."

"I'm still here. I'm just …"

"Lost," he finishes for me.

"Exactly. It's difficult because I have to pretend to be you the majority of the time now. I swear you're more popular than you were before. Are you—" I pretend to gag "—nice to people now you're in a happy relationship? You're gross."

"Your face is gross."

Suddenly, Harrison lifts his head from the other side of Benny. I didn't even know he was there.

"You're both immature and loud."

Benny and I smile at each other. "We love you, Harrison," we say in unison.

"Still not used to that," Harrison grumbles and tries to go back to sleep.

"Is there a reason you two are here and not at Harrison's?"

"Marshall and Felix decided to pay us back for having loud sex the other night," Benny says. "I don't even think they were fucking. They were probably jumping on the bed and moaning."

"They were having sex," Harrison says. "I've heard it enough times to know."

Any hope I had of Benny possibly moving in with Harrison and giving me my own room is dashed now.

"You should go for it with whoever you had sex with though," Harrison says. "Take a chance."

He wouldn't be saying that if he knew who it was.

"It was just sex," I say.

And it was. I can't have more.

It's too complicated, and I've decided I'm no longer going to be chaotic because if shit keeps happening to me, at some point, I have to realize that I'm the common factor in it all.

Is it me? Am … I the drama?

jonah

IT CAN'T BE a coincidence that after Cullen has hockey practice, I have a spring in my step that lasts through to the following morning.

Dalton coaches three times a week, two days of classes and one day of private coaching one-on-one. Cullen only does the classes, but I'm seriously contemplating signing him up for the private sessions. Dalton did say I should encourage Cullen's love of hockey, after all.

And maybe that's getting desperate, considering ever since we slept together, all the interaction we've had revolves around Cullen, hockey, and fleeting looks.

Damn it. It's been a long time since I've been infatuated with someone, but I can't get Dalton out of my head.

It's clear he wants me too. I see the way he checks me out. But whatever it is that's holding him back hasn't changed, and I'm trying to be respectful by not asking what it is—so I can fix it, get rid of it, do whatever I have to do with it—or if he's changed his mind yet.

It's Friday, which means I won't see Dalton again until

Monday. I wish I knew where he hung out or had his number so I could—

I shake my head at myself. It doesn't matter what kind of mood he puts me in; I can't be the type of guy to chase someone unobtainable.

He was up-front about what he could give me. It would be greedy of me to ask for more.

That's what I tell myself as I get in line at the Bean Necessities coffee cart, my permanent smile still in place.

All that good mood sinks when I see who's in line about four people in front of me. My gut churns. My heart stops.

Because I'm starting to think I know the real reason why Dalton couldn't have more than one night with me. He shouldn't have even had that with me.

I knew I'd recognized him. I knew I'd seen him somewhere before.

For whatever reason, he lied and said he didn't know me.

That fucker was in my class last semester, and the guy he always sat next to, the redheaded grad student auditing my class, is his boyfriend.

And there they are, mere feet away, kissing. In public.

I can't believe I didn't put it together before. I guess I was used to seeing him with his boyfriend permanently by his side.

Disappointment turns to anger.

I need to walk away. I'm undercaffeinated and can't be late for class. I can't get involved. And I did promise to never speak of what happened between us to anyone, but when does a deal like that become void? If I knew it was because he wanted to cheat on his boyfriend to carry out some fucked-up professor-student fantasy, I would never have invited him back to my place.

Damn it. Everything makes sense now.

His hesitation.

The way he called me Professor Brooks.

The way he lied about being kicked out of an entirely different school.

The man is psychotic.

Which is exactly why I shouldn't march up to him and his boyfriend and cause a scene, especially in front of people who are in any of my classes.

And I won't do it. I won't.

Walk away, Jonah.

Walk. Away.

My feet half listen. They start walking. Just … in their fucking direction.

Don't do this.

Do not risk your career, your reputation, or your dignity.

Do. Not. Do. This.

"Dalton," I bark.

I guess we're doing this.

Both Dalton and his boyfriend flinch.

The hazelly-bluey-green eyes I've had dreams about widen at me. Dalton's gaze flicks between his boyfriend and me. "Y-yes, P-professor Brooks?"

"Oh, going to try to act all innocent? Like you're not a cheater?"

Dalton's mouth opens and closes rapidly. His boyfriend glances around frantically at everyone in line and those close by who might want to see a show.

"Maybe we should, uh, go somewhere to talk about this?" the boyfriend says.

I turn my attention to him. "Y-you knew? Was it some kind of sick game to both of you?"

"I-it's n-not a game," Dalton stutters.

"A bet? See if you can sleep with your professor?" I'm not going to comment on anyone's relationship. If they're open or whatever, that's none of my business, but this is … this is—

"What? I didn't." He turns to his boyfriend. "I definitely did *not*."

"Oh, so now you're a liar as well as a cheater. Got it." I turn on my heel to leave.

"Wait," the boyfriend says.

I don't know why I do it, but I turn back around.

"Harrison, I honestly don't know what he's talking about," Dalton says.

"I'm pretty sure you do." Harrison stares at his boyfriend like he's waiting for him to get it. "This isn't the first time this has happened."

Dalton's mouth drops. "Emmy."

What, he thinks he deserves an acting award for this bullshit? "Emmy?"

"Emmett," Dalton says, like it's obvious, but then ... then he does something completely unexpected. His shoulders slump. "Emmett didn't happen to mention he has a twin brother?"

T-t ... twin?

It's my turn to stutter. "B-brother. He mentioned a brother. Ben. Goes to Franklin."

Ben raises his hand. "That's me."

"I'm guessing it's your last name that's Dalton, then."

His nod is slight.

I run my hand through my hair. I had this all wrong. And now ...

I glance around at everyone staring at us. At the drama.

Fuck, I did everything I said not to, and worse, I did it for nothing.

"I-I have to go." This time, when they try to stop me, I don't let them.

I practically run from campus, and it's not until I'm almost home that I remember I was on my way to class, so I send out a class-wide email.

Hi all,

Won't be in class today.

Do some of the formulas in your textbook and come see me during office hours if you have any questions.

Professor Brooks.

Why wouldn't Dalton—fuck, Emmett—tell me he was a twin?

The memory of him saying "A little bit" when I asked if they look alike flits through my mind, only this time, it's a hell of a lot more sarcastic than I originally took it.

I'm an idiot. The biggest idiot.

And I can't believe I did that.

I caused a scene. Got upset over someone I have no right to get upset over. Made a complete fool of myself and have no way of getting in contact with Emmett to apologize in advance. His brother is going to tell him what happened, how I acted, and then I'm going to have to walk into that hockey rink on Monday and pretend like I'm not unhinged.

Sorry, Cullen, I think I'm coming down with a case of terminal embarrassment. I can't take him back to hockey, or I will die.

Maybe I can convince Cullen to take up tennis or basketball or any other sport he hasn't tried yet. Anything but hockey.

emmett

BENNY:

911. Harrison's house.

ERGH, it's my day off. I get to sleep in on Fridays. What could be so urgent that he's making me drag my ass out of bed and go to his boyfriend's house.

ME:

I better not get there and find U 2 stuck together in a super glue/ lube mix up. That sounds like an ER kind of 911 call.

His reply is quick. Way too quick. And his message doesn't make me want to rush over there any faster.

I'll rephrase: YOU SLEPT WITH PROFESSOR BROOKS AND FUCKED US BOTH IN THE PROCESS?

If it wouldn't make everything ten times worse, I'd avoid it. Oh, who am I kidding, I'm going to try anyway.

New fone. Who dis?

Knew it wouldn't work. His number appears immediately, so I answer. "Calm your balls. I'm on my way."

"I can't believe you did this to me," he says, and whether it's that I'm tired, over having to pretend I'm him, frustrated that I haven't gotten anything I want for the last six months, or maybe I'm defensive because I know what I did was wrong, I don't hold back.

"To you? Everything I've ever done has been for you."

"You slept with my professor for me?"

Okay, no. That was selfish of me, and I don't have an answer for him for that one.

"Get here already," Benny says and ends the call.

I'm in trouble. So much fucking trouble. But worse than that is Ben obviously ran into Jonah, and I have explaining to do all around.

Did Jonah tell Ben about my coaching job?

Did Ben tell Jonah I used to take his classes for him?

I doubt Ben would've done that, but I have no idea what happened, and I have no idea what to do from here.

I'm so sick of being deceitful.

I throw on some clothes and can't be bothered climbing out the window, so I walk through the DIK house.

The guys wave to me as I walk by, but Big Wally's gaze narrows as he sees me. "Didn't you leave half an hour ago?"

"Probably."

He accepts my nonsensical answer, and this is exactly why no one in this house has realized they've been living with two entirely different human beings for half the year and how they've known Ben for three years but never noticed anything off about him.

It's so depressing thinking I've been part of these guys' lives for that long, but they don't know I exist.

For the entire walk over to Harrison's, I let myself play the victim. I was lonely. It's not easy being two people. He saw me as me, not as Ben.

I go through all the things I've been telling myself as an excuse for what I did, but at the end of the day, I did something to jeopardize Ben's position at Franklin U. Sure, we've both done that by cheating our way through school, but that was a joint decision. I did this on my own.

It was reckless and selfish and … I must be still those things because I don't regret it. I'm more upset that it can't happen again.

I don't even get the chance to raise my hand and knock before Benny opens Harrison's door with a scowl on his face.

"Down, tiger. It's not the end of the world." I step past him and head for the living room. I've been here before, while Harrison's roommates were out, but that's not the case this time.

I walk in to see two guys staring at me. Blinking.

"Holy fuck, there's two of them," a dude with curlier hair than mine says. Though his curls are a lot neater than the mess on either Ben's or my heads.

The bigger of the two leans in and says, "That's what twin means."

I wave awkwardly. "I'm Emmett."

"Do you mind giving us three some privacy?" Harrison asks his roommates.

"I don't get to watch the drama?" Curly-headed dude whines.

"Can they stay?" I ask. "You know, witnesses to my murder will be helpful in putting Benny away."

"We'll go." The tall guy drags the little one out the front door.

The fact Benny hasn't said anything is unnerving. I'd feel a lot better if he was yelling. Telling me to eat shit and die like our brother Asher would.

"You slept with your professor," he finally says.

I throw myself on the couch, defensively crossing my arms across my chest. "Technically, I slept with yours."

Benny paces in front of the coffee table. "What the fuck, Em?"

What the fuck, indeed.

"I don't know what to tell you." I throw up my hands. "He didn't recognize me as you, didn't know you were in his class, he's hot, I was lonely, so—"

"You were lonely?" Ben stops pacing, his face falling.

"You know I love Harrison—"

"I am pretty loveable," Harrison says.

"But with you and him spending all your time together, me not really having a life outside of being you for the last six months, not really knowing what I'm going to do with my life ..."

"I'll give you that," Benny relents. He joins me by my side and puts his arm around my shoulders, giving me the support I haven't felt for a while. It's not Benny's fault though. It's mine for not telling him sooner, but I didn't want to put a damper on his newfound happiness with Harrison.

"I didn't realize it was getting to you so much," he says.

"Most days are fine, but others, it's like ... I don't fit anywhere here. Jonah caught me in a weak moment, and you've seen him. He's hot."

"Am I missing something?" Harrison asks. "Is Professor Brooks hot? I don't see it."

"It's a whole hot, nerdy vibe," Benny says.

"It was only a onetime thing," I say.

"How did you even meet him?"

I wish my brother hadn't asked that. I swallow hard and look away. "At the beach." My voice betrays me, going up at the end like a question.

Benny knows I'm lying.

So I relent and let it all out there because I may as fucking well. "I met him at work. I have a job."

"A job?"

I shrug. "Since a few months ago."

"Is that where you've been sneaking off to?"

"I wouldn't call it sneaking."

"Why aren't you telling me what it is?" Benny asks and seems genuinely hurt. He probably already suspects what I'm doing. There's only one thing in the world I'd keep from him.

Harrison steps in and puts his arm around Benny's shoulder. "Cool it with the twenty questions. Em will explain everything." His eyes meet mine. "Won't you?"

The way he's glaring at me, the way his eyes say "You owe me" ... I admire him for wanting to protect my brother and stick up for him. That's usually my job.

"I refuse to go back to school. I hated engineering. Hated the courses I was taking. Didn't really connect with anyone. I knew early on college wasn't right for me, so when my roommate accidentally set that fire, I ..."

"You took the fall," Benny says for me. "Of course you did."

"It was my way out of a situation I didn't know how to quit. It was a solution from feeling like I didn't belong." I make eye contact with my brother. "There's really only been one thing that has given me that feeling before."

Benny stares at me, and in the most serious tone he has, he says, "Is it sex stuff? Are you a stripper? Hooker? Did Professor Brooks pay you to do nasty, nasty sex acts with him?"

I shove him.

He laughs and holds up his hands before his whole demeanor slowly fades into disappointment. "It's hockey, isn't it?"

"I'm coaching kids how to skate, how to shoot, you know, all the basics we already had down by three years old, thanks to Dad."

"Emmy …" Ben's gaze turns soft. "You could have told me."

"Anytime I suggest we go skating or try to join a local social team, you make a face, so … I stopped asking and stopped talking about hockey altogether."

"I thought you hated it as much as I do?"

I stare at the ground as I admit, "I never hated it. I hate the media like you do. I hate all the comparisons we got coming up in the juniors, but the sport? It has my whole heart."

"I didn't know," my brother whispers.

"How could you? I never said anything."

"Why? We tell each other everything! Or, I thought we did. Then I find out you love hockey, you're sleeping with our professor—"

"Your professor." I need to keep making that distinction. "And it was once. Once only."

Benny's head snaps up. "You should go for it. It's not too late."

At first, I think he's giving me permission to chase after Professor Brooks, but then I realize what he actually means.

"I've been out of the game for too long."

"Bullshit. You're twenty-one. Get West to pull some strings. Asher. Hell, Ezra Palaszczuk or any other queer dude who played in the league. You could go AHL or ECHL, and—"

"And leave you?"

His face falls.

"Exactly my point. The thought of not being in the same state as you …"

"I don't want to be responsible for holding you back," Benny says, and I know he means it. I'd hate to be the same for him.

"You're not. Just because I miss hockey, that doesn't mean I have to follow in our big brothers' footsteps and go pro. I'm perfectly happy coaching, skating, and being on the ice again. It doesn't pay much, and I'm only working three days a week, but

I'm hoping if my hours increase, I could get my own place, and then we wouldn't have to hide who I am anymore, and we could be Ben and Em again. To everyone."

"This might be a wild idea," Harrison says, "but what if you tell everyone now? Will the DIKs really care all that much?"

"That our shared pool of house dues have been going toward feeding both me and my brother? That if the school found out we were housing someone who wasn't a student, they could shut down the whole fraternity? That—"

Harrison holds up his hand. "Okay, I get it. What if I ask Felix and Marshall if Emmett could take our spare room that we're using as storage space for all our crap at the moment?"

"I can't ask you to—"

He cuts me off. "You're not asking, I'm offering, and sure, I'd need to talk to the guys about it, but you're earning some money now, aren't you? You can chip in for rent, food, all of that?"

I jump at it. "I can. I just don't earn enough to get a place of my own, which would be needed if we were keeping up the one-person charade."

"You really hate being me that badly?" Ben asks.

"You're emotionally draining." I crack a smile.

"Fuck you, am not."

"I once got asked by one of your frat brothers if I was okay because I was smiling way too much."

Harrison laughs. "Sounds about right."

"Fine. You can be boring, happy Em again."

I put my hand on his forearm. "It's not actually that bad being you, but by needing to be you all the time, I started losing myself, and outside of you and Harrison, I've had no one. You two have each other, and I—"

Benny squishes me in a crushing hug. "Aww, Emmy."

"Ugh." I shove him off me. "Out of curiosity, if I'm going to always be Em and you're always going to be Ben from now on ..."

Benny glares at me. "No, you can't fuck my professor again."

"Damn it. He was so good in bed, you have no idea. We did this whole—"

Harrison puts his hands over his ears. "I don't need to know this. La la la la la."

"I don't want to tell you who you can and can't sleep with," Benny says, "but if he ever found out what we did—"

"I know. It's too risky. Our brothers are going to have a big enough coronary when they find out I'm no longer in school."

"Though both of us getting kicked out does seem on brand for us."

True. So fucking true.

CHAPTER ELEVEN

AFTER SPENDING the weekend literally hiding in my apartment, too scared to go anywhere near campus, the coffee shop, hell, even to a store for food, there's no being able to hide now.

Or is there?

I glance at Cullen in my rearview mirror. "You know, if you're starting to get over hockey, you don't have to play anymore." It's usually a couple of weeks in where we have to keep encouraging him to go to the rest of the lessons we've already paid for, but this time, I'm going to be so supportive of his decision that I'll let him piss that money away.

"I love hockey."

Of course he does.

"You wouldn't rather go for ice cream?"

"After."

"I was thinking now. I'll get you the biggest one in the store." That will take so long to eat he might miss his class.

"But we'll still go to hockey right after, won't we?"

"Or we could not. It's entirely up to you."

"Ice cream and then hockey." My nephew can be so bossy.

Now, how do I stall for even more time? Then, a brilliant idea hits me. I drive past the nearest ice cream place.

"I thought we were getting ice cream," Cullen yells from the back.

"We are, but there's a better one I want to take you to."

"No, I want that one!"

"Well, with that attitude—"

Then my nephew plays dirty. "Please, Uncle Jonah?"

Damn it.

I make a U-turn and then pull into the parking lot. He wins. This round.

I get him the biggest ice cream they have, but he's a growing boy and is finished within a couple of minutes.

"Let's go."

"Wait. I have to finish mine first, and I really need to savor the taste. I'm not like you. I don't inhale my food."

He giggles but sits impatiently.

"Mm, cookie dough."

"Can I try?" he asks.

"Sure." Anything that will keep us here longer than we really need to be.

He takes over eating my ice cream too, but this time, he's a lot slower. Maybe his bottomless pit of a stomach isn't so bottomless anymore.

When he finishes that off too, I look at the time.

"Oh no, it's probably too late to take you to hockey. You'll be walking in late. Want me to call them and tell them you'll be—"

"No. I still want to go to hockey."

When did Cullen become so stubborn?

"Okay," I relent. "We'll head there now."

And as if the universe couldn't hate me any more, we get green lights all the way to the rink, meaning we arrive on time. Well, after he goes and puts his gear on, he'll be late, but we're at the rink on time.

"I'm going to wait in the car for you today, okay? Are you able to get one of the coaches to help you get into your gear today? You can come out as soon as you're done. You don't even need to get changed again. Just come out in your hockey stuff."

"Why are you being weird, Uncle Jonah?"

"Weird? I'm not weird. You're weird." I get out of the car and pull Cullen's gear bag out of the trunk. "Go have fun."

I watch him walk up to the doors, making sure he gets safely inside before I cower back into my car. This is going to be a fun hour.

I take out my phone and look through my school emails that need actioning.

Professor Brooks,

 I didn't make it to class this morning. Can you tell me what you went over?

 Jayden

Sure. Why don't I teach all two hundred students individually while I'm at it?

Jayden,

 Unfortunately, I don't take notes of my own classes. Maybe one of your peers could share their notes.

 Professor Brooks.

Professor Brooks,

 Is it too late to drop your class? When is the cutoff?

 Tori

Tori,

 The cutoff was two weeks into the semester, which was stated in the course outline, and during every class for those two weeks. If

*you drop the class now, you'll get an incomplete and have to repeat
it if it's a requisite of your degree.*

    Professor Brooks.

I'm about to click on another ridiculous email when there's a knock on my window, and I jump a mile high.

It's Emmett's boss, Fletcher.

I put down my window.

"Uh, you might want to get inside," he says, and my heart tries to fly out of my chest.

"What happened?" Worst-case scenarios fly through my head. He took a skate to the face, the neck, his carotid artery was slashed—I've seen videos of this happening in games before.

"He's okay, but he's feeling sick. He only made it one step off the ice before he was throwing some milky liquid up."

What was supposed to be my escape from Emmett has only brought me right to him.

Stupid giant ice cream. Who knew that would backfire? Probably every parent ever. In my defense, he was supposed to get so full and take so long that he didn't want to go to hockey at all.

I'm out of the car and following Fletcher inside in a split second.

Cullen is on the bench just off the ice, with Emmett rubbing his back and a pile of puke in front of him. The other kids are still on the ice, skating without any real direction or supervision.

"Hey, buddy." I slink next to him.

"Ice cream before hockey ... not good," he whines.

"Yeah, that's my bad." Instinctively, I go to rub his back as well, but Emmett's hand is still there, and my fingers brush over his.

We lock eyes.

My breath stalls.

He breaks first. "How about your uncle takes you home, and I'll see you again on Thursday?"

Cullen whines. "My tummy hurts."

"Lesson learned, huh?" Emmett smiles at me over Cullen's head. "No more ice cream before practice. It not only made you late today, but it's cut your lesson short and disrupted the others' lesson."

Damn, do I sound that condescending when I tell my students they're wasting my time?

"Won't happen again," I promise, which only seems to amuse him more. "Time to go."

I help Cullen up to walk out, and Fletcher joins me on the other side. He's milking it for sure, but also, I feel bad for being responsible.

"Fletch," Emmett calls and catches up to us. "I can help out if you could watch the class for five minutes?"

His boss cocks his head at him.

"I get the feeling Cullen's uncle isn't taking his hockey career serious enough, and I want to have a talk with him."

"All right," Fletch says. "It's under tens intro hockey, but you're NHL royalty, so if you see something in Cullen, go for it."

Emmett cringes. I don't know why.

But then Fletcher is gone, and Emmett's there, helping me walk Cullen out to the car.

I expect him to bring up the moment that I never want to relive ever, in the history of ever, but he doesn't.

"Can I come by later tonight?" he asks me.

"I'll be fine," Cullen answers him. "My mommy will make my tummy feel better."

"That's good. Moms are amazing at making their kids feel better." There's something sad in his tone as he says that, and knowing he lost his mom when he was young and being raised by two older brothers, his underlying hurt is evident.

Maybe that's why I agree to let him come over. Or perhaps I'm hoping his twin didn't tell him about the stupid scene I made.

Who am I kidding? He knows.

But I should apologize for how I acted.

"I'll be home from dropping Cullen off at seven," I say.

"I'll see you then. Hope you feel better, kiddo." Emmett opens the rear seat door for us.

Cullen starts buckling himself in, and as Emmett slowly closes the door, he follows it to lean against it.

"And I'll see you tonight."

Nerves punch me in the gut, but I owe him an apology. I owe him an explanation of why I got possessively caveman over thinking he had a boyfriend.

Ugh. I don't want to do this.

emmett

I SO DON'T WANT to do this.

But Jonah is obviously avoiding me—I can't say I blame him —and I don't want our situationship to affect Cullen. The ice cream sabotage was an obvious attempt at dodging me, as well as staying in the car for Cullen's skating lesson, which he hasn't done before.

It's impossible to tell if he's pissed at me or embarrassed about the scene he made in front of half the student population. Which is already going down as one of the school's juiciest scandals this year, other than that whole baseball mess that we don't talk about. Gossip, good. Felonies, bad.

I knock on his door and hold my breath while I wait an eternity for him to open up.

There's shuffling around inside and then silence, and even though I can't see him, I imagine him on the other side of the door, doing the exact same thing as me.

When he does finally open it up, he has his head slightly angled down and a sheepish smile on his face. "Come on in."

He steps aside, and as I pass by him, the urge to touch him, reassure him, do something is overwhelming. But I don't give in. Touching him is a right I don't have. Not when there's mistrust between us.

And I know for sure that it's mistrust. Regret.

If only he knew the full truth.

It's something that can never get out. I could never throw my own brother, my twin, my other half under the bus for a one-night stand. A crush.

I'm here to set the record straight, and that's it.

"Want a drink?" he asks in a tone that really hopes I say no.

"I'm good. This won't take long."

"Sit." Jonah gestures to the couch. The couch where we sat two weeks ago and I decided to fuck everything up.

Reluctantly, I sit back where I did that night, almost like a punishment. A reminder of what I did to my brother. I risked his schooling all because I wanted Professor Brooks's dick.

Jonah sits next to me, and at the same time, we both say, "I'm sorry."

"Why are you sorry?" he asks. "I'm the one who attacked your brother and his boyfriend."

I huff. "I wouldn't call it an attack ... per se."

"He told you about it, then?"

"Him and half of campus."

He runs his hand through his hair.

"It's okay. You didn't know. And that's why I'm sorry."

His lips quirk on one side. "Yeah, it might have been helpful to know your brother Ben is your identical twin. When you said you looked alike 'a little,' I didn't pick up on the sarcasm."

"It's a bad habit we have, and it's reflexive to be vague about it, but I should've made the effort with you. I ..." I'm done lying, but I can't tell him the whole truth either. "I knew you were my brother's professor."

His brow scrunches. "Y-you did? You didn't say anything. At all. When I asked at the rink if we'd met—"

"There's something you have to understand." I turn so I'm

facing him completely. "You know that I got kicked out of San Diego, but what you don't know is none of my family knows other than Ben. I don't have enough money to rent somewhere on my own, so I've been staying with Ben in his frat house ... where no one knows because—"

"You can't stay in official student housing if you're not a student. So this whole time, you've ... your frat house all think that you're ..."

I nod. "They think Ben and I are the same person. And you, when you came into my job at the rink, I couldn't pretend to be Ben because Fletcher knows me as Em, and I couldn't tell you I knew who you were because—"

"Because I'm faculty, and I'd have to report you."

"And now you know the truth—"

"It's my duty to. This is why you could only have one night. This is why ..." He runs his hands through his warm brown hair again, this time gripping at the roots. "Why did you come home with me and risk all of that?"

"Another reason why I'm sorry. I did it because for the last six months, everyone on campus has known me as Ben. I was losing myself in being him, and you ... You were the only one other than Ben's boyfriend to know me as me. As Emmett. So even though it was risky, I took something I selfishly wanted because you were the first person in months to bring me back to myself."

"Technically, I thought your first name was Dalton."

I laugh. "I know. And I didn't correct you because, well, like I said, it's become a habit. Being vague about who I am. Needing to act like Ben around other people. It was tiring, and you ... you breathed life back into me."

Jonah's warm brown eyes meet mine, and I have to blink away the blurriness of tears trying to form.

"Aww, Emmett. I ..."

The sound of my name breaks me.

Consumes me.

And even though this wasn't the plan, I've only told him half the truth, and I promised Ben I wouldn't repeat the same mistake, here I am. Falling into Jonah.

Taking what I want.

Again.

I lean in, wanting to bring my lips to his, but he tenses when I get close. "Kiss me," I whisper.

"This is already so messy. We shouldn't."

He's right, but in this moment, I don't care.

"I know, but I want to feel it again. Feel you. I want you to want me as me. As I am."

His second hand cups the other side of my cheek. "I do want you. Much more than I should or thought I would."

I think he's about to give in when his hands drop completely. I immediately feel the loss and want to lower my head and rub against him like a cat, wanting that connection again. Luckily, I have some sort of restraint. Granted, it's close to snapping, but I still have a hold on it. For now.

"When I saw your brother with his boyfriend," he says, "I became filled with rage. Rage I had no right having. I tried to convince myself it was because I was appalled over being the other person, someone he cheated with, but when I found out he wasn't you? You have no idea how much I was thankful for it. I understand why you said only one night, but if we do this again, where do we go from there? You can't be seen with me, and even if I'm willing to keep your secret so you can still live with your brother, if anyone found out I knew, then I could be fired."

"It's okay now," I say. "Ben's boyfriend offered me a room at his place at a price I can afford from working at the rink. I don't need the DIK house anymore. There's really only one *dick* I want."

I still shouldn't take it, but it's so difficult to resist him. I move, hesitantly, leaning up on my knee, and then slowly throw my other leg over his lap so I'm straddling him. "You can say no, and I'll walk out of here right now." Please don't say no. "Or we can ignore the outside world for a minute and give in to what we both obviously want." I rotate my hips, loving the feel of his hard cock under my ass.

His hands find my hips, and he throws his head back. "Fuck, I want to say something about needing more than only a minute, but you've barely touched me, and I already want to come so bad."

"So we'll ignore the outside world for ... ten minutes? Twenty?" I rub against his cock again.

"All night?"

I still on top of him, staring down into his eyes as I say, "I seem to recall we made that promise before."

"But this time, I know why. I know your situation. We could have the night we wanted, but there was too much in our way. You could stay the night instead of slinking out of here right after. We could talk. We could—"

"You can stop trying to convince—me. You had me the second you said 'but.'"

He snickers. "Butt."

"Aren't you supposed to be the mature one? You're a professor."

His face falls. "Yeah, we're not going to play that game this time. No more professor-student fantasies after realizing your identical twin was my student."

I wince. "Deal. Definitely okay with that."

"Good." Jonah leans in and kisses the tip of my nose. "Tonight, it's going to be you and me. Coach Emmett and Uncle Jonah." His lips move to my cheek. "Two guys who met at hockey practice and have no other ties."

I shudder on top of him.

He pulls back to look at me. "Are you in?"

"So in. Now, hurry up and get me naked."

Jonah's smile is wicked, and I can't wait any longer. I slam my mouth down on his and drink him in, swallow his moan, and embrace the mistake we're about to make.

Uh, again.

CHAPTER THIRTEEN

Jonah

WE MAKE OUT LIKE TEENAGERS, both of us frantic without making a move to take it further. My cock is hard and complaining, but I don't want to stop Emmett from what he's doing. It's unclear if he's trying to torture me or kill me, but the way he writhes on top of me, it would be a travesty to stop him.

His breathing is harsh and loud, and it only turns me on more. My hands can't decide where they want to be. Taking off his clothes? Cupping his face or his ass? One on his hip, the other supporting his back? They want to be everywhere, doing everything, and I'm good with that. It allows me to explore all of him.

I pull away from his mouth to take his shirt off and immediately go back to kissing him and trailing my fingertips over his bare skin.

His muscles are tight, and he's the definition of lean but toned. His wild hair is out tonight, curly frizz flying everywhere.

Emmett breaks away this time to get out, "More. I need more."

I go to stand and do that romantic carry them to the

bedroom while their legs are wrapped around my waist, but I don't take into account that Emmett is basically all muscle and only an inch shorter than me, so there's no way I can lift him. Slim, yes. Heavy, also fucking yes.

We're lucky we don't land on the coffee table as we go down, but at the same time, we're so lost in each other that we barely pause.

I'm on top of him now, frotting against him hard but kissing him harder.

In our frenzy, he taps my shoulder. "If I'm going to come like this, I want our pants gone. I want your skin on mine. I want—"

He doesn't need to say more. I lift up on him only to get rid of my clothes. I ditch my shirt and then struggle out of my pants while he gets rid of his jeans.

When we come back together, it's even more explosive, and while the little voice inside my head tells me to slow down, savor it, maybe even take a breath or two to calm down so this won't be over so soon, I'm too horny, too close, and way too into this to care how we come or when.

We have all night, and if he's staying, there's a good chance we'll be able to have a second round later. After we talk some more.

It must have been difficult for him these past six months, pretending to be someone he's not. Keeping secrets from his family. From what I know of them so far, they're really close.

Which only brings more questions about why he got kicked out of school and why he has no desire to go back.

I want to know everything about him, even if that's not the point of doing what we're doing here.

The point of this is to get off. Feel his hard cock sliding against mine and keep going until we both find that high we're chasing.

Emmett grips my shoulder, his fingers digging into my skin. He thrusts upward, meeting my hips over and over again.

"Are you close?" I rasp. "I don't know how much longer I can—"

He interrupts with perfect timing. He stills, his whole body tensing as his warm release paints our skin.

Lifting his head, he puts his mouth back on mine and kisses me through his orgasm. He grips the back of my hair and holds tight, continuing to roll his hips as he empties his load.

Sensing the energy about to leave from him, I thrust hard and fast, hoping to come by the time he stops pulsing between us.

"Here, let me." He works his hand between the slapping of our bodies, and the second he wraps his hand around my cock, I unleash.

My mess joins his, and white-hot pleasure swarms my veins. My whole body. I push through his grip, his hand milking me for all I have, and by the time I slump on top of him, breathing heavily, he's already caught his breath.

"Fuck," I croak.

"Yeah, that was pretty amazing."

"You're amazing," I breathe and roll off him.

The legs of the coffee table are in the way, so I push the end closest to me away so I'll fit, not caring that it's now crooked in the middle of the room. After that, my furniture could be upside down for all I care.

Our legs are still intertwined as we lie on my carpet and revel in that sated feeling. The sense of satisfaction.

"I didn't think it would be over with that quickly," he says.

"I did. Ever since you walked out of here the last time, all I've been thinking about is getting you back under me." I turn my head to look at him. "But who says it's over? You're staying the night, and I have at least one more round in me."

"Do we lie here and recover or shower and then recover?"

"If we lie here awhile, maybe round two can be in the shower."

He smiles, and he looks so ... pure when he does. "I like the way you think."

"You're not going to in a minute."

"Uh-oh."

"What did you do to get kicked out of school?"

And yep, as suspected, he looks at the ceiling and sighs. "The official story is I started a fire in the dorms."

"On purpose?"

He snorts. "No, it was an accident, but it was by doing something stupid and reckless."

That doesn't sound like Emmett. Sure, I don't know him well, but playing with actual fire?

Slowly, he turns his head back toward me. "The thing is, it wasn't me who did it. I just took the fall for it."

That aligns so much more with how I see him, but ... "Why?"

"The guy who set it. He was a scholarship kid, and it truly was an accident. He was trying to show everyone how to make a flamethrower with a lighter and a can of deodorant—"

"So really stupid and reckless."

"Yup, but in his defense, who knew dorm buildings that are old are basically like tinder?" He makes a "whoomph" noise. "Went straight up in flames."

"Was anyone hurt?" I'm scared to know the answer.

"Nope. Everyone was evacuated, but half the floor had damaged rooms, which meant needing to rehouse students, and it was a big mess."

"I'm still failing to see why you took the fall for someone else's stupidity."

He shrugs. "I hated school. Simple as that. I didn't want to be there. He did."

"What were you studying?"

"I'm really good at numbers but shit at writing, so I figured engineering would be a good field to go into, but it wasn't long before I realized … I fucking hate engineering."

Sounds like a typical student to me—not knowing what they want to study and doing something because they think they *should*. "Fair enough. What do you want to do instead?"

Emmett throws his head back. "Ugh. You sound like Ben."

"You don't have to tell me. I just like getting to know you."

He smiles again, this time rolling his body toward mine and pressing himself up against me. He still has cum on his stomach, which is now smearing across mine, but I don't care.

"I know a good way to get to know each other." He works his way between our bodies and wraps his hand around my cock. It tries to respond, but it's too soon.

"It's not ready for that shower yet," I say.

"Damn."

I lean up on my elbow so he can see how serious I am when I say, "Why don't you like talking about yourself?"

He sits up now. "Don't think we should open that can of worms tonight."

"Why not?"

He leans against the couch so I mirror him by leaning against the angled coffee table. It's not the most comfortable, but I want to be facing him. I don't want him to keep dodging me.

Our knees touch on one side, like neither of us want to lose that connection completely, but the time for being wrapped around each other is done, apparently.

He lets out a loud breath. "Because I don't know where to even start. With living in the shadows of my two eldest NHL brothers or physically having to pretend I'm my twin so I don't end up homeless in California or moving back to Vermont where I would get put back onto that hockey prodigy conveyor belt Ben and I turned our backs on?"

"Wait, West and Asher play for the NHL? Is that why your boss said you're hockey royalty?"

"*That's* what you took from what I said?"

"No. It ... It's a lot to take in."

"I told you. Don't get me started."

emmett

HE GOT ME STARTED.

"Wait, you and Ben used to switch places on purpose to confuse West?"

"Not specifically to confuse West, but he's the one it worked on most. It was as if Asher could smell the difference between us." I lift my hand to show him the scar I got when I was younger. "Now all West has to do is ask to see our hands."

"How did that happen?"

"Hunger Games, sibling edition."

Jonah laughs. "No, really."

"Nine-year-old me had an accident with a sharp knife at Christmas dinner. Benny tried to replicate it once but couldn't cut deep enough."

"You were that desperate to keep confusing him?"

"It's ..." I'm walking into dangerous territory here, and I'm not even sure I can explain it well enough for him to understand, but defending my relationship with Benny is something I've had to do my whole life. "It wasn't so much that. It's ..." How do I tell him my brother means everything to me. He's my comfort zone.

Jonah leans forward and runs one fingertip down my arm to the inside of my elbow where my intertwined tattoo is. "Does Ben have this too?"

"On his other arm. We got them last semester after ..." Fuck.

"After what?"

After we decided to stop cheating with school. Yeah, I can't say that.

"We wanted to see how long it would take his frat brothers to notice. Spoiler alert: they haven't yet. One time during a party, Big Wally got so drunk he stumbled into Ben's and my room, saw both of us, and said, 'I'm so drunk I'm seeing double' and then he ran to the bathroom to puke and never mentioned it again."

"What would you have done if they did figure it out though? Like you said, you couldn't tell me because I'd have to tell the school, but—"

"Eh, after months of pretending to be Ben, I needed something that was mine. Even if it meant I'd have to face my big brothers back home. It's a contradiction, I know."

"Yet, Ben got the same tattoo."

This is something that not a lot of people understand. "You know how there are those twins you see articles about where they know when their twin is upset or hurt or they can basically read each other's minds? Ben and I have that. He's my other half. In the future, our partners, whoever we end up with, are going to have to accept that we're a package deal. I don't want to be apart from him ever. So even though his tattoo is the same, having it on a different arm is enough for me to remove myself from him. It's the same but different. Like us. It makes no sense, I know, but it doesn't need to because it makes sense to me."

"I'm not going to pretend I understand what it's like to be a twin or how your matching tattoos are different if they're not, but like you said, I don't need to understand."

Even though we've said this can't go past tonight and I try to ignore the pang of disappointment in my gut, the wish for him to want to understand is there.

I knew from the beginning that Professor Brooks wasn't the guy for me, that it would be impossible to have anything real with him, but this only cements it.

My person would understand the way Harrison understands Benny and me.

"Did I say something wrong?" he asks.

"No. You said the truth." Yet, I can't stop the bitterness from seeping into my tone, and that's annoying because my emotions aren't his issue.

"Then why are you suddenly checked out?"

I force a smile. "I'm realizing that I'm screwed."

"How so? And please take note that I took you seriously and didn't make a joke about not being screwed yet. I still have plans for that later."

This time, my smile is genuine. "Why don't we get to that now?"

"Not until you tell me."

"Why do you want to know so much about me if this can't go past tonight?"

"Well, I'm wondering why it can't? I didn't pick up on it in my horny haze before, but you said you're not staying at the DIK house anymore, right? You're going to be moving off campus. I'm no longer your brother's professor, there's no conflict of interest. There's—"

I hate that I get excited. "I can't. I just … can't."

"What's holding you back, Emmett? You can be who you want with me. You can be yourself."

That's the thing. For the first semester of this year, I wasn't myself around him. I was Ben.

I can't start something on a lie. I couldn't continue to lie.

And there's no way I could watch what I said every minute of the day. I'd totally slip up, I know it.

"You said you'd never understand me, so I think one night should be all I selfishly take."

He frowns. "Is that what I said? Or did I say that I don't need to understand because it makes sense to you, and that's what's most important? Because if I told you how to think, wouldn't that be someone else telling you who you should be? You're you for a reason, and I respect that reason."

Fuck a duck.

I'm so screwed.

"I think I just fell for you a little bit," I blurt.

"Good. Then, my plan is working. How about that shower now?"

There's no need to say yes. Not when I'm on my feet and running for the bathroom as fast as I can.

I could really get used to Jonah's dick being inside me. With my chest pressed against the shower wall, my ass sticking out, my hair drenched and hanging over my face so I can't see, it's easy to let go.

I wasn't lying when I said I might have fallen for him a little, and how messed up is that? Why? Why would my body, my head, my heart choose someone so unobtainable?

I can't go home to Benny tomorrow and be all, "I've decided to risk your everything for a guy," and I can't tell Jonah the real reason I can't be with him.

This whole situation is a mess, and I hate it.

But I also love how much Jonah's turning me out.

"Fuck, Emmett, you feel so good."

The way he says my name, the way he respects me and my

way of being me … I almost ask him to stop so I can go home and cry myself to sleep. Because I want more than this with him.

I want tomorrow. Next week. Next month. Anything after that.

I want a chance.

I wish we could hold out and do this all night, but that's not possible when he's making me come unglued.

Nothing else exists other than his cock, my ass, and the poor decisions that got me here.

"I need you to come." He grunts. "Really, really soon. Or now. Yup. Right fucking now."

I'm so close, but as Jonah stills and comes inside me, I know I'm not close enough.

I reach for my cock and jerk off as fast as I can get there.

Jonah keeps fucking me through his orgasm, and as his thrusts get slower, the deeper he goes. His cock passes my prostate. Once, twice. My hand moves more frantically.

And when he stills inside me and leans in to kiss the back of my neck, I unleash. Something about the hard sex reduced to a tender moment makes me let go.

But with the end, the reality of tomorrow moves closer.

Ben's gonna be pissed when I tell him where I've been, but just because I spent another night with Jonah, that doesn't mean he's going to find out what we did.

He can never find out.

And he can never fall for me because I couldn't stand to hurt him if he ever did figure out I was the one who used to sit in his classroom.

I remain where I am, resting against the tiles, while Jonah slowly washes me down. I'm so boneless I let him clean all of me and focus on catching my breath.

When he's done, he leans in close. "Let me take you to bed."

Bed sounds perfect. Sleeping in a bed instead of on a

mattress on the floor is even more enticing. I haven't moved completely out of the DIK house yet, but even when I do, my mattress situation won't change. I don't have the money for furniture as well as rent, and there's no way I'm going to call home and ask for some cash. Not because West or Asher won't give it to me, but they will want to know why I'd need so much when all of my tuition and meals are paid for on campus.

I might be ready for things to change, for me to do me, but I think until I have a proper plan or an idea of what I want to do with my life, what West doesn't know won't hurt him.

We dry off in a sated haze and don't bother putting clothes back on before crawling between Jonah's sheets.

We naturally curl into one another, my head landing on Jonah's shoulder, and I fall asleep to Jonah running his fingers through my wet hair while ignoring the sense of pending guilt.

jonah

EMMETT WON'T TELL me why he can't date me, why he has to leave in the morning, or what I can do to change his mind, but in the meantime, I refuse to sleep so I can enjoy him while I can.

He's so closed off. Not only with dating me but everything about him. He talks about himself, sure. He gives little pieces. His family, what it's like being a twin. But that only came after I made a fool of myself and found out the hard way that there's a duplicate of him out there.

He hasn't volunteered anything too deep other than losing his parents, and when he talks, it's almost as if he has to think of his words carefully.

He's still holding himself back, which I thought now the twin thing has been exposed, that he'd have no reason to remain vague and closed off.

Apparently, I'm wrong.

So if it's not the twin thing, what else is he keeping close to his chest?

Emmett shifts in my arms. For a moment, I worry he's trying to pull away, but he doesn't. He settles in closer, but the whole move reminds me that come morning, he really will be pulling away, so I try my best to clear my mind of all the thoughts, doubts, and assumptions surrounding Emmett and enjoy holding him.

Eventually, I fall asleep, but I'm woken up by my phone buzzing first thing in the morning.

Emmett is still curled into my side, his frizzy hair a mess, his lips parted while he snores softly.

I reach for my phone, trying not to wake him, but when I see an email alert from one of my students, I groan, and Emmett's eyes open.

"Sorry. Didn't mean to wake you."

"What's the time?" He yawns and stretches, and he's so fucking cute.

"I almost want to lie and say it's early so we can stay in bed, but I have to leave for class in an hour."

He whines and throws his pillow over his head. "Wake me in forty-five, then."

I lean over and kiss my way along his shoulder blade. "I was thinking I could make you breakfast before you leave."

Emmett's head appears again. "Food?"

"I take that as a yes?"

He shifts again, this time leaning up on his elbow as he brings his lips to mine. "Yes, please."

"Coming right up." I kiss him again and then stand right as my phone vibrates again. I hang my head. "I don't want to look."

"Who's messaging you?"

"Students. The first one's email subject line asked a question that is outlined in the syllabus."

"You can't expect all of your students to be able to read, can you?" He smiles.

"Honestly, I'm starting to question how some of them even got into college."

His smile falls. "What does this one say?"

"You can look if you want. I haven't had any caffeine to help me deal with excuses yet. It's probably something ridiculous."

He reaches for my phone and holds it up to my face to unlock it. While he entertains himself, I leave the room to the sound of him laughing.

"Do I want to know?" I call out while I take out eggs from the fridge.

"The subject line is the best. *Hi, I'm dying today.*"

Of course it says that. College kids are dramatic. "Tell them they can die today so long as they're back in class tomorrow."

"Oh, shit," Emmett says and sounds genuinely worried.

I head back to my bedroom and lean against the doorjamb. "Don't tell me they're actually dying."

"No. But, umm, another email came through. I thought it was another student, so I opened it, and ... umm ..." He bites his lip and then turns the phone toward me. "It's from the dean, and it's about the scene between you and my brother on campus on Friday. She wants to see you in her office after your morning classes."

"Fuck," I hiss.

"You can't get in trouble though. I'm not really a student."

"You technically don't exist," I point out.

"I can come out."

I can't help smiling. "Come out as ... a human being?"

"As someone who's real. I don't have to rely on Ben for a place to stay anymore, and I'm sick of pretending to be him in front of others. You can't lose your job because of an honest mistake."

"Even if it was you with Harrison that day, I should've acted more professionally. Now everyone on campus thinks I slept with a student of mine."

"Even if you had slept with a student, he wasn't in your

class when you did it, so it's not like they can say he slept his way to a good grade."

"No, but they could claim I used my position to be inappropriate. I looked your brother up and noticed he dropped the class, meaning he got an incomplete. What if they say I—"

"But you didn't. And Ben would tell the truth."

"What is the truth? Why did he drop my class last semester? He was doing well, had one bad exam and then, what, decided it was too hard?"

Emmett licks his top lip and glances away. "That's a personal Ben issue that I don't feel I have the right to talk about without his permission."

That makes me feel marginally better that it didn't have to do with me, but ... "It still looks bad."

"I know. I promise we'll stand behind you though. I'll make Ben do it if I have to."

"Why would you have to make him? It's the right thing."

He shakes his head. "No, I know that. I just ... I—" He stands and starts throwing on his clothes. "I'll make this right. I promise."

I want to believe him, but there's a small part of me that's panicking over having the shortest career as a professor in the history of the school.

emmett

ME: I am so sick of drama and chaos.

Also me: I messed up someone's career, put my brother's degree on the line, and am lying to nearly every single person in my life, all because I wanted Jonah's dick.

It's official. I really am the drama.

I don't get to stay for breakfast with Jonah as planned, which sucks because getting dressed and leaving his place so fast means I didn't even give him a proper goodbye. Instead of being on my knees or being pounded, I'm pounding pavement with my feet as I run back to the DIK house.

I'm calling Benny nonstop, but he's not answering, and he's probably still asleep. I'd normally climb in the window because the rest of the house isn't allowed to see me, but fuck that. It's time.

Plus, there's a large chance he's not sleeping but having sex with Harrison, and I don't need to see that. Uh, again. Not that I've seen them fully going at it, but close enough, and that's already too much.

When I finally reach the DIK house, I try him one more time before barging inside. He finally answers.

"For fuck's sake, what is it?"

"Love you too, Benny Wenny, but we have a problem. A really big problem. It's time."

"Time you let me sleep? Great. Bye."

"Time to tell your frat brothers and everyone else at this school that I'm not you. I'm walking up to the porch, and you can't stop me." I end the call before he can protest.

I enter the house, where no one pays attention because there is always someone coming or going in this place.

The usual breakfast traffic is in the kitchen, so I make my way in there so I can tell everyone to stop calling me Ben.

My brother appears from the hallway at the exact moment the guys lift their heads to say good morning to me.

Ben lands beside me. Every single pair of eyes staring in this direction widens. Some mouths drop open. And then an eerie silence settles over the frat house.

"What the fuck?" Big Wally finally says.

Ben shakes off the shock and brings out the jokester. "Help! Someone cloned me in the science lab!"

I fold my arms. "Benny."

"See! He just admitted I'm the real Ben!"

"Don't make me bring out the photos from when we were twelve and you wanted to be so different to me you cut your own hair and had the world's shortest bangs." I turn to the guys. "So, I'm Emmett, Ben's twin brother. I've been homeless for the last six months, so I've been living here and kinda been pretending to be Ben. We're sorry for deceiving you all, and you don't need to worry, I don't live here anymore. I just needed you all to know of my existence."

"Wait up," Big Wally says and glances at Ben. "You've been a twin for six months?"

"Technically my whole life, big guy. He's just been here for the last six months."

"That's what I meant. How do I know who I've told what to? You know secrets, man. All my deep, dark secrets."

"Don't worry," I say. "I haven't told anyone how you have a recurring dream where you're trapped in a *Where's Waldo* book and no one can ever find you."

Everyone in the room snickers.

"See! I told you that in confidence! And now you're telling me you're not even Ben?"

"In Benny's defense, he had to tell me that story, so if you brought it up, I'd know exactly what you were talking about."

Timmo rubs his temples. "Wait, did he tell you or Ben?"

"Ben," I say. "And if we really want to get in on technicalities, I'm still the person you see as Ben, but I'm delightful and fun. I smile more."

Ben growls at me. "I told you not to smile so much. You're always trying to ruin my reputation."

"Did anyone have any idea?" Timmo asks.

Big Wally walks over to us. His name comes from his height, and not going to lie, he's intimidating standing in front of us. He points at me and then at Benny. "I saw you two once."

I nod. "You did. You were drunk off your face."

"I knew it. Everyone said I was crazy." He holds his hands up. "Vindication tastes so sweet."

We laugh at his antics.

"Are we all cool?" I ask. "I can give you guys back rent or whatever. It'll take me a while because I'm on minimum wage and only work three days a week—"

"That's up to the pres," Big Wally says. "But I'm cool with it. We didn't even know you were here, so can we really be pissed?"

"Speak for yourself," Jayden says. "It's creepy. It's like ... trickery and a betrayal."

Benny and I share a guilty look. Because this goes way

beyond only the last six months, but if we only take the last six months into account ...

"I really am sorry about having to trick you, but I had nowhere else to go, and I don't even go to this school, and other than going home to Vermont, I didn't really have any other choice."

"Where were you living before here?" Jayden asks.

"San Diego State. Until I got kicked out."

"For?"

"That doesn't matter," Benny says. "I told him he could stay with us, so if anything, it's my fault."

"This puts our whole charter at risk," Timmo says. "Pres is going to be pissed."

"What am I going to be pissed about?" Ridge enters the room, and like he has the rest of this year, he doesn't even notice there are two Bens.

"Them." Big Wally points to us.

Ridge turns to us, doing the same double take when he takes us in. "You're a twin?" His eyes dart between Benny and me. "Which one of you is Ben?"

"They both are. Apparently," Jayden says.

And okay, I get it. They're bitter and feel tricked.

"We really are sorry," I say. "Or, I am, at least."

"I'm sorry too," Ben says. "Sorry that my brother has been here for six months and not one of you has been smart enough to notice."

Big Wally goes to open his mouth, but Ben keeps talking.

"You don't count. Everyone told you that you were too drunk and seeing double, and you believed it."

"No, I didn't," he mumbles. "Well, I did, but only because Ben having a clone seemed too far-fetched."

"Love how you immediately jumped to clone and not twin," I point out.

"You suck," he says, pouting.

"You're all allowed to be pissed. You can ask me for money to pay my way, and I'll pay it off in installments or something, but—"

"You don't need to pay us," Ridge says. "Accepting money from you would be admitting we had a non-student stay with us. Are you moved out now?"

"Completely." Well, mostly.

"Then if anyone asks, the most Ben's twin ever did was crash here a couple of times. That's the official story, and if any of you fuckers go and ruin that, it's all our asses who wouldn't have a place to live when we get shut down. Got it?"

There are murmurs of reluctant agreement before the president is back on me.

"And you're never allowed to sleep here again."

"Deal," I say quickly. "I wasn't here last night at all, so I'm already acing that rule."

Beside me though, Ben stiffens. "Where *were* you last night? I know you weren't at Harrison's because he told me."

"Uhh ..."

Ben slumps. "You were with Professor Brooks, weren't you?"

"Professor Brooks?" Big Wally exclaims. "Wait, is that what all that drama was about last week? Everyone thought you slept with the professor! Man, having a twin sounds like so much fun."

Yeah, you'd think that, but it's gotten to the point that I wish we didn't have each other's persona to fall back on. Would I change things if I could? Fuck no. But it would be easier if we didn't resemble each other so damn much or know each other inside and out that it's too easy to wear that mask. If we'd never started switching places, we never would've gotten ourselves into half the situations we do.

"That's why we need to go," I say. "He has a meeting with the dean to talk about what happened in the quad on Friday because everyone is spreading shit. Everyone thinks Jonah slept with his student."

Ben glares at me in the way I can tell what he's thinking. I don't even need to be his twin to know what he's trying to say. Technically, he *did* sleep with his student.

Ergh. Maybe I shouldn't have forced Ben to tell his frat brothers, but if I'm taking back who I am, I can't be Ben anymore. With anyone.

I drag Ben into the administration building because even though this is the right thing to do, my brother is in selfish mode.

"You know, if we let him take the fall for this, they won't question why I dropped his class, and then we won't be risking having everything exposed."

I let him go and stop completely. He has to be joking.

"Actually, I'm having issues in my ethics class too. Can you sleep with that professor too?" He's smiling and carefree, but I can't help thinking he's actually being serious. You know, one of those jokes that actually holds truth.

"Do I really need to explain to you—"

He holds up his hand. "I'm joking. As much as I'd love to use this as an excuse to get out of the mess we made, I know I need to face the truth eventually, but I was hoping I could face the truth at home in Vermont and never reveal our complete history here."

"You want to do it where we don't face any consequences."

"We never have before, why start now?"

Because we're not only fucking up our lives but now other people's. Jonah could lose his job because of us, and if he gets fired his first year teaching, does that mean his entire career is over?

"When do you plan to tell West and Jasper that you were diagnosed with dyscalculia?" Thinly veiled threats? Me? Never.

"When do you plan on telling them you got kicked out of school?" he throws back.

"Touché."

"If I tell them about me, you know they're going to fly out here, so you better be ready for that."

Also true. Damn it.

"So if you really want me to be completely selfless, I could call them right—" Damn him calling me on my bluff.

"Fine. You win. But you're not getting out of helping Jonah because he did nothing wrong in this scenario. We're the ones who dragged him into our fucked-upness."

"Correction, *you're* the one who did that. I was happy to leave his class and never interact with him again. You're the one who sat there pretending to be me and then decided to sleep with him as you."

Benny still isn't taking this situation seriously, and it pisses me off so much. Only, I don't think it's him I'm mad at. It's me. It's just easier to take it out on him.

I step closer to my brother, the one person I've always vowed to have his back. "The only reason I was in that class in the first place was *for you.* And now because of that, I can't date the one guy I've been interested in since we moved to California. So maybe don't throw that in my face when all I've ever done has been for you. If it weren't for you, I'd—" I cut myself off because I can't blame Benny for my decisions. Sure, I'd probably be in the NHL by now or preparing for it, but it was my choice to follow Benny to California. "Sorry. None of this is your fault alone. I just can't bear the thought of ruining Jonah's life."

Benny blinks at me. And then some more.

"Sorry," I say again.

"No, you're not. But that's okay because I've decided something."

"You hate me and are disowning me as your brother?"

"No. That this guy must mean a lot to you for you to be this uptight. For you to get in my face like that. Therefore, Jonah means a lot to me, and even though doing this is bringing unwanted attention on both of us, I'm going to stand by you. Because you've stood by me on way many more occasions without question. Even when you should have questioned me."

I hang my head.

"Like giving up hockey. You didn't stand up to me then, but you did for Professor Brooks? I need to acknowledge that."

"Hockey's different," I mutter. "I agreed with you on, like, ninety percent of what you said."

"You gave up the NHL for me, and now that I know it, I'm going to make it up to you. By getting you the man of your dreams, even if it means risking my degree."

And this is what it's like to be part of an unbreakable bond. We get pissy, we disagree, and we can even fight sometimes, but when it's something important—like giving up hockey or how I feel about Jonah—we'll always have each other's back.

Behind us, the doors open and Jonah walks in. His skin is pale, and he looks nervous, and when his eyes meet mine, he does a double take and then glances at Ben. Back and forth, back and forth, his gaze darts between us.

I know it's a shitty thing to be hopeful for, and I can't expect everyone to automatically know the difference between Benny and me. Harrison picked it up quickly, but that doesn't mean Jonah will.

His eyes settle on me, and his lips quirk. "Did you have to drag him kicking and screaming like you thought you would?"

Ben's mouth drops, but mine breaks into a smile.

"How did you know I'm me?"

Jonah scoffs. "Please, you look nothing alike."

I glance at our arms to make sure our tattoos aren't showing.

"Fine. I was only eighty percent sure it was you."

Eighty percent is still more than a lot of people in our lives can tell. It might sound crazy to some—that the biggest turn-on for me is someone who can tell the differences between Bennett and me—but it plays into the whole being unable to use each other's identity as a crutch.

Everyday individuals can't hide who they are, Photoshop and catfishing aside. In an everyday situation where they have to go into work and speak with others, they don't even have the option of hiding behind a twin, and I think Benny and I have taken that for granted.

It's codependent as fuck, and I'm finally in a place where I can't do it anymore. I don't want to do it.

Jonah turns to Benny. "And, Ben, I want to say I'm sorry for confronting—"

He puts up his hand to stop him. "Don't need to apologize. It's not the first time we've been mistaken for the other, and if anything, this has blown back on you more than me. I'm the dude who slept with his professor; I'm a legend. Or, I was, until Emmett went and ruined it by telling all my frat brothers he exists."

"I'm so sorry my existence is an inconvenience for you," I snark.

"It's okay. You're forgiven. Now, who do we have to tell we're twins so you don't get fired and you did nothing wrong?"

"The dean," Jonah says.

This is exactly the type of situation we try to avoid—bringing attention to how easy it is for us to switch places.

"It'll be a quick prove who we are and get out, right?" I ask.

Jonah touches my arm. "Are you having PTSD from getting kicked out of San Diego? You do know you're not going to get in trouble, don't you?"

"Sure. I mean, of course." I do know that, logically. But my brain isn't being very logical right now. For some reason, I have it in my head that if we bring attention to the fact we're twins, people will automatically assume we cheated in classes.

There's no jump in which that makes rational sense, but I think because we'd gotten away with it for so long and did it so often that I expect to be caught out eventually. What if today is that day?

Ben doesn't seem to have the same hesitance. "Let's do this, then."

Okay. Doing this.

Doing it.

Going. To. Do. It.

Neither Jonah nor I move.

"Okay, I'll do it." Ben turns on his heel, forcing us to follow him. Because if I know my brother at all, he's going to go in there and say something stupid.

Too late.

"Hi, Dean Kirwin. I want you to know that even though Professor Brooks accused me of cheating on my boyfriend with him, I can assure you that I didn't. Uh, cheat. I wouldn't do that to Harrison. Wait, no. I didn't sleep with him at all. My twin brother who doesn't go to this school did. Not me."

I facepalm. Could he sound like he's lying any more?

CHAPTER SEVENTEEN

DEAN KIRWIN STARES AT ME, unblinking, as I enter the room.

"Ma'am." I curse at my awkwardness because even though I'm not from the South, my ma'am came out as if I'm from the bowels of Texas.

"Brought reinforcements, did you?" She smiles.

"No. They came here on their own, but I figure this will be a lot easier to clear up with both of them here."

"Take a seat, gentlemen. I have a feeling this story is going to be far more interesting than the telenovelas my daughter makes me watch."

"There's really not much story," Emmett says as he sits next to me while Ben takes his side. "I met Jonah while coaching his nephew in hockey, and we hit it off. I knew he was a professor at the same school as my brother."

"But neither of us knew Ben was in my class," I say because he seemed to have left that part off.

"And I had no idea my brother was even coaching hockey," Ben says. "All three of us didn't know anything until I was suddenly being yelled at by my old professor."

Not helping, Ben.

I run my hand through my hair. "That was obviously unprofessional on my part. I thought Emmett had looked familiar, but I couldn't pinpoint where I knew him from. It wasn't until I saw Ben that I jumped to all the wrong conclusions. Emmett had told me about Ben. I just didn't realize they were identical twins. It was all one big misunderstanding."

Dean Kirwin presses her lips together. "On one hand, I'm glad it wasn't as convoluted as I was expecting, but I don't need to tell you the kind of rumors that are flying around this place."

"I know. I've heard," I say.

"You don't want to get a reputation your first year that will follow you everywhere you go."

Everywhere I ... I ... "Am I still being fired?"

Dean Kirwin leans back in her seat. "No. You're not being fired. If that happened, it would be even worse for your reputation. I'm satisfied this was a misunderstanding and no ethics were smeared. I won't have to take this any further."

I let out a loud breath, and Emmett reaches over for my hand and squeezes.

"That will be all," Dean Kirwin says.

All three of us stand, but before we can make it out the door, she stops us again.

"Oh, one more thing. Mr. Dalton, can you tell me why you dropped Professor Brooks's class so late in the semester if it wasn't about relationship drama?"

I frown because that's something I wanted to know after looking him up. He was doing well in my class up until the last test he took before dropping it.

"Too much on my plate. I know it's a prerequisite for my degree, and I do intend to make it up."

"Make sure that you do if you want to graduate next year with the rest of your class."

"Will do." Ben is practically already out the door when he replies.

Emmett slips his hand in mine as we leave the dean's office, and I furrow my brow at him.

"You know, for someone who says he can't date me and that last night was another onetime thing, this is the second time you've grabbed my hand."

He smiles and looks up at me out of the corner of his eye. "Are you complaining?"

"Hell no, but I am wondering why."

"Can you two hurry up?" Ben asks. "I hate authority, and being in this building is giving me the heebie-jeebies."

"Is he always this dramatic?" I ask.

"Yes."

When Emmett and I reach Ben outside, Ben turns to us. "All right, where are you taking me for lunch?"

Emmett looks at me.

I look at him. "I think he's talking to you."

"Nope. Both of you," Ben says. "You two owe me for that."

"For doing the right thing?" Emmett asks.

"Exactly. Don't try to turn me into a good human or whatever."

Emmett leans in close to me. We're still holding hands, and while I want to ask him what's going on, I want to keep this glimmer of hope a little longer.

"He's lying," Emmett says low. "He's actually a decent person when I'm reminding him he shouldn't be selfish."

I don't know Ben well, but that sounds about right. "He has to be reminded not to be selfish?"

Emmett cocks his head. "I think everyone has the ability to be selfish sometimes. Sleeping with you was definitely selfish on my behalf."

"Because Ben was in my class?"

Emmett's lips purse.

"I'm hungry," Ben whines. "If you two are going to date, Professor Brooks should at least be trying to win me over already."

My head swivels so fast, glancing between the twins. "D-date?"

Emmett squeezes my hand. "I thought Benny would hate the idea and not let me—"

"Let?"

"Hmm, wrong choice of words. Basically, if Benny said no, which I thought he was going to, I wouldn't betray my brother by doing it. Which is why—"

"Why you said you could only give me last night."

"But the good news is, apparently, he doesn't care if we date." He stares down at his feet. "So if you still want to ..."

"I so want to."

"Good."

"Ugh." More complaints from Ben. "Is this what Harrison and I are like? We're so gross. Stop giving each other undress-me eyes and put food in my belly."

"We better feed him so he doesn't change his mind. Now that I've been given permission to date you, I'm going to date you so hard."

"Can't wait."

"Let's start now." He drags me toward his brother.

"Should I be worried our first date is going to be with you and your brother?"

"Most people would love that," Ben says. "Actually, a scary amount of people would. It's honestly disturbing how into twincest people are." He shudders.

"Are you serious?" I ask. That can't be true. Or, I don't want it to be true. That's ... that's—

"Hey, we aren't here to kink shame," Ben says. "So long as everyone understands that while I find Emmett to be the most handsome man in the world, we are not into that."

"You don't have to worry about me in that department." It's my turn to shudder.

"Good." Ben grins. "You win some bonus points."

"Points? Are you keeping score?"

"Duh, and you being a professor means you're already negative twenty points, so you still have a lot to make up." Ben starts walking in the direction of the beach, where there are some cafes and small restaurants.

I lean in and whisper to Emmett. "I can't tell if he's joking or not, which means I don't know if I should let myself be scared or swallow that shit down."

Emmett smiles. "Maybe a bit of both?"

"Great."

"You can always back out," he says.

Considering I've been obsessing over this man since I first met him, there's no way in hell I'm doing that. "Not a chance."

"Right answer."

emmett

WHEN WE ENTER SHENANIGANS, we get more than a few stares. It's the first time Benny and I have been out together anywhere near campus, and it's so weird walking through the place with everyone staring at us.

"Are they staring at me or you?" Jonah asks.

"Probably both. You slept with Ben, and now there are two of him. Maybe your cum has cloning properties you're unaware of."

Jonah snorts.

This is what I wanted—to be seen. But now that it's happening, it's too much attention.

"Let's get a booth in the back."

No sooner do we sit down than Benny's tapping away on his phone.

"Who are you texting?" I ask.

"Harrison. Who else would it be? He's on his way."

"Does he really need to be here for this?"

"Yes. Who else is going to grill Professor Brooks about his childhood, his intentions, and whether or not he qualifies as being fucked-up enough to be part of our family?"

Jonah looks like he's about to throw up.

"Could you maybe not scare him off? I didn't scare away Harrison."

"No, just pretended to be me while I was dating him."

"What?" Jonah shrieks.

Before either of us can explain, two of the DIK frat brothers who don't live in the frat house approach.

"So it's true," Tre says. "Big Wally texted me, but I thought he was drunk again."

"It's true," Ben says. "This is Emmett."

I wave awkwardly at them.

"This is trippy," Colin, the other one, says.

"Have you never met twins before?" I ask.

"Yeah, but like, together," Colin says. "We've known you for three years and no idea. Nothing."

"Because people stare at us like that." Benny waves his hand over the two of them.

"Shit. Sorry." Colin shakes off his stupor and composes himself while he turns to me. "Nice to meet you, man."

Tre slaps the back of Colin's head. "You've known him for six months."

"Oh. Right. It's nice to know you're ... not Ben? What am I supposed to say here?"

Benny and I burst out laughing.

"We're all good," I say.

When they leave, Jonah leans back in his seat. "If that's how people look at you all the time, I can see why you don't like to tell people about each other."

"Not everyone looks at us like we're robot clones," Benny says. "But a lot do."

"That must be so weird."

I shrug. "The people we keep in our lives get over it really quick."

"So do you guys switch places often? How did Harrison find out you're twins?"

Both Benny and I stiffen, our gaze darting right to one another.

We're going to have to get our story straight, but for this, I can be vague.

"Uh, I'd met him around the same time Ben did, and neither of us realized we both knew Harrison."

"Wait, he was unknowingly dating both of you?" Jonah seems horrified at the idea.

"No!" we both say.

"Ben was dating him. I was his friend. I thought it was weird that he would invade my personal space more often than he normally would? But it wasn't overtly sexual, so I didn't put two and two together. Benny told me he was dating a guy named Harrison. I only knew Harrison by his nickname Bowser."

"Well, I'm kind of happy I'm not the only one who got confused by you two." It's the self-deprecating way he says it that upsets me.

My smile is tight, and Benny is silent.

"The good news is there's no reason for us to switch anymore," I say. "I'm out of the frat house and in my own place."

Colin and Tre are back already. With drinks this time.

"Colin would like to offer you drinks as an apology for all the awkward staring," Tre says.

"Seriously, it's okay," I say at the same time Benny reaches for the beers.

"Thanks," he says and takes a sip. "You're forgiven."

"They were forgiven anyway. We're the ones who tricked them for ye—months." Months. Not years.

"I can totally see it now. Emmett is the nice one," Tre snarks.

"Guaranteed," Benny replies. "Anytime I've been nice to you, it's actually been Emmett."

Harrison appears out of nowhere, obviously overhearing the conversation as he walked in. "Ignore Benny. He's actually a snuggly wuggly love monster."

Jonah and I laugh while Ben threatens death upon his boyfriend.

"But then you'd be single, and you wouldn't have anyone to snuggle with you." Harrison slides into the booth and kisses Benny's cheek.

Their relationship is so enviable, and I hope one day to have something like what they have.

I wish it could happen with Jonah, but deep down, I know it's not possible.

If I come clean and tell him the truth, I lose him. If I keep this a secret forever, there's no way I could have anything real with him. It would all be built on a lie.

Already as it is, I'm finding it hard to find the right words. How long will it be before one of us slips up?

"What did I miss?" Harrison asks when Colin and Tre make themselves scarce again. "Has the interrogation started yet?"

"There will be no interrogation," I say. "But you're here in time to order food. I want a burger and fries." I turn to Jonah. "What will you have?"

"Club sandwich looks good."

"It's amazing," Harrison says. "I want that too."

"Off you go, Benny." I smirk at my brother.

"No. This was supposed to be you treating us after my gallant sacrifice."

"It's such a sacrifice to tell the truth," I deadpan. "But fine. You did warn us."

"I don't mind paying," Jonah says.

"I'll come with you to order and pay." I stand.

We shuffle out of the booth and head for the counter to

order, ignoring Benny's protests because we don't know what he wants.

"Should we, uh, go back?" Jonah asks.

"Depends. If you want to be on his good side, probably. If you want to be on my good side, you'll follow me." I step closer to him. "And if you're on my good side, I might spend the afternoon with you. In bed."

"Pissing off the brother, it is." Jonah continues to the bar.

It's our turn to order, and the guy behind the bar gives us an up-nod.

"Hey, Benny, what can I get you?"

Reflexively, I swallow the correction before I realize ... "It's Emmett, actually. Benny's brother."

His brown eyes crinkle in the corners. "No way. I didn't know he had a twin. Nice to meet you, man. I'm Perry."

"You too." I literally can't wipe the smile off my face. It's like coming out all over again. That sense of self. Old me is already coming back.

We give Perry our orders, and I'm a nice brother and order what I know Ben loves, even if I'm tempted to order him tofu and vegetables. There's nothing wrong with that, but Ben thinks vegetables are the devil. Especially green ones. I almost order a side of broccoli but refrain.

Jonah goes to pay when I grip his hand.

"I'll get this. I still owe you after risking your job."

"You didn't risk my job. I jumped to the wrong conclusions."

"I should've told you."

"I'll give you that, but I still didn't have to confront Ben in front of everyone on campus. I want to pay for our first date."

"Even if it's a horrible double date where my brother will pretend to be tough and ask you inappropriate and way out-of-line questions?"

He licks his lips. "Something tells me you'll be worth enduring all that."

I wish he was right.

I turn back to the cashier, and Jonah pays. When we reach the table again, Harrison is looking over Benny's shoulder at his phone.

"Are you ready?" Benny asks Jonah.

"Ready as I'll ever be. Shoot."

I'll give him one thing: he's being a good sport about it.

"What are your intentions with young Emmett?" Benny asks.

"I'm older than you, jerk."

"Two minutes doesn't count," Benny argues.

"I bet that's what Harrison says to you a lot."

Jonah cuts in. "I'll just answer before you two have a twin breakup over it. I want to date him."

"Does that mean you're exclusive?" Ben asks.

I hang my head. Jesus fucking Christ.

"Well, I'm not dating anyone else," Jonah says. "I don't date a lot, but I know that might be different for Emmett, so it's really up to him."

You'd think after months of not hooking up because I had to pretend to be Ben would have me craving all the sex with anyone who'd want me, but Jonah makes me want something more.

"I'm the same with dating," I say. "Kind of hard when everyone thinks I'm a dude named Ben. I'd never hook up with anyone who thought I was him."

"That's one hard rule we've always had," Ben adds.

"Good to know. Though I can totally tell you two apart now." He winks at me.

"It's the tattoos, isn't it?"

He laughs. "Little bit. Although you're putting a lot of faith in whether I can tell my rights from my lefts."

"You're a college professor."

"Of statistics, not direction."

Harrison leans in closer to Benny, and I don't think we're supposed to hear what he says, but I do. Even if I don't take my eyes off Jonah, who's staring back at me with amusement.

"They're really cute."

"This feels weird," Benny says.

"Aww, is all their gooey, lovey-dovey eyes making that heart of yours melt?"

We finally draw our attention away from each other in time to see Benny shove his boyfriend. "Fuck off, is not. I mean … I think this is the first time Em and I have been with people at the same time. And it's weird because I get to be me, and he gets to be him. There's no confusion."

I want to slash at my neck because why would there be confusion if I've only been pretending to be him for the last six months?

"What about when Em was in San Diego? It's not that far away." Yup, on cue, Jonah is asking questions.

I give Benny a "look what you did" stare while I try to come up with something to cover for it.

Benny, on the other hand, already has an answer prepared. "When we decided to go to different colleges, we agreed to trying to make it on our own. To have that separation we've never had before. Separate friends. Separate classes. Separate lives."

Hey, that's not a complete lie. "But we still wanted to be close enough to see each other if we needed to. Like … when someone sets a fire and I take the fall and get kicked out of school."

"Exactly," Ben says.

Harrison shakes his head. "You two are more codependent than I even realized."

"We are not codependent," Benny argues.

And I wish I could agree with him, but I can't. "We're totally codependent."

"You say it like it's a negative thing."

I know, technically, codependency can cause a whole lot of emotional issues and affect having healthy relationships with others, but look at Benny and Harrison. They're as healthy as the relationships we saw growing up. Our parents before they died, our brothers and their partners ... they have it.

And I want it.

I internally sigh because I know I don't have it.

Even though I know I'm wasting my time by dating Jonah and putting my heart, and his, on the line, there's absolutely no way I can make myself bail out.

Not yet.

It's impossible to know when that point will come, only that it needs to happen before either of us gets in too deep.

*Email to: **Stats B students.***
*From: **Professor Brooks***

I'm taking dick leave. This afternoon's class has been canceled.

AS SOON AS I hit Send, I see the autocorrect mistake and want to die from embarrassment. It's as if autocorrect knew what I was really planning on doing with my sick leave. Sick. S-I-C-K. I quickly follow it up with a professional:

As I hope you're all aware, my last email was supposed to say sick leave. Regards, Professor Brooks.

But of course, that doesn't stop the slew of replies.

"Dick leave is good for the soul, professor."

"So sorry you are dick. Oops autocorrect here too."

Each reply is as immature as the last, and a couple skirt that edge between making a joke and crossing lines, but after all the drama that has surrounded me with Ben and Emmett, I'm going to let it all slide.

"Dick leave? Really?" Emmett says, reading over my shoulder.

We're walking home from lunch, which he has apologized for numerous times already, but I don't mind. It's not like Ben was actually interrogating me, but even if he was, I want him to like me, so I'd answer any ridiculous question he wants to throw at me.

I have nothing to hide. I'm a simple man who has an infatuation with someone I never would have gone for in the past.

Emmett is twenty-one. Gorgeous. But again, twenty-one. Most people his age are too immature for me. I'm only four years older, but the difference between twenty-one and twenty-five is a stark contrast. At least in my life, it was. At twenty-one, I was carefree, drinking every weekend, being a typical college student. My master's made me grow up a lot, and then in the blink of an eye, I'm a full-blown adult and have a real job.

Emmett is an outlier though. He's not a typical twenty-one-year-old. He can be immature, but it's as if the weight of the world sits on his shoulders, like maybe losing his parents so young meant he needed to grow up sooner. He has so many admirable traits. He's loyal to his brother. Kind. Selfless. He wasn't willing to date me at all because he thought Ben wouldn't approve. And yes, I think he's hiding some scars, some things he doesn't want me to know, but I'm hoping with time, he'll pull down those walls and let me in completely.

He's still laughing and muttering about "dick leave," and while I should be appalled that he can't let it go like many of my students won't, on him, it's cute. I don't know how that works, but it does.

"Someone was distracting me while I was typing," I protest.

"How was I distracting you? I've been walking six feet ahead of you this whole time because while I'm determined to get you back to your place and naked, you're strolling along like you're out for a relaxing walk. Less slowy slow more fasty fast."

"Why do you think I was so distracted? Your ass was right in my line of sight. So if anything, it's your fault I'm so *slowy slow*."

"I'm starting to think you're not as desperate for me as I am for you."

I grab his hand and pull him against me. His chest hits mine with a thump. "Do you really think that?" I ask. "Because I canceled an afternoon class to be with you. I'm so desperate for you it was either cancel class or spread even more rumors about my hard-on for students. Teaching while trying to hide how hard you make me would be impossible."

Emmett's eyes flutter closed. "This is not helping me with my patience."

"Or lack thereof."

"Exactly. Let's go." He takes off walking again, dragging me with him.

I love how impatient he is for me, and I decide to be mean and play into that. "You know what I'm going to do as soon as we're inside?"

"If the answer is anything but strip me down and make me come, I'm not interested in hearing it."

"I was thinking I could take my time with you. Take off all your clothes one piece at a time. Kissing your skin as it's exposed." I'm assuming he won't want to be fucked right after eating a giant burger and fries, so I'm going to give every other part of his body my tongue.

Emmett whimpers and continues to drag me toward my apartment.

"And when you think you can't take any more teasing, I'm going to swallow you down and drink all your cum."

"Okay, now you're officially mean."

Turns out I also love it when he pouts.

My determination to drag it out goes out the window as soon we're inside. It doesn't help that he doesn't let me get close to him to make sure I can undress him slowly.

"That's cheating!" I say as I watch him strip down as fast as humanly possible. He kicks off his shoes while he takes his shirt off.

I try to catch him when he bends his leg to take off a sock, but he hops out of my grasp and then runs while undoing his pants.

"You do know that the longer you run from me, the longer I'll drag this out? When you think you're going to come, I'll back off. When you think I'm going to put my mouth on your cock, I'll kiss you somewhere else."

"Why are you being mean?"

"Because I wanted to take my time with you, but you're adamant on driving me so crazy that I might not make it."

An evil smile takes over Emmett's face. "So, you mean, if I refuse to go over to you and do this ..." He drops his pants and underwear, kicking them off, and now he's naked, standing in the middle of my living room with his hair a mess of wild curls and his eyes trained on me while he touches himself. "You might snap and give us what we both want faster?"

I'm going to be strong. I'm going to be strong.

He strokes his hard cock, and I know without a doubt that I won't be able to hold out.

"Screw it." I race over to him and immediately drop to my knees.

My hand wraps around his dick, taking over from him, and as I open my mouth and look up at him through my lashes, that evil smile hasn't wavered.

"That was easier than I expected."

"Just so you know, one day, where it ends with us here again, I will be able to hold myself back and torture you slowly. But today is not that day."

I close my lips over him and bob my head, swirl my tongue around his shaft, and then deep-throat him all the way to the base of his cock.

"Holy mother of fuck."

That reaction is almost worth giving him the upper hand. And as much as I wanted to drag this out and take my time, there's no way.

Being where I am feels too good. Bringing him to orgasm is all I want.

I'm so hard it's painful, and I'm regretting not getting undressed when he did.

I work him over with my mouth while I undo my pants and reach inside my underwear to get some relief.

His hand finds my hair, gripping tight to hold my head in place. When his hips surge forward and he starts fucking my face, I jerk myself harder and faster.

The second the first spurt of warm cum hits my tongue, I follow him over the edge.

What I planned to be a long, slow, drawn-out orgasm has turned into a quick release instead, and I don't regret a single thing.

emmett

JONAH and I reluctantly pull away from each other when he has to get to his morning class the next day.

I wander home via the beach, and even though I'm sated from an amazing night of sex and I'm happier than I've been since moving to California, I'm still not feeling like I could call the West Coast home. The sand, the water, all of it is pretty, but it's a long way away from the thick summer foliage and winter snow back in Vermont.

I miss Vermont, and I miss my older siblings, but where Benny goes, I go, and that's the way it's always been. The way it always will be. Not out of expectation but want. No matter what, we factor in each other. We chose to come to California together, and I do like it here, but ... I don't want to live here forever. I know if I told Benny that, we'd work something out, but I've always been the follower. Benny would never hold me back, and he'd want me to be happy, but what if he wants to stay here and I'm not ready to leave him?

I'm not sure what Benny's plans are after graduation other than wanting to become a sports reporter. He could get a job anywhere in the country, and if that's the case, will I follow him there too?

Who knows?

At this point in my life, all I know is I want to do something hockey related with my future, and when this thing between Jonah and me blows up, I will want to get as far away from California as possible.

As if being homesick summoned my big brother, my phone rings with West's name flashing across the screen.

I answer with a dry "Hey, Dad."

"Cute. Quick question. Why hasn't your tuition come through for this semester yet? I got the email from Franklin a few weeks ago, paid it, and then forgot about it. I only realized last night while going over the financials with Jasper that we haven't gotten anything from San Diego."

"Oh, really?" My voice cracks. "That's so weird. Maybe they're running behind schedule or something."

"Mm, maybe. Can you go to the administration building and see if you can get to the bottom of it?"

"Or you could revel in free tuition until they realize their mistake. Go spend all that money on you and Jas and make it up when it finally catches up to you."

"Emmy ..." That's his cut-the-shit tone.

"I'll look into it."

"Thank you. How is school?"

"Eh, next question."

"How are you?"

"Good. How are you and Jas? How's home?"

"We're great, home is great. I'm still trying to convince Jasper to get a dog now all you kids are out of the house."

"It's been two and a half years since Benny and I moved out. If he hasn't caved yet, he's not going to. Move on. Maybe adopt a cat."

"Cats are assholes."

"Probably why I love them."

"Dating troubles?"

I want to roll my eyes. "I'm not talking about my love life with you."

"Why not?"

"Because it's weird. It really would be like telling my dad how I hooked up with a totally hot guy who's kind of nerdy but not."

"So there is a guy!" West sounds way too excited about that.

"Yeah, but I already know it won't go anywhere. It's just fun. You should talk to Benny about love and all that other crap."

"He and Harrison still together?"

"Sickeningly together. I'd hate it if he wasn't so damn happy."

"You deserve happiness too. Have you told Benny about the hockey coaching yet?"

"I have, and you were right. He was supportive." Eventually. Of course, he was more pissed off that I'd slept with Jonah, but I'm not going to get into that with West.

"I told you he would be."

"Yeah, yeah, you were right and whatever." I reach Harrison's place—or my place, I should say—and just like the beach, this doesn't feel like home either. "I've gotta go, but I was thinking of coming home for spring break? If you'll have me."

"You know we will. Send me the flights you want, and I'll book them for you."

"Will do."

We end the call, and I let myself inside, where my new roommates Felix and Marshall are snuggly on the couch with their morning coffees.

"Where have you been?" Felix asks, sitting up with the biggest smile on his face.

"Out."

"Who were you with?"

"Who are you, my mother? Oh, wait, no, she's dead."

Felix doesn't even flinch. "Your brother does that, too, when he doesn't want to answer stuff."

"We learned that trick from our older brother Asher, but I'm guessing it doesn't work on you?"

"Nope. I want details."

A door opens down the hall, and my brother appears, shirtless and only in his boxers. "He's fucking my stats professor still. Even my interrogation yesterday didn't scare him off."

"Don't you have a frat house you should be sleeping at?" I ask.

"Don't you have classes you should get to? Oh, wait, no you don't."

I flip him off.

"What are your plans today?" Benny asks.

"Dunno. I have the day off, but I was thinking of heading to the rink anyway for a skate."

Benny's lips turn down. "Can I come? I only have a morning class, but I'm free after that until this afternoon."

"Who are you, and what have you done with my brother?"

"No, seriously. I was thinking about what you said and how my hatred for the media ruined my love for the game, but ... I do miss it. Maybe I'll find my love for it again without the pressure of being the Dalton Duo, without so much expectation breathing down my neck."

"Hell yeah, man." I hold out my hand for him, and then we pull each other into a hug.

He has no idea how much it means to me that he's not only supporting my choice to be involved in the hockey world but wants to be a part of it with me, even in the smallest capacity.

He's compromising. I love Benny to death, but he's headstrong, so when we disagree on something, I'm usually the first to back down.

Maybe I should've told him sooner about coaching, but I didn't want him to think I was betraying him or the decision we both agreed to when we moved to Cali.

Benny nudges me. "It'll be fun to kick your ass on the ice again."

"Oh, bring it."

Being back on the ice with my Benny gives me an indescribable high. Because it's in the middle of the day on a weekday, all the kids are in school, and the rink is practically empty. It's open for people wanting to skate, but it's not the most popular thing in California, I've found.

Fletcher and another coach join us for a game of pickup. They've volunteered to play goalies for us because they want to see us pitted against each other.

Hey, you and the rest of the NHL world, Fletch.

Both Fletcher and Scarlett seem way too excited, and I get the feeling it's because they know who we are. The Dalton Duo. The next generation of Daltons. The biggest disappointments in the draft's history, quitting the game before even giving it a chance. I think our decision will make sense to him after he sees how rusty we are.

We have all the practice padding from the rink's scheduled social games, so we won't have to worry about getting rough with each other.

Harrison, Felix, and Marshall came to watch Benny play, and I ignore the pang of jealousy that looms over me when I see the connections Benny's made during his college years.

I haven't even heard from anyone at San Diego other than the initial texts asking why I left. My friends were more acquaintances than anything. My best friend has always been my brother.

It irrationally makes me want to kick his ass, and here's my chance.

"Do you even remember how to play?" I taunt.

"It's like riding a bike." To show off to his spectators, he skates forward and then jumps, turning backward and skating circles around the rest of us.

"Toxic display of dominance over with then?" I cock an eyebrow at him.

"Please. That was only the start."

Figures.

"Let's do this."

Fletcher and Scarlett take their positions in between the goalposts while I throw the puck center ice for a face-off. We don't have someone to drop the puck for us, but Fletcher has a whistle for us to go on.

"Which way you skating?" Benny asks. "I'm tempted to make you try to score on your boss, but considering your penchant for older dudes, you might take it the wrong way."

"Hilarious. So funny. And just so you know, I'd totally sleep with Fletcher if he was into it, but he's not. He has a wife."

"Sucks to be you."

"I can still score on him though."

"Not worried about being fired?"

"Nope. He loves me. You ready, or you going to keep stalling?"

We take our positions, bent over, sticks out, ready for that whistle to come. When it does, we both fight for the puck until I get it loose and chase after it.

Benny checks me, and I almost trip, but there's no point calling penalty when it's the two of us. By the time I've righted myself, he's already at the puck and flying down the ice toward Scarlett.

He's right. He's taken to it like riding a bike, and he's as fast as he ever was.

I chase him down, but he's faster than me. Back when we were playing together, him on left wing, me on right, he'd speed down the ice and set up the perfect shot for me to snipe it into the net. Now that I'm on the opposing team, his speed is going to tire me out faster than you can say *What hockey career?*

Turns out, coaching kids doesn't keep you in peak physical shape. How Benny can still be so fast is disheartening because for a teeny tiny second, I'd been contemplating what West had said. That if I go home, I could recondition and maybe get back to where I was.

And just when I think there's no hope of catching him, it seems he might still be fast, but he's forgotten how to stop smoothly.

I almost run into him as he tries to take a slap shot. Instead of hitting him, I do pull to a quick stop, and then I easily knock the puck out of his way.

It goes sailing toward Scarlett, who stops it with her stick. "Uh, which one of you is on my team? You look identical."

I laugh. "Me. Blue helmet. Benny has the black one."

"No, he's lying. I'm Emmett. Black helmet."

Her head swivels between us.

"Scar, it's me," I say.

"No, it's me," Benny argues.

Harrison yells from the sidelines. "Benny is the one in the black helmet!"

"Traitor!" Benny calls back, but by that point, Scarlett's already passed the puck to me, and now it's his turn to skate after me.

We take it in turns stripping the puck off each other, skating up and down the ice. I get one shot on Fletcher, but I really am rusty, and it goes wide. He dives for the puck and misses, and if

I had a teammate right now, it would be an empty net with a free shot.

Unfortunately for me, this is one-on-one, and Benny gets possession again. Then we're on our way back up the ice to my defensive zone.

When we were growing up, our coaches and older brothers were divided on what position we should play. As the Dalton Duo, the coaches wanted us to be a defensemen pair because we make such a great team, but our brothers wanted us to be on that first line, trying to score as many points as possible and being on top of that point leaderboard. The same as they were and where Dad pushed them to be.

We've been trained in both defense and offense, so we've got skills in both areas.

Benny starts to tire, or I pick up my pace. One or the other. Either way, I'm able to catch up to him easier now. He tries a quick wrist shot, but Scarlett is on her game, and she knocks it right back. He tries for the rebound and, like me, is way off aim, so I'm able to intercept it.

I get on the breakaway from him, and then it's me versus Fletcher. This time, as I skate toward the blue line, I concentrate on my game plan.

The way Fletcher moves in front of the net, side to side, waiting to see where I'm going to shoot, there's really only one safe place to go. I slow enough to get control of my stick and the puck and send a shot right into the five-hole.

Boom. Score.

I fist pump the air and revel in the high before reality comes crashing down.

Chasing my dream of hockey means I'd have to sacrifice a lot. I'd have to move. Benny's place is here. He has the DIKs, Harrison, his degree, his whole future that he's working toward. He wouldn't follow me the way I followed him here, and I wouldn't expect him to.

I'd have to live without my twin for the first time ever, and it's impossible to know if I'm ready to do that, but I can't keep denying the draw to this game that has my whole heart.

This is where I belong, but I also belong with Benny.

It's going to be impossible to choose between them, but there's going to be a time where I'll have to, and in my gut, I know this game is it for me.

This is my home.

On the ice.

CHAPTER TWENTY-ONE

jonah

AS I RELEASE my last class for the afternoon, I have the urge to text Emmett to see what he's doing tonight. Getting addicted to spending time with him? Guilty.

Though I'm worried about being too pushy. Maybe I should be playing this more cool than I am.

I decide to leave it until at least tomorrow—I'm going to see him when I take Cullen to practice anyway—but on my way out the door, I realize I don't have to play it cool. Not with Emmett.

Because he's standing right there with two coffees and wearing the most heartwarming smile in the universe. He has his hair out, and his wild, blond curls sit just above his shoulders. I think the only other time I've seen him with his hair out is while we've been fucking, and it's possible I'm associating that image with how he looks right now, but he's absolutely gorgeous. And way out of my league.

His bluish-green eyes sparkle at me as he hands me one of the cups. "Drink up. You're going to need it."

"Should I be scared?" I take it and sip.

"Nope. You should be excited." Emmett's all bouncy on his feet, like a hyperactive puppy.

"What did you get up to today to put you in this very peppy mood?"

"I played hockey with my brother." His grin widens. "It was so awesome and fun, and it reminded me of old times. It got me out of this funk I've been having."

"You've been in a funk?" Should I be offended by that? He must see the worry in my face because he puts his hand on my arm as we start walking toward the street exit of the school.

"Not when it comes to you, but with life in general. Ever since getting kicked out of school, I've been trying to think about what I want to do. I love coaching, and I love having kids like Cullen who just get it, but ..." He bites his plump lip. "I miss playing."

"What's holding you back? The pressure?"

"There's that, and I've most likely left it too late to try to make it professionally anyway, but at least I know what direction I want to go now. I could become a full-time coach and join a social team, or West mentioned me going home to Vermont and playing for CU. Maybe I'll catch the eye of an agent, or my brother can pull some strings and I'll get put on a farm team that might one day pick me up for the NHL. The world is my oyster ... or whatever that saying is."

My heart has no right to, but it twinges anyway. "You're thinking about moving back to Vermont?"

"Don't you ever think about moving back to ..." He frowns. "Where are you from originally?"

"Super-duper far away. So, so far."

"Oh, right. Cali boy. I forgot about that. You're from San Diego, aren't you?"

"Yup."

We reach the parking lot, and he takes out his phone. "Have you ever lived outside of California?"

"No. What are you doing?"

"Getting a ride share. We're going out."

"We are?"

"Yup. I'm too wired. I should be exhausted because I reckon we ended up playing three periods' worth of ice time, but I used to always be like this after a game. It takes a while to wind down, so I figured you can entertain me while I do that."

I wrap my arm around his waist and pull him against me. "In that case, I'm in. What's the plan? Early dinner? Movie?"

"No, that would involve me needing to sit still."

He's cute when he's excited. Actually, he's cute all the time. The idea of him moving to Vermont fills me with the kind of longing I should definitely not have this early into our ... dating-ship. I can't call it a relationship because we just started dating. But these feelings are there, strong and powerful.

I'm probably setting myself up for heartache, knowing he's most likely going to leave, but I'm holding out hope that he won't because I know it would be difficult for him to leave Benny. Is it horrible to hope for his unhealthy codependence with his twin to stay strong? I should probably start thinking about it.

"Are you going to tell me where we're going or keep it a surprise?" I ask.

"Surprise."

"Am I at least dressed appropriately?"

Emmett pockets his phone again and places his hand on my chest. "Maybe too appropriately. Ditch the blazer. And while we're at it, the shirt too. Ooh, pants."

"Emmett," I warn. If he keeps going, we won't be heading out at all but back to my apartment.

"You look fine, and there's no dress code where we're going."

"To clarify, is there no-dress code or no dress code? As in, it's not a rule to be naked or anything?"

"No, do you know of places like that? We should change our plans." He jumps up and down on the balls of his feet again.

"I wanted to be sure after you asked me to get naked right here in the parking lot."

The sun is beginning to set over the school, the sky turning a burnt orange.

"We're going somewhere super fun."

Now I really am scared.

Our ride shows up, and we slip into the back seat. Other than a hello, he doesn't speak. Instant five stars.

I try to figure out where we're going, but I'm kind of excited for the surprise.

Though when we pull into an industrial area full of warehouses and nothing else, I'm back on the scared bandwagon.

Emmett is quick to say thank you and jump out of the car, still having that kid-like energy about him.

It's not that I don't like enthusiastic people, but I haven't had anything in my grown-up life that makes me that level of excited. Emmett looks like a kid at his own birthday party, and if I truly think about my life, nothing has ever come close to that.

I haven't had that … spark, that urge to throw myself into something wholly and completely in a really long time.

"You ready?" Emmett asks.

"To be taken inside an abandoned warehouse to do god knows what? You're not one of those people who like trashing old, run-down places, are you?"

He smiles, but it's too innocent for my liking. It's so innocent that it's … not. "Would someone as sweet as me do something like that?"

"Granted, I still don't know you well, but you did get kicked out of school for setting a fire."

He goes to open his mouth, but I keep going.

"Even if you say it wasn't you, how am I to know for sure? You might actually be a thirty-five-year-old married dude who is pretending to be student age."

He laughs. "Want to see my ID?"

"No, this is all hyperbole, but still."

Emmett takes my hand, gentle and soft. "It's not abandoned, and we're not breaking any laws. I promise. I bought tickets for this."

"Okay." I relax. Marginally.

But then he says, "You know how to parkour, don't you?"

I stare to where our ride share left. "Wait, come back!"

Emmett laughs again, and I like making him do that. "You're way too easy to rile up. Come on. This will be fun."

He leads me down the side of the buildings, past some cars parked in a small lot, and to the very end warehouse that has a very makeshift sign saying "Snow World" above two doors.

"How did you find this place, exactly?"

"Google."

"So, you've never been to the big scary warehouse that might as well be a van that says 'free candy' on the side?"

"The photos made it look awesome inside."

"Well, if it was on the internet, it must be true."

"That's how the world works, isn't it?" He pushes through one of the doors.

Inside the small reception area isn't much better. There's a rack of thick jackets lining the wall and a small desk with an old man behind it. He stands from his seat and smiles. "Come in. Come in." He waves us closer to him.

I still have no idea what's going on, but Emmett shows him his online booking, and then we're told to find jackets that fit us.

"Still scared?" Emmett asks as we put on the winter clothing.

"Yup."

He pauses at the hanging plastic flaps that they have in refrigerator trucks to keep everything inside cool, and as he moves one aside, we're blasted with freezing cold air. Emmett has no hesitation, but when he says, "Oh, wow," it gets me moving too.

The outside might not be much to look at, but inside …

"Holy shit. It's like a winter wonderland." One side of the warehouse has a fake snow mountain with people on sleds, to the back there's a pit of snow, and right in front is a small ice-skating rink. The walls are lined with frozen ice sculptures, lit up by colorful lights from underneath them, and to the right of us, there's even a slide made of ice for the little kids. A mother and a toddler are over there, and the child slides down and then runs back around to go again.

"I told you the photos looked good."

"Yeah, but I was fully expecting you to be scammed."

"So pessimistic."

"I prefer the term realist, but I have to admit, I never would've come here if you didn't bring me. Even if I saw it online. I guess I'm always under the impression if something looks too good to be true, then it is."

He stares at me for a moment, an expression I can't read on his face, but then he turns back to the ice. "Where do you want to go first?"

"Well, I'm guessing the ice skating is out because you could do that at work."

"Hey, I will never say no to skating. I could teach you. Maybe you're a natural like Cullen."

"Or maybe I don't want to embarrass myself in front of you yet."

"You mean—"

I put up my hand, knowing he's about to mention the scene I created on campus. "Technically, I didn't embarrass myself in front of you but your brother. You heard about that second-hand, so it doesn't count."

"How'd you know what I was going to say?"

"Because I'm smart." I glance between the sledding and the snow at the back and really think back to when I was a child and how much I wanted to see snow and throw a snowball. "I know what I want to do. Snow angels?"

"Perfect."

He takes my hand again, and I will never get sick of that. We head toward the back of the warehouse. There are only a few families here with small kids, and I get the impression that maybe we're a bit old for this type of place, but it's an amazing venue.

Emmett throws himself down on his back on the man-made snow, arms and legs wide.

Little does he know I can be just as immature as him sometimes. Okay, never, but what can I say, he brings it out in me. Instead of joining him, I bend down and get a handful, squishing it into a ball.

He sees it before I throw it at him, but it's too late. It hits him in the stomach.

"Oh, I know you did not just do that."

I hold my hands up. "Wasn't me."

He jumps to his feet. "You don't realize what you've done."

I step closer to him. "What have I done?"

"Only challenged the Dalton family snowball champion to a snowball fight."

"I'm really scared. Let me guess, you and Ben would team up and pretend to be one player."

Emmett's face falls.

"Ha, I knew it. Let's see how good you are without your brother helping you."

"It's on, Cali boy."

I didn't see his hands when he stood from the ground, so when he smushes snow onto my head out of nowhere, I know I've made a big mistake.

But it's one I'll make again and again because that excited feeling I've been missing since I was a kid? I have it with Emmett.

emmett

WE CAN'T STOP LAUGHING as we throw snow at each other. It's not like real snow. It's hard as fuck and hurts like hell, but I love every second of it.

It's not long before the place starts filling with school-aged kids and teenagers. Guess school has let out for the day.

"Okay, okay." Jonah holds up his hands. "We should probably stop before we knock out a kid."

"Sure. That's why you want to stop. It has nothing to do with me kicking your ass."

"Not at all. You really think I went into this intending to win? I've never been to the real snow, and my major in college was statistics and data analysis. I'm under no delusion that I know how to throw a snowball."

"So you like being pummeled?"

He doesn't miss the innuendo in my tone. "Actually, I prefer to do the pummeling, but in this instance, I knew it would be the other way around."

I smile up at him. "Good. I usually like to be the one being pummeled."

"I can't tell if we're talking about snowball fights anymore."

I close the gap between us, pressing my body against his but keeping my hands to myself very PG-like because we're now surrounded by children. "We're not."

"Is this place suddenly feeling too crowded?" Jonah rasps.

"Yup."

"Ready to get out of here, or do you need to burn some more energy by sledding down that hill over there?"

"I can think of a better way to burn some energy."

Jonah groans. "Let's go."

It's like we can't keep our hands off each other. We rush outside to return our rented jackets, and if there weren't so many families and children about, I'd be tempted to push Jonah up against the wall of the building and have my way with him.

I take out my phone to order a ride, but the nearest car is about fifteen minutes away. "Stupid industrial area with no drivers. Don't they know I'm desperate for di—" I glance around, but the parking lot is empty. "—ck?"

"Maybe put that in the notes section. Someone might take pity and get here faster."

"Ooh, good idea." I pretend to type on my phone.

"Please tell me you didn't actually—"

"Of course not. I don't go around telling everyone how much I like dick, unlike certain professors who like to email their entire class about it."

This time when Jonah groans, it's not in desperation. "I am never going to live that down."

"How were classes today? Did anyone say anything about it?"

"When I walked into the room, there were a few snickers, but I told them all to get it out of the way now until it didn't become funny."

"Oh no. Did you get through any coursework?" My sympathy might be dry, but I do feel sorry for him.

"They were still laughing as they left when the lecture ended."

"I never would've guessed you'd be the type of professor to have so many scandals."

"Maybe I'm not cut out to be a professor." Jonah says it so seriously that I have to do a double take.

"You're joking, right? You're a great professor. You let your students go at their own pace and explain things when you need to. You're informative and charismatic, and—" Fuck.

"Have you been spying on me?" He smiles, but my heart rate increases to the point it's hard to breathe. Because this is exactly why I shouldn't be dating him. And now, I'm going to have to lie to him. Again. Just to cover that I know firsthand what a great professor he is.

"H-Harrison raves about you."

"But not Ben?"

"Hell no. He hates statistics. Sorry to burst your bubble."

"It's all good. I know the majority of my students don't like statistics and are only doing it because it's a prerequisite to get their degree. And maybe that's why I'm not so sure about this being a professor thing. Because I want to help people who want to be helped. Who want to be there. The bullshit excuses I get from some of them is insane."

It's views like that why it took so long for Benny and me to admit something wasn't right with us. "I get where you're coming from, but you know, some people aren't wired that way. I was not made for college, so it made my experience challenging, especially when I could barely understand what I had to do."

"What do you mean?"

"I've never been tested or anything, but we're pretty sure I have a form of dyslexia." I shrug. I wish I could talk more about it, but it's a dangerous subject because if I even breathe a word about Ben having dyscalculia, we're all fucked.

"You didn't want to get it checked?"

"Nah. I got through high school fine, and I mean, Benny helped me do that, but college is a whole other ball game, and it was way too much for me to handle. Numbers I understand. Words? Not so much."

"You could get diagnosed now and get extra learning materials to suit your particular needs. I could talk to the dean at Franklin—"

"The thing is, it's not only because I found writing the engineering reports difficult; it's that I didn't enjoy it. At all. Just because I understand numbers doesn't mean I want to make it my career. I studied that because I thought I had to do something math based."

Jonah nods, and I hope he's getting it. I don't want him to be the type of guy who hears one thing but thinks his idea is better because I do not want to go back to school. At all.

"So you're set on this hockey thing?"

"Honestly, I have no idea what I want to do with my life. Hockey, yes, but in what capacity? No clue."

He smiles. "If it helps at all, I have no idea what I want to do with my life either. I kind of fell into teaching because I was the right student at the right time when Professor Aves was retiring. It was an opportunity that literally fell into my lap, and while I appreciated it at the time, I'm wondering if I took it because I was too scared to find something else. Or too scared to acknowledge that I didn't have the passion for data that I thought, and therefore, I spent all my time and money earning a useless degree. At least I'm getting to put all my student knowledge to use."

"It kind of feels like a waste, doesn't it?"

"Yup."

"Well, now that we've completely depressed the fuck out of each other, how about we go somewhere for a bite to eat before heading back to your place."

"Stupid cockblocking ride share taking too long and making us talk about real issues."

"Yup. All the ride share's fault."

I'm in trouble with Jonah. I like him way too much and love waking up next to him. His arm didn't move from where it was draped over my stomach all night, and while I have no idea what time it is, I know it has to be close to when he needs to get up to go to class.

Confirming my suspicions, his hand finally tries to leave me as he pulls himself away, but I quickly roll over and hold on to him for dear life.

He chuckles quietly. "I was only going to get up and use the bathroom and make coffee. It's still early. Sleep more."

Jonah kisses the top of my head and slips out of bed.

See? He's perfect.

Ugh. Why does he have to be so perfect?

I drift back to sleep and am awoken again by freshly brewed coffee and a half-naked Jonah. The only thing that would be better is if he wasn't wearing any underwear at all.

"Here." He hands me a mug.

I sit up and take it while he climbs back into bed next to me.

"I was thinking ..." he starts.

"Nothing good ever comes from thinking."

"Maybe for you, but I want to point out something I picked up on yesterday."

My heart pounds, and I feel sick. I wait for him to call me out on cheating in his class for my brother, but would he really go to the effort of making me coffee if he suspected that?

I stare down at my coffee. Maybe it's poisoned.

"You really do belong on the ice," he says, and even though

the weight on my chest doesn't lift, I can breathe again. "Not just as a coach. You should give your all to try and make it, or I think you'll regret it."

"I've been thinking the same thing recently."

"Does that mean you're giving more serious thought to moving home?"

I get the impression he's fishing for something. "It's one of many plans I'm considering."

"Anything in particular holding you back?"

I side-eye him, and his face falls.

"Shit. That sounded like I was asking for me, like will you stay in California for me, and that's not what I was going for at all."

Is he sure about that?

"I'm more asking so I can prepare myself for whatever you decide. Like, for instance, if it's your brother holding you back, you wanting to be here with him, then what happens if he decides to go with you? Do you just ... leave?" His shoulders slump. "Shit, that makes it sound like it's about me again."

Not going to lie, the flustered look on his face somehow makes me like him more.

"You are allowed to do whatever you want. No, not allowed —it's not like you need my permission. What I mean is—"

"You want to know if there's any chance of a future here or if I'm planning to run home without so much as a goodbye."

Jonah sighs into his cup. "I'd at least hope for a goodbye fuck."

"Oh, I'd leave you with at least that. I'm very selfless and giving in that way."

"I don't want to put pressure on you when it comes to you and me. You were adamant nothing could come from this at all, and I'm not asking you to marry me or anything, but ... I guess I want to know where I stand or where I will stand if things keep going the way they're going?"

If the rate at which I'm catching feelings for Jonah continues, I'm going to be a mess of guilt by the time I have to end it. And I will have to end it eventually.

"I've completely freaked you out now, haven't I?"

I force a smile I don't feel. "No, you haven't. I promise. It's just ..."

"How about this? I won't ask you again so long as you promise that if things change for you, you tell me. I don't want to play games, so if you're interested in someone else or—"

"I'm not. It's not that. I can't offer you anything when I have no idea where my future will take me, and I also don't think that we should stop seeing each other now because of that. I'm loving every moment we're spending together. I'm excited when I get to see you, and I've stayed over two nights in a row now. I'm so into you."

"That's all I needed." Jonah leans over and kisses me briefly, tasting like coffee and disappointment.

"Then why do I sense you didn't like my answer?"

He knows I'm holding something back. I should tell him there's no future. That there can't be one. But when he asks why, what am I going to say? Because I have a secret that could affect your career? Like he'll drop that.

"I'm not disappointed. I can't expect you to know your plans when you're twenty-one. I'm almost twenty-six and still don't know if I'm on the right path. I also wasn't asking so we could label whatever this is between us, but ..." He hesitates.

We're so good at this communication thing.

"I'm going to be frank." He turns to me, and I can't help myself.

"Can I still be Emmett?"

"Ignoring your lame joke, but here's what's up. I really like you, but I can't shake the feeling you're hiding something from me, or you're not in this fully. And if that's what this is, then that's totally okay. I would just rather you be up-front about it before I catch feelings that will be hard to get over. That's what I'm trying to say."

He wants to know the truth. He's asking me to let him off the hook. And as much as I don't want to, I can't keep being selfish.

CHAPTER TWENTY-THREE

EMMETT SITS THERE, trying to find the words to say that will let me down gently.

I get it. He said from the start there were things that he couldn't offer me. I thought it was because his brother was my student, but it's obviously more than that.

What it is, I have no idea, but if I'm going to continue to sleep with him, I need to readjust my hopes.

We have fun together, and while I might have stronger feelings for him than he does for me, I can handle that. As long as I know ahead of time that if I allow myself to fall, it's my own fault because he has promised me nothing.

He's still staring with a scrunched brow, and while I'm tempted to hear what he has to say, I know it's not going to be the words I want to hear. You don't hesitate this long if there isn't something major standing in your way.

"Your lack of answer is answer enough," I say. "Can we forget I said anything? Let's see where this goes and try not to think about any future." I drink the rest of my coffee in one gulp and get back out of bed. "I'm going to get dressed and head to campus."

"Jonah ... I ..."

I avert my gaze. I can't look into his eyes if he's going to end things all because I got ahead of myself. But because I'm me, I completely ignore that voice telling me not to turn back to him, and when I do, it's not pity in his eyes. There are fucking tears.

"Shit, what's wrong?" In a split second, I'm by his side, unable to help myself.

"I can't do this."

My heart sinks. "Wait, we don't need to put a label on anything, and I know you feel like I'm pressuring you, but—" I run my hand over my hair. "I shouldn't have brought it up. I've been happy with what we have, and I went and screwed it up because I haven't liked anyone the way I like you in a really long time. And there I go again with the pressure. I'm sorry. I really am. Maybe ... maybe we need to take a step back. Then I won't be crowding you and you—"

"You're not crowding me," he croaks. "You have no idea how much I want to give everything to you, but I can't. I literally can't."

"Why? What's standing in your way? I don't understand."

Emmett buries his head in his hands. "I'm not a good person. Benny and I ... we're not ... I'm not ..."

"What are you talking about?"

"There's another reason I took the fall for that guy who set fire to the dorms, but I can't talk about it."

"Ever?" I squeak.

"Even if we were to fall in love, become boyfriends, get married, I would never be able to tell you without betraying my brother, and when it comes down to love and relationships or having Benny by my side, it will always be Benny. Do you understand?"

Not in the slightest. I am starting to think Ben might have killed someone, though. That's probably being dramatic.

Or is it?

"So if I want to be with you in any capacity, you're saying I have to ignore this giant secret you have, and it will never be a piece you will share with me?"

"I can't expect you to be okay with that, which is why ..."

"Why you've been holding back."

"Exactly." Defeat laces his voice.

I don't want to lose what we have, but at the same time, I don't think a relationship can build if two people aren't being completely open and honest with each other. But in a sense, he is being honest. He has told me there's something he can't say, will not say, and can never say.

So I guess the question is, will I be able to accept that and still trust him?

It would be easy to say we're at the beginning of this, we could see where it leads, and the big stuff isn't important, but what if we do this, and I fall past the point of no return, and then I realize this void between us is too big? Do I protect my heart now or risk having to pick up the broken pieces in the future?

"I ... I need to think about this," I say. "I'm sorry—"

"Don't be sorry. It's fair. This is exactly why I said I can't date you. Why I wanted only that first night, but then you'd bring your nephew to hockey practice, and I couldn't fucking help myself. You know, if you weren't so irresistible, this wouldn't have become an issue."

As much as that thought warms me, it just makes me sad.

Emmett stands. "I'll let you get ready for classes and give you the space you need."

My heart tells me to beg him to stay and forget about whatever secret he has that was done in the past. It has nothing to do with me. Yet, my gut instincts hold me back.

So I only watch as he gets dressed and then approaches me, kissing me softly on the cheek and then walking out the door.

When did this all become so complicated?

I'm nervous walking into Cullen's hockey practice that afternoon because I still don't have any idea how I feel about the whole situation.

But when I do go inside, Emmett is already on the ice, his hair tied back in his signature messy bun, his powerful legs pushing him around like he's gliding on air.

I give him a wave when he looks in our direction, but it's as if he wasn't paying attention because he snaps out of whatever trance he was in, puts on a weak smile, and waves back.

He doesn't come near us though. "Go get dressed and get out here, Cullen."

Emmett's either giving me the space I said we need or has decided I'm not worth the effort of keeping. Which would make sense. He's been nothing but truthful about us having no future from the beginning, and maybe my "I really, really like you" speech was his wake-up call that it is time to cool it.

I wish I had someone to talk to about this, but all of my college friends moved on after graduation. Some went on to do their master's at other schools; some went straight into the workforce.

I could call my sister, but we don't really have that type of relationship. I love Lauren, but I don't trust her judgment when it comes to men.

When I began the year, I was assigned a tenured professor as a mentor, but I don't think asking for love advice was included in the mentoring. Then again, the best piece of advice he's given me so far is "Don't get a lap dance from a student," so maybe not all hope is lost?

So, while Cullen has his lesson, I take out my phone and text Dr. Sinclair.

ME

You want to go out for a drink tonight?

DR. SINCLAIR

That would be completely inappropriate. But tell me, you had sex with a student, didn't you?

ME

No. But I do need some advice. It's not strictly professoring related though.

DR. SINCLAIR.

I'm in. Just tell me when and where.

I'd normally meet up with friends at Shenanigans, but I've noticed the shift in vibe ever since becoming a professor instead of a student. Almost like I'm not welcome there anymore. It's possible I'm reading into it because I'm me and I'm not entirely the smoothest of people, but either way, I don't want to have this conversation in a bar with a million students.

ME

There's a bar near the Navy base called Bottom's Up. You heard of it? It's a gay bar that has all the nice sailor eye candy.

DR. SINCLAIR

Now I'm doubly in. Though, I can only look. No touching.

ME

Same. But I just can't go to Shenanigans.

DR. SINCLAIR

You definitely slept with a student.

ME

At least that would be a clear answer—cut and run. This is more complicated than that.

DR. SINCLAIR

Instead of meeting there, let's ride share so we can get you drunk.

I'm starting to think my mentor might be a bad influence on me.

When Cullen's class is done, Emmett doesn't come near me. I take Cullen into the locker room to help him out of his hockey gear, and then Emmett is nowhere to be seen when we're done.

"Ready to go?" I ask Cullen but still glance around for Emmett to show his face.

"Yep. Hockey is so much fun."

So he's not getting sick of this sport as quickly as I thought he would, and I can't help thinking it's because he wants me to suffer as payback for putting him through every other sport under the sun.

Why else would he attach himself to the one sport that has Emmett in it?

Totally selfish on his part.

"Let's get out of here." I steer my nephew toward the exit, but I'm walking so slowly people probably think I'm moving in slow motion.

We get to the door before I hear Emmett's voice.

"See you next week, Cullen. Good job today."

"Thanks, Coach Dalton," Cullen calls back but keeps walking.

I hesitate for a minor second before turning back to Emmett.

He gives me that small smile of his, and all I can do is return it before walking out.

Where we stand, I can't be sure, but until I figure out whether or not I can accept his situation, it's better this way. Even if it fucking hurts.

emmett

AFTER GETTING home from what was the worst day at work since I started there, I grunt at my roommates and brother, who are hanging out in the living room, and make my way to the cupboard I call home now.

It's not a literal cupboard, but with the cluttered mess the guys haven't cleaned out yet and the small mattress I was sleeping on in Benny's frat house, I have no room to move. So instead, I flop down on my stomach and wallow.

Ignoring Jonah was the worst because all I wanted to do was tell the kids to skate and have fun while I ran over to him and kissed the fuck out of him.

I stayed strong though, and I need to.

He asked to take a step back and get some space, and maybe we both need it.

I was getting way too comfortable with him, and that was only after staying over at his place twice in a row.

He needs to walk away from me. He needs to save us both because I'm not strong enough to end things myself.

It's inevitable, so why are we even contemplating sweeping this under the rug? Why is he dangling hope in front of me when we both know a secret between partners is unhealthy and will only lead to resentment? And then if he found out what that secret was? It would ruin everything and hurt Benny.

And the last thing I ever want to do is hurt my brother.

"Yo, mopey fuckface. What happened?"

Okay, *now* I want to hurt him. Physically anyway. I settle for giving him the finger instead. I don't turn my head, don't acknowledge him in any other way.

The idea of him being punished for a mistake we both made ... I can't live with that. I don't want him to get hurt academically because he has dyscalculia. We both already feel guilty enough for holding each other back. We thought we were helping, but we only cheated each other out of a proper education. We took the protective route when we might have needed to be more supportive and tried to teach and share our strengths instead of doing it for each other.

But hindsight is 20/20 or whatever that phrase is. We didn't know we were making things worse by trying to make them better.

It took me until this morning to realize the other reason I took the fall for the fire, and it's that I don't believe I deserve to be in college.

Yes, I hated it, and I don't want to go back, but it wasn't just that. I welcomed the blame, the expulsion, the consequences, because I knew I hadn't earned my spot.

Guilt hits in the weirdest ways. At random times. Benny and I had been switching for years. We even cheated on the SATs, for crying out loud. We tested at separate centers, on different days, and in the short break between the math and English portions, we met up in the bathrooms, swapped clothes, and no one was any wiser.

The amount of trouble we went to so we could keep taking the easy way out is now astonishing to me, and it's no surprise both of us only have a middle-grade grasp on our poorer subjects.

"Is this normal for him?" Marshall asks Benny. "This is what he's done all day since he came home this morning from being out all night. Then when it was time to go to work, he got up and left, and now …"

"He's imitating a dead fish. Probably practicing for all the sex he has with Professor Brooks."

Why am I protecting him again?

Oh, right. Love and all that crap.

"I'll talk to him."

I don't need to lift my head to know Benny is ushering Marshall and probably my other roommates out so he can tell me to snap out of this toxic funk.

We both know his speech won't work, but it's what we do for each other. The door closes with a resounding click, and then Benny kicks my foot.

"Move over so I can sit down somewhere."

Instead of sitting up, I roll so I'm horizontal, my head still on the low mattress but my legs lifted to rest on some boxes stacked on top of each other. Don't know which roommate they belong to or what's in them, but they're sturdy, so that's all that matters.

Benny mirrors my position. "What's wrong?" He draws out the word and puts baby talk into it. He might be being condescending, but this is how Benny shows he cares.

"Your face is what's wrong." I, too, am amazing at expressing how I feel.

"So, your face? Is that what you mean?"

"Yes."

Benny turns his head to me. "Wait, is it really our faces that's the issue?"

"Yep."

"Because we're so good-looking?"

"Because it's the fucking same. Can you imagine what our lives would've been like had we not been identical?"

"Completely boring." He answers so quickly. "Imagine how many times we actually would've been in trouble for all the crap we did if they could tell us apart and knew who to blame?"

"Imagine getting the help we both needed in school and being able to actually function like every other human being."

"Emmy …"

I shake my head. "Sorry. I'm in a really shitty headspace. Jonah basically asked if we have a future, and I had to tell him no. So now he needs space, and he's going to decide I'm not worth the effort, and—"

"Whoa, whoa, whoa, slow your roll. What did you tell him exactly? Why can't you have a future with him?"

"You can't be pissed at me, considering I did it to protect you."

"I don't understand."

"Think about it, Benny. Say we end up getting serious. He meets the family. We fall in love and have a big queer wedding, and then one day, he finds out you have dyscalculia and there's no way you could've gotten your grades in his class."

"So tell him after I get my degree."

I huff. "And then make him feel tricked? Like, ha ha, my big secret is we cheated our way into a degree for Ben, and now he has his diploma, there's nothing you can do about it. Come here and give me a kiss. Love you."

Benny's silent, and so am I because I think we're both finally getting those consequences we've avoided for so long.

To protect my brother, I have to give up someone I really could love.

In years to come, will I look back at college and think I'm an idiot for even wanting Jonah to begin with, or will I look back and only see resentment for my twin?

It's impossible to know, and I'm scared to find out the truth.

Only time will tell.

"I'm so sorry, Em," he whispers, and I know he is.

Because "I am too," I whisper back.

"We really fucked ourselves over, didn't we?" he says.

"Yup. Any regrets?"

"Nope." Benny's mouth pops on the *P*. "Actually, yeah. I regret that we've held each other back for so long thinking it was for the best. Without that, none of this would have happened, and you could be as happy as ..." He slams his mouth shut.

"You were about to say you're happpppy," I taunt.

"Was not. You lie. We should be doing things to make *you* happy. Let's go out tonight."

Pass. "Does it look like I want to move?"

He laughs. "Yes, actually. How are you comfortable?"

"I'm not. But I deserve it, I guess."

Benny grabs my arm. "No, no, no, none of that. Up we get. You know what will be super fun? Taking Harrison to Bottom's Up. You know that gay bar where all the Navy SEALs are drunk and shirtless a lot of the time? I'm about to open that baby bi's eyes to the awesomeness that is half-naked sailors."

"Is there any point in saying no to you right now?"

He tugs on my arm harder, trying to get me to stand, and it's all the answer I need.

I shake off his grip. "I'm getting up. I'm getting up."

"Good. Because you stink. Did you not shower at the rink?"

"Nope. Couldn't be bothered."

"Go shower, then we'll have pre-drinks before we go have all the drinks."

"Is tonight going to get messy?"

"You betcha."

Great. Just great. But hey, maybe drinking my weight in alcohol will make me forget my problems.

If only that was possible.

CHAPTER TWENTY-FIVE

BECAUSE IT'S the middle of the week and it's still early, the bar is quiet, which is good.

"What will you have, Dr. Sinclair?"

"What have I told you? When there are no students around, call me Silas."

I purse my lips. "I was about to say it feels too unprofessional to do that, but here we are, getting drinks and about to talk about my dating life, so really, what is professionalism anyway?"

His lips turn upward. "You're still not going to call me Silas though, are you?"

"Silas," I say to make a point, but my voice cracks. It's weird because he's kind of an authority figure, but not really, so it's messing with my head.

Dr. Sinclair is in his thirties, already tenured, and if it weren't for his tattoos down one arm, I would've said he was the most straitlaced person ever. He's usually clean-shaven, but on occasion, like tonight, it looks like he hasn't shaved for a couple of days, and it gives him a sexy, scruffy look.

A few months ago, I would've said he is the type of guy I

157

usually go for. Mature, put together. But after meeting Emmett, I'm starting to think those men were my type because it's who I thought I *should* go for.

Maybe when it comes to relationships, I need to be the serious one.

We order drinks and find a cocktail table in the corner we can stand at.

I take a sip of my beer, but Silas just watches me.

"Are you going to start talking, or do you need something stronger than light beer?" He swigs his grown-up drink of liquor with no soda in it, which makes it palatable for me.

Maybe I am closer to the students I teach in mental age than I thought. Emmett sure as fuck can bring out my playful side. I'm in that age where I haven't got everything figured out yet but am too old to be doing stupid shit.

I take another sip and then rest my elbows on the cocktail table. "Those rumors about me, about being with a student—"

"Dire, indeed. Tell me everything."

"I wasn't with my student, but I did sleep with his twin brother. Only, I didn't know at the time that he had a twin or that his twin was in my class because how are you supposed to keep two hundred students in two different classes straight?"

"You don't. Half the time when I'm lecturing, I'm asleep."

"Exactly. And at least I thought I knew him from some-where, but I didn't put two and two together until I met Ben, who's Emmett's twin. But anyway, this isn't the point. This is merely the background."

"Got it. Continue."

"Emmett and I have been sleeping together, dating, and doing all that mushy gushy crap you do in the beginning of a relationship. Seeing each other any chance you get, staying over. He slept at my place twice. In a row."

"Oh, wow, so you're practically married, then."

"I'm not finished. Anyway, I knew I was getting ahead of

myself, and I brought up the *where do we stand* conversation, and it was obviously way too soon because he freaked the fuck out."

Silas winces.

"I know, right? Shit move on my part, but the thing is, he wasn't freaking out because I was pushing him for something he wasn't ready for. He was freaking out because he has this huge secret, and he told me he will never be able to say what it is. He can't give himself to me wholly unless I'm okay with always being kept in the dark."

"Damn, those are some red flags right there."

"So you think it's a red flag too?"

"I do, but who doesn't love a good red flag? I'm trying to think of what kind of secret it could be, why he told you about it in the first place, and how he expects you to be all cool with it."

"It has something to do with his twin brother, and he says he's protecting him."

"From what? Did they kill a man? They were originally triplets and killed off the third?"

Maybe I'll take back what I said about Silas being mature. Even if murder was the exact same thing I was thinking when Emmett first told me.

Silas takes a drink and then licks his lips. "If it has to do with his brother and not you, do you think you could move past it?"

"I get the impression it does have something to do with me."

"Conceited?"

I scoff. "Paranoid and insecure."

"Ah, I see." His long and lean finger taps the side of his glass. "Could you try to figure out what the secret is on your own and then decide whether or not you can forgive it?"

"Where would I even start with that?" Something Emmett

said comes back to me. "Wait, he said it had to do with the fire that got him kicked out of San Diego State."

"You're dating someone who set a fire and has big secrets? I should tell you to run far, far away."

I wave him off. "He didn't set it. His roommate did, but Emmett took the fall ... for some reason."

"Or he's lying to you, he and his brother did it, they killed someone, and—"

"No one was hurt."

"Are you sure?"

My eyes widen. Fuck, am I sure?

Silas smiles. "Let me find out for you. I went to college with Professor Turner, who's teaching biology there." He takes out his phone and sends off a text.

"What am I supposed to do while we wait for his reply?" And why am I so suggestible? All it's taken is for Silas to question one thing Emmett has told me to start thinking he's a liar and I can't trust him.

One little doubt has me questioning everything we even had.

And this is why Emmett has been adamant about having no future. Because he knows that I will never trust him. Not fully.

I could say that I do, even believe that I do, and then something will happen, or he'll say a white lie or something doesn't match up exactly with what he's saying, and I'll go back to this —questioning what he's keeping from me and if it's about me. About us. If it has the potential to destroy everything.

"On second thought," I say, "I don't need to know. Not knowing the answer to it is enough of a warning sign that you're right. I should end it. Too many red flags and not enough answers."

"So go digging for answers. Do a deep dive on him."

"At this point, I'm not sure I even want to know the truth." Not to mention, that's a huge breach of privacy.

Across the bar, near the entrance, there's a loud ruckus as a group of guys enters. I almost swallow my tongue when I see who it is. The red hair catches my attention first—Harrison. There are two other guys with him who I don't know, but where Harrison is, Ben will be, and where Ben will be—

Yup. On cue, I see the twins. One of them looks gleefully happy, while the other looks like he'd rather be anywhere but here with his hoodie up and one blond curl hanging down by his face. I'm hopeful the sad one is Emmett, but Harrison throws his arm around that one and kisses the top of his head, pulling him toward the bar.

Guess Emmett really doesn't care, then. Avoiding me this afternoon, happily going out partying tonight ... Can the world please open up and swallow me whole?

"Fucking hell," I grumble.

"What?"

"They're here."

Silas lifts his head, scanning the room. "Who?"

"Emmett. And his twin brother and a few other guys."

"Ooh, where?"

I point them out.

"Which one is yours?"

Even though I'm sure it's the one smiling with one of the other men, maybe he's on a first date in a group or his brother is setting him up with someone more appropriate for him, I can't shake the instinct that Emmett's the one currently at the bar with his brother's boyfriend's arm wrapped around him. But how does that make sense?

"The two at the bar are boyfriends, so I'm guessing Emmett's the one flirting with the other guys."

Silas cocks his head. "Would we call talking flirting?"

"Probably," I mutter and drain the rest of my beer.

His phone lights up on the tabletop, and as Silas reads, his brow creases. "That's a dead end. Your boy was telling the truth. Accidental fire. The school wanted to kick both him and his roommate out, but they were both top students, and Emmett was adamant it was all him. There was an official hearing, and when Emmett had a chance to defend himself, all he said was, 'I deserve this.'"

"Why would he say that if he didn't do it though? Sure, he was covering and taking the fall for someone else—allegedly—but why wouldn't he say he's sorry for doing it? Why would he say he deserves getting kicked out of school?"

"Part of the covering act, I suppose."

At that moment, one of the unfamiliar guys locks eyes with me. I audibly gasp and quickly look away because I'm that smooth.

"We should get out of here," I say.

"Already? You're not drunk yet."

"I don't want him to see me. Or talk to me."

"Even though you know he told you the truth about the fire?"

I think long and hard about that because he was telling the truth. It was my insecurity that let my imagination get away from me, and that's not his fault. It's mine.

But that doesn't change anything. Our relationship would always be like that. I will always have doubts, and he will always have his secret.

I woke up this morning thinking I'd found such an amazing man. Someone I was excited to see. Who was sweet, hot as fuck, and damn, the sex …

Now … Now I'm starting to think all that superficial stuff is just that—surface-level bullshit.

We'll never have a future; I agree with him on that now. We could've worked through it together instead of what this is, but he made his choice to not let me in, and I can't keep chasing someone who's unavailable.

"I want to get out of here before he sees me."

But as if his ears were burning or he could hear me all the way across the bar, blue-green eyes meet mine, and I want to mentally high-five myself for not trusting the obvious answer when it comes to Emmett. He is the one being consoled. It's written all over his face when our gazes meet.

"Uh," Silas says, "too late by the look of it."

Fuck.

emmett

WHY IS JONAH HERE, and why is he with someone so damn hot? Someone who's the complete opposite of me.

I tear my gaze away and turn to Harrison, who's taken pity on me like one of my big brothers would. "He's here."

"What? Where?" He lifts his head and swivels it around like he's a fucking gopher.

Real subtle, Harrison.

"Don't look! He's at the back with some hot guy."

This time, when Harrison looks, he tries to be more subtle. "That's not some hot guy. That's Dr. Sinclair. Biology professor."

That doesn't fill me with any kind of relief.

This is my own fault though. I knew telling him I had a secret would create this huge wall between us, and I was delusional to think he'd be okay with never knowing, we'd ride off into the sunset, and live happily ever after, but I couldn't keep pretending like everything was okay. He was asking about a future, and I couldn't lie to him.

"Can we get out of here?" I ask.

"He's already seen you."

I glance back where Jonah and his professor date person put down their empty drinks and head this way. Jonah's stare bores into me.

I hold my breath. My heart thuds. And then, when Jonah breaks eye contact and ducks his head, slipping right past us and heading for the exit, my heart stops completely.

Even though I wanted to do the exact same thing just now, it stings like a bitch. At least he got the chance to walk out on me first. If he feels even a fraction of what I do for him, I wouldn't want to hurt him like I hurt in this moment.

How did it go from being so happy to complete misery, all over a guy I'd barely started dating?

What is it about Jonah that makes me this gooey-eyed love monster? Am I really that self-sabotaging, that guilt-filled, that I went for a man I knew I couldn't have so I could hurt like I'm supposed to?

Did I subconsciously do this to myself so I could experience the punishment I never got and dragged an amazing man into my guilt-filled bullshit at the same time?

I have to go apologize. Or make it better somehow. If I could make it better for him, maybe my gut would stop churning.

Benny comes to my side. "Are you going to chase after him?"

I should, but my feet won't move, and I know I'm going to chicken out. "What's the point?"

"You really like him, and I've never seen you this torn up over a guy."

"I can't keep lying to him. It's not fair to him, and I'm getting a stomach ulcer from the stress and the guilt."

"Question. If you could tell him the truth—"

"I refuse to throw you under the bus."

"Let me finish. Take me out of the equation. If you could tell him the truth, do you think there could be a real future with this guy?"

"If he forgave me ... possibly?"

Benny sighs. "Let me put this in more simple terms. If you had a chance at a future with him, would you want to take it?"

"Not if it meant—"

"Your answer is obviously yes, so I'm going to fix something for you this time." Benny turns to walk away when I grab his arm.

"What are you doing?"

"Something I should've done last semester. No, something we both should have done years ago."

I'm too stunned to stop him.

That is until his boyfriend says, "Where's he going?"

Then, the thought of years and years' worth of consequences comes crashing down on me. "To ruin his life," I growl and chase after my brother.

I move so fast my hood falls off my head, but when I catch up to him, he's storming his way toward Jonah and Dr. Sinclair, who are watching one of their phones, and I assume they're waiting for a ride share.

Jonah looks up and sees Benny first. "Em ... no, wait, Ben." Then his gaze flicks to mine.

"If Emmett won't tell you the truth so he can protect me, then I'm going to do it for him."

"Don't," I say. "You're throwing your whole future away."

"I'll start over if I have to. Do college all over again."

"Benny ..."

He turns to me, gripping my shoulders. "It's the right thing to do."

"Start over?" Jonah asks.

I'm about to physically put my hand over Benny's mouth when he says, "I wasn't in your class. Emmett was. He did my math classes for me."

Jonah stumbles backward. "He *what?*"

"Jonah," I say. "I can explain."

His face is contorted in shock, and he shakes his head, blinking rapidly. "It was you. You were ... it was *you* in my class."

"So you did sleep with a student," Dr. Sinclair says to Jonah.

"I ..." Why are words not working?

"You cheated your way through my class by doing your brother's work for him? Why would you—" He slumps. "Because you're good at math." Jonah turns to Dr. Sinclair. "And you said your friend said Emmett was a top student, but he has undiagnosed dyslexia."

And here it is, the moment I've been dreading. The moment where it all implodes. His mind ticks over in real time, with each revelation written all over his face. From shock to anger to finally heartbreak.

He turns to Benny. "Let me guess, you're better at English. You've been swapping the whole time." Then, his normally warm brown eyes become cold as he pierces me with his harsh stare. "Was anything you said real?"

"Jonah, please." I'm begging now.

Jonah's shutting down on me, and there's nothing I can do to stop it.

"You know what normal kids with learning disorders do when they're struggling?" Benny asks. "They get help because their teachers can tell that they're having trouble. But when you have a twin ... it's easier to pass off the responsibility, especially when we could help each other. We didn't think we could get away with it forever, but we always found a way."

"How long has this been going on? Since freshman year? Before then?"

I look down at my feet. "Since middle school. You have to understand. Our parents had died, and it was clear that Benny and I had different talents and lacked what the other had, so ... we decided to stick to what comes naturally to us."

"Swapping places comes naturally?" Jonah yells. "Wait, of course it does. You two lived in the same frat house for six months pretending to be the one person, and no one picked up on it. How have you never been caught?"

Benny and I look at each other.

"People are dumb?" Benny snarks.

"No." The disdain in his voice kills me. "You two are sociopaths who are good at their craft."

Benny lunges for Jonah, but I hold him back. He's already screwed his life up enough as it is by even telling Jonah anything; adding an assault charge to the list of shit we need to own up to is the last thing we need.

Jonah backs away from us. "You were right, Emmett. This is something I would never be able to get past, and now I have all the answers I needed. This thing is over."

And just like that, my heart shatters.

"Fuck you," Benny hisses and tries to break free of me. He's almost successful, too, because suddenly, holding on to him is too difficult. Harrison grabs his other side though.

"You know nothing about what Emmett has been through." Benny's still yelling. "Fucking nothing. You have no idea how much this has been eating at him, but he has stayed loyal to me because that's the type of guy he is. He should be choosing you, but you won't let him. If you can't see that he's a decent person under the blanket of our mistakes, then you don't fucking deserve him."

"Bennett," I yell. I never use his full name. Ever. It's what makes him stop.

"You know what I don't deserve?" Jonah asks, eerily calm. "To be put in the position of having to choose between reporting this or keeping my mouth shut. You've both put my career on the line."

I glare at Benny because he had to have known this is where this was heading, right? All his hypotheticals inside about wanting a future with Jonah don't fucking matter when there is no way to work through this all.

Dr. Sinclair grips Jonah's forearm. "Hold on before you go running to the dean about this."

Jonah turns his head toward his colleague, his eyes wide. "What? Out of everyone, I thought you, Mr. Stickler For the Rules, would be the first to run to Dean Kirwin."

"I'm not saying what they did was right, but I am saying they have a right to explain themselves completely first."

"I don't owe either of them anything." A car pulls up to the curb right where they're standing, and after Jonah checks his phone against the license plate, he climbs into the back seat.

Dr. Sinclair looks at us, his mouth open like he wants to say something, but eventually, he, too, slips inside the car, and they drive away.

My legs buckle, and I almost fall, but Benny's there to hold me up.

He's always there for me like I am for him.

The water in my eyes refuses to go away no matter how hard I blink, and then Benny and I are standing there, on the street, holding each other.

"So ..." he eventually says. "That didn't go to plan."

I pull back. "What was your plan? Do you really think you could've told him that you have cheated your way to your degree, even your high school diploma, and he'd be like, 'Oh, your secret is that you've made a mockery of my whole career? Thank you so much, now I can be with your brother who tricked me into thinking he was you for months.' You really think that?"

"Well, no, but I figured he'd be angry at me, not you. I'm the one who cheated in his class."

"But I'm the one who actually took his class. This is why I knew I shouldn't act on any attraction I had to the guy in the first place. Because it would never work out, and now you've gone and screwed up everything for yourself. What are West and Asher going to say when they find out we've both been kicked out of college and have no plans for the future?"

"I was serious," Benny says. "I want to start over. I'll do my whole schooling again if I have to."

"If any college will have you after a cheating scandal."

He smiles. "Daddy Jasper will accept me. He's head of the math department."

I wipe my nose with my sleeve. "You'd go back to Vermont?"

"It's not my first choice, but I do know it would be yours. I could get the schooling help I need. You'd be able to play hockey, coach hockey, do whatever you want."

"What about Harrison?" I glance over Benny's shoulder, where his boyfriend is standing, watching this all unfold.

Harrison's hands are in his pockets, and he's avoiding eye contact with me. "Benny and I have already spoken about it, and if he moves, I move."

"You're leaving?" Felix shrieks.

"Not definitely. We don't know. My plan was to finish my master's first, but maybe that timeline has been bumped up due to a certain someone not thinking his actions through."

"You'll get used to that with Benny," I say, and my brother punches my arm. "Why you punching me? You know it's true."

"That doesn't mean you have to say it out loud."

The tension crackling in the air is broken with some laughter.

"Well, that was a fun shitshow," Felix says. "How about we go back inside and drink all those emotional booboos away?"

Earlier tonight, I had no desire to go out drinking. Now? I'm hoping drinking my weight in alcohol will make me forget everything that happened today.

jonah

EVEN THOUGH SILAS tells me not to do anything rash tonight, I can't help pacing my apartment when I get home. My phone is in my hand, email open and addressed to the dean, but as I try to contemplate where to even start, I have no clue.

Identity swapping, cheating, me being the one too oblivious to see the guy I'm fucking is playing me for a fool.

Did he purposefully try to make me fall for him so I could be guilted into not reporting him and his brother?

On a scale of one to murder, cheating in college is nowhere near as bad. But cheating in my class and then dating me?

Memories of Emmett and Harrison sitting in my class—always together—fill my mind, and whether they have warped since finding out the truth or are even clearer, I don't know, but I can picture with perfect clarity Emmett's eyes on mine. His small, bashful smile. Back then, I would've assumed it was because he was sitting next to his boyfriend, who was hovering over him and probably murmuring sweet nothings in his ear, but thinking about it deeper, it was always Harrison who was close to Emmett. Not the other way around. Harrison would read Emmett's work, but I don't recall any touching or affection. I must've seen Harrison and Benny on campus and assumed the couple thing in class.

Unless there's an even sicker layer to their swapfuckery and they like to share partners.

I shudder. The thought of sleeping with Benny, thinking he was Emmett ...

A few days ago, I would've said it wasn't possible. Now, I don't know what the fuck is happening.

In every relationship, there's a moment where you realize your partner isn't as perfect as you thought they were. Sometimes it can take years to discover it. With Emmett, it was all over before it truly began.

Luckily too, because while my feelings for Emmett are strong, it's not like we were in love. A few dates and sleeping together on the regular are easy to get over.

At least that's what I'm trying to tell myself to stop me from sending an impulsive email that will ruin lives. Real lives. Hell, even my reputation and job could be put on the line because I didn't know cheating was going on right under my nose.

That doesn't stop the angry urge to email the dean and tell her exactly what they did, but I have to ask myself something. Do I want to email because it's the right thing to do or because I'm so mad at them I want them to hurt like they've hurt me?

Silas was right. I need a clear head when I bring this forward. Doing this fueled by emotion will make everything worse. For the twins and me.

I close out the email draft, but as I do, an email from a student address comes through. It's Benny's address.

Dear Proffesor Brooks,

U might not rememebr me being in ur class as me, but I will always remeember. I sat there every day, Enamurd Enamired? Why isn't spell check helping meeeee.

You captivated me

You were the best math proffessor I'd had at both Franklin and San Diego.

I never thought Id meet u outside of class or that I'd so quickly become obsessed with hanging out with u.

I new we couldn't be together, but I couldn't stay away. For that I'm 100% sorry.

I shouldn't have dragged u into my mess. If I could take it all back, I would. Maybe. Ok, maybee I wouldnt. Know Y? Because you were the britest thing in my life for the last six months.

I was spirilling. U grounded me. NOw I'm back to spirilling and I hate myself 4 hurting U.

Twincerely yours

Em.

PS. I'm drunk. Everyone said not to send this, but I wanted to get it off my chest.

I can't tell if the email has made me angrier or sadder. The misspellings are atrocious, and sure, it might be from being drunk, but it might also have to do with him suspecting he has dyslexia. If he can't spell simple words, forgets punctuation and simple sentence structure, there's no way he would be a "top student" at San Diego. Even though they already said as much, this is visual proof of what Benny and Emmett did.

From the outside, it would seem impossible. How did they do exams in school? How'd they get through the SATs?

And when I think about the effort they must have gone to just to get away with it all, I have to ask why they didn't come forward sooner.

Ben's words come back to me. They started doing it after their parents died.

I haven't met West or any of their older siblings, and I

understand it would've been a difficult time, but to keep it going?

The schools, me, everyone else affected were all collateral in their self-sabotage because they really are the two who have suffered most from their actions.

I want to hate them, I really do, but I'm not sure I can. If anything, I feel sorry for them.

I'm angry at what they did and can't help thinking of myself as just another target for them to play their mind games on. But I also know, in the big scheme of things, this isn't about me.

It's about two little boys who had their parents die before they hit puberty, could see their older brothers struggling to keep everyone together, and instead of asking for help, they turned to each other.

I try to imagine Em and Ben at nine years old, going through a time of grief, feeling the pressure of doing badly in school—hell, not even understanding school. I can see how they fell into using each other as a crutch and how they became so code-pendent.

But I can't see how they could bring themselves to continue to do it for so long. Where was their conscience? Where was the guilt? From where I'm standing, I can't even say they were remorseful for it.

The way they spoke about it, it was as if Benny was telling me about facts on a fact sheet. And I don't believe for a second that Emmett is truly sorry.

He was willing to choose keeping his secret over losing me. Well, he chose. And I seem to be the only one hurting.

emmett

"EVERYTHING HURTS, AND I'M DYING," I complain. My mouth is dry, I feel like I've been hit by a truck, and … why is my side aching? And what the hell is that fuzz I'm lying on?

Snickers from somewhere ring in my ears, but when I lift my head and the room comes into focus, I realize I'm in the living room, face down on the carpet instead of in my bed.

"Wha—"

"Morning, sunshine," my brother sings. He's on the couch, his feet right next to me.

"Did … did you step over me to sit there?"

"In my defense, we put you on the couch last night. You're the dumbass who rolled off it."

I manage to flip onto my back, but shooting pain stabs me in my ribs. "What happened?"

"You got delightfully shitfaced." Benny grins.

"That's obvious. I meant with my ribs."

"Oh, you were certain you could jump one of those light posts things that line the sidewalk along the beach. Spoiler alert: you couldn't. You ran right into that thing." He laughs again.

"You're the worst brother ever."

"Hey, I'm the one suffering from your hangover. You get no sympathy." He rubs his head.

"You were drinking too!"

"Not as much as you."

"I still can't believe you two share hangovers and other side effects." Harrison appears above me. "Do you want ice for your ribs?"

"Are they broken?"

"Felix checked you over. He thinks they're just bruised."

"Is Felix qualified to do that?"

Harrison shrugs. "He's becoming a vet. It's in the medical field."

"Well, it's comforting to know if I were a dog, I'd be in good hands."

"Want me to take you to the hospital?"

"Nope. Don't need that kind of paper trail for my dumb-assery. We're still on West's insurance. I'm fine." And as if trying to convince even myself, I try to sit up. I wince in pain and want to scream out, but I don't. Because I don't want them to think it's as bad as it is.

"About West ..." Benny bites his lip.

"No. We're not telling him anything."

"I don't think we're going to have a choice soon. Wouldn't it be better to tell West and Asher that you're no longer in school and I'm about to be kicked out before they find out on their own?"

"I'm thinking it might be better to move to Mexico, get new identities, and never have to face them."

"Emmett ..."

Ugh. "I guess it's time. I didn't want to tell them until I had a plan, and then I didn't want to tell them because of Jonah, but I guess that's all gone to shit now."

"Do you have a plan?" Benny asks.

"Hockey. That's as far as I've gotten."

"Great plan," Benny deadpans.

"It won't be much of a shock to West. He knows I've been coaching."

Benny shifts. "He does? Since when?"

"He was asking questions about why I was so hard to get ahold of. I had to tell him something other than 'I've been avoiding you for months because I don't want to disappoint you by telling you what's really going on.' He's offered for me to transfer to CU and play for him. He thinks I could recondition and try to get a spot in the AHL or NHL if Asher could pull some strings, but I don't want to get my hopes up. I've been out of the game for three years. That's almost the length of an actual hockey career for some. It's probably impossible to bounce back from that."

I have to give Ben credit—even though I know he's hurt that I told West before him, he swallows it down.

"We were huge names in the hockey world once upon a time. If nothing else, a team might give you a chance for the publicity. Maybe Buffalo."

I shake my head. "That would scream nepotism, and I'd want to earn my spot on my talent over my name."

"Then yeah, that might not be a solid plan."

"What are you going to tell them?" I ask.

"The truth. Like you, I want my degree because I earn it. I'd only need a passing grade for all my math classes."

"So … how do we do this? Are you calling, or am I?" My ass starts vibrating, so I reach into my back pocket—carefully because twisting my torso hurts—and pull out my phone.

"Apparently, he's calling us." I show Benny West's name on my screen.

We both stare at it, slack-jawed.

"Hey, maybe your older brother has that twin ESP thing too." Harrison might be joking, but that doesn't make the freak-out lessen.

"Answer it," Benny says.

I accept the call just as it cuts out. "Oh no. Missed it. We have more time to come up with a game plan of what we want to say." It starts ringing again. "Persistent fucker."

"Here, I'll do it." Benny snatches my phone from me and answers it on speaker before I can stop him. "Hey, big bro."

"Benny?" West asks hesitantly.

"Still can't get us straight after all these years."

"Definitely Benny. Em's with you?"

"Yup. We're just hanging out."

"Hi," I say. No, I squeak.

"Haven't you got classes?"

"Nah, not until this afternoon," Benny says.

"Both of you?" The accusation of skipping classes isn't new for him, but there's something more in his tone this time. It's probably paranoia, but I can't help thinking he *knows*.

But how much does he know? That I got kicked out? That Benny is screwed when it comes to his degree? Maybe Jonah went on an email rampage last night and everything is already in motion. The dean knows, called West, and Benny's paperwork is being drawn up as we speak.

We're so fucked.

"West?" I croak. "You need to come to California." That's all I get out before the panic takes over.

"Yeah, no shit," West says, sterner than I've probably ever heard him. "I'm already here."

Another voice joins him. "So am I, dipshits."

Benny and I snap our attention to each other, our eyes wide.

"A-Asher?" Benny says. "You're in California?"

"Don't you have a game?" I ask.

"Yes, but because you're morons, I'm here," Asher says.

"Asher," West scolds. Ah, they're going to play good cop, bad cop. Fun.

"You're allowed to ask for time off from the NHL?" I ask, deflecting.

"Not ... technically, but I told Coach I had dumbass little brothers and needed to deal with something, so he did me a favor and put me down as a healthy scratch. The press is going to have a field day with that."

"So, where are you?" West asks.

"We're at my apartment," I say.

"Real helpful," Asher says sarcastically. "Considering we thought you were still in the dorms at State, we have no idea where that is."

"Maybe we don't want to tell you until you stop being angry at us," Benny says.

"We're not angry at you." West sounds genuine, but is he?

"I am," Asher says. "At both of you."

West's voice becomes muffled, but he does a shit job of trying to hide what he's saying. "Dude, we're trying to get them to tell us where they are. Stop antagonizing them."

"You know that Benny is in on it," Asher whispers back.

Yeah, can still hear you guys.

I glance up at Benny and mouth, "What do we do?"

"Here's the deal," Benny says. "We'll tell you where we are if you promise not to yell at us until we explain everything."

Our older brothers are silent for a beat.

"I can't wait to find out how you explain a dorm fire and getting kicked out of school and keeping it a secret for an entire semester. Give us the address."

And even after that, Benny still gives them the address. Probably because they didn't mention anything about our cheating scandal.

Then, as they end the call, Benny grips my shoulder. "It was really nice being your twin. I'll miss you when they kill you."

"That implies they're not going to kill you too. Especially once we come clean about *everything*."

"About that …"

I point at him. "No. You can't get out of this. If I'm going down, you're going down with me."

Of course, as I say that, Felix makes an appearance, running his hand through his wild curls and talking through a yawn. "That sounds like some hot twin porn stuff."

"We should really ease them into this," Benny says. "One chaos twin drama at a time, and they obviously already know about you. They can stay in the dark about me."

"I have a question," Felix says. "Are your big brothers really that scary? They're not actually going to hurt you, right?"

"Of course not," I say. "But …"

"We don't want to disappoint them," Benny says. "West gave up his NHL career for us, and we always felt like we had to do well at everything so it would be worth him doing that."

"Ah. I can understand not wanting to disappoint parents."

I stand. The pain in my ribs has somewhat subsided. Maybe I rolled on my side before I woke up and aggravated it. It still hurts, but it's not a sharp stabbing pain when I move now, only a dull ache.

"They're on their way. I'm going to go shower and try to get all this hangover off me."

I walk away to Harrison's voice, but he's not talking to me. "I don't think your brother knows how hangovers work."

Maybe not, but at least in the shower, the water will cover my tears.

I want to take it all back. If time traveling was a thing, I'd go all the way back to middle school and slap past me upside the head. Then maybe bang Benny's and my heads together and tell them to speak up. To ask for help. To turn to people who can actually help instead of each other.

It sounds like the beginning of a joke: What do you get when two dumbasses are dumb? A whole fucking mess.

Oh, wait. Jokes are supposed to be funny.

To give them credit, both West and Asher let us get the whole story out before they react, just like they promised. I only worry that it isn't on purpose, and now they're in some joint catatonic state.

We didn't hold back. We told them *everything*.

My roommates made themselves scarce when West and Asher arrived, even Harrison. Though I assume Harrison is close by for when Ben needs him afterward. Benny didn't want Harrison to see our dysfunction. Like that didn't already happen when we went home for Christmas break. On the other hand, that was regular dysfunction, not life-altering drama like this. I also spent most of that trip coming up with excuses and distractions from all the questions about school.

"This is all my fault," West mutters and leans forward on the couch, his forearms resting over his legs.

"Wait, what?" I frown.

"I should've done better. I should've known you were struggling. I should've—"

"As much as I would love to blame you for it all," Asher says, "this is the fault of our circumstance."

"When did you get all insightful?" Benny snarks.

"I don't know. Maybe when you were cheating your way through life?" Asher snarks back.

Those two are so much alike. Fight snark with snark.

"Asher's right though," I say. "It was a mistake we never

should've started because once we'd gotten away with it, we realized it was easier to keep it going than deal with it. We were already dealing with so much."

"I don't understand why you didn't ask for help," West says. "Well, I do understand. We were all going through so much back then, and—"

"And you were coming to terms with being a guardian of kids who you barely had anything to do with," Asher adds.

"On top of losing our parents," Benny chimes in.

I hate that it's all come down to this. "We knew you were struggling with us from the beginning. You couldn't tell us apart, and you were always so frazzled, and Asher was chasing after Rhys half the time, who kept sneaking out with his girlfriend."

Benny hangs his head. "I went to Rhys for help with my math, but even the math genius couldn't help me."

"We took the easy way out, and it might have taken us a long time to learn our lesson, but once we'd been doing it for most of high school, we realized we were both too far behind to own up to it. And then with the SATs, we knew there was no way we'd get high enough scores to get into college without cheating. It was something that got away from us, and if Harrison hadn't found out about it, I have no doubts we'd still be doing it."

Asher runs his hand through his hair. "Okay, that's one clusterfuck we need to work out. What about the other one? The fire. Why did you take the blame for your roommate? If you hated college so much, you could've told us and dropped out. I'd never planned to go to college, you know that, so why—"

"Again, it was the easy way out. I saw an opportunity, and I took it. I didn't want to tell you and disappoint you until I had a plan, but then I met Jonah, and coming up with a plan was put on the back burner."

"He's skirting the real issue," Benny says. "Yes, he hated

classes and the whole college experience, but I half think he hated it because he never truly believed he deserved it. If we had gotten here on our own—"

I cut him off. "You're wrong."

He cocks his eyebrow at me. "Am I?"

"Mostly. You're right that I think I don't deserve to get a degree, but I also don't want one. At least, not in engineering."

"What do you want to do?" Asher asks.

"Anything hockey related. Coaching. Playing. Anything. All I know is three years was way too long to go without it."

"You could come home and go to CU to get a teaching degree with a coaching-specific certificate and play for us in the meantime," West suggests. For, like, the fifth time since I told him about my coaching job.

"Screw that," Asher says. "I'll talk to Buffalo. As soon as you're back in good shape, you're signed."

"And to get back in good shape, you could play D1 college hockey," West says.

I glance at Benny, who's already staring at me. "If you finish your degree in Vermont, West can bribe Jasper with sex so he can teach you math."

"Jas is going to be so pissed when I tell him," West says. "The kid he helped raise since ten years old cheated in math. He's the head of the math department, for fuck's sake."

"Hey, yeah," Benny says. "How come he didn't notice us switching?"

"Too busy making sure West was okay while West was trying to make sure you were all okay," Asher says. "With five kids to make sure they're not drowning in grief, it was easy to miss it. Plus, you two were pro con artists from birth. You even used to pull that switching shit on Dad."

True.

"But that's all in the past now," Asher continues. "So that's behind us, and what we need to focus on are steps to work toward a goal. Is the goal going to be moving back home to finish off degrees and train to get back in your best physical shape?"

"I was kind of hoping I could stay and do most of my degree here and pick up the math subjects back home," Benny says.

"If you don't get expelled first when Jonah goes to the dean," I point out.

"You think he will?" West asks.

"I dunno. He's really pissed at us, and I don't see why he wouldn't. Another professor was there when it all came out too, so if Jonah doesn't, Dr. Sinclair probably will."

"Okay," Asher says, a concentration line forming on his forehead. "Where can I find Jonah and this other professor?"

"Why?"

"Because I'm gonna go talk to him."

"Talk or threaten?" Benny asks.

"Talk. If the cheating news is going to get to the dean, there's no way Benny could finish his degree here, and we'll know what our next step is—moving you both back home where West and Jasper will be able to keep an eye on you so you don't fuck everything up again."

Even though West is the oldest, Asher has always been better at problem-solving. West gets flustered way too easily and overwhelmed. Asher has so much chaos inside him that he thrives under pressure because it's just another day for him.

Where Benny takes after Asher, I take after both of them. I'm chaotic and flustered.

Well, didn't I win the genetic lottery?

jonah

IT'S BEEN a whole night of no sleep, of tossing and turning and not knowing what to do. If I found out that any other student was cheating, it would be a no-brainer. I would've emailed the dean last night. I would be sending mass emails to every single class I have, letting everyone know that I have a no-cheating policy, but I can't exactly email them today saying, "Unless it's my boyfriend, I don't allow cheating." And then everyone would laugh because they'd assume I was talking about my personal life and not actual grades. After the "I'm taking dick leave" email, I'd never live that down.

There has to be a reason I'm not running to put any academic consequence in motion, and that reason won't be short of being a massive double standard. As angry as I am at both Emmett and Ben, there's that part of me that acknowledges if I rat him out, there's no way we'd be able to put it behind us and find a way to move past it all. Which also tells me that even though Emmett and his brother are both walking red flags, I still want to be with Em.

I'm glad I only have one midmorning class to get through today. Friday is a light load for me, other than office hours in the afternoon, but I can cancel those and tell anyone to email me if they need something urgently. Which, of course, will mean I'll have students emailing me to ask what time class starts next week when it's the same time every damn week or asking if when they take off for spring break early, they'll be penalized. Their dog died, their grandma is sick, all of the excuses under the sun. But I'm okay with that if it means I don't have to be on campus any longer than a few hours.

Grudgingly, I shower to try to wake myself up, gather my stuff, and head for the door. The temptation to cancel class is strong, but because of Em, I've already done that a couple of times this semester.

I did it so willingly too. It's hard to tell if it's because I don't think I'm cut out to be a professor or if it's because Emmett Dalton has a magical dick and ass. Or maybe it's that from the moment I first saw him ... Then I remind myself of one indisputable fact.

I'd seen him before that day at the skating rink because he'd sat in my class twice a week for almost an entire semester, pretending to be someone else.

His awkwardness when I asked if we'd met before wasn't imagined like I'd thought. It's because we had. Because he was Ben. And Ben was my student.

Emmett always had this closed-off vibe to him. He was up-front from the beginning that he couldn't give me a future, and I can't believe that even after that, I still wanted it. Still wanted him.

I'm an idiot.

The guys who don't care about hurting your feelings don't tell you that you don't have a future. The ones with legitimate issues who are up-front about it are the ones you're most likely to fall for.

I've never been a "want what I can't have" kind of guy. Or at least, I didn't think I was. This proves otherwise.

Just before I leave, my phone goes off, and I pull it out of my pocket to see it's a text from Emmett.

> I'm so so so so sorry 4 evrything that's bout 2 happen.

I blink at it for a moment, trying to figure out if he means with the dean or something else. If they go to the dean first and come clean, then she will assume I was hiding this for them. If it weren't for that rumor about me sleeping with Ben and we didn't have to go in and explain it to her, I might have more plausible deniability. I'd have none if they get to her first.

All right. New plan. I'm going to stop by the dean's office and tell her everything before I go to class. I'm on a time crunch though. I'll have to skip the coffee I was planning to have to keep me awake, but this is more important.

I barely make it out my door when I'm stopped by two men, one who's as tall as me but is muscular and the other who is taller and leaner but still has more muscles than me. Not that it's hard. Both have dark hair and bright green eyes. They're vaguely familiar, and as soon as I think that, I remember where I'd seen them before. On Emmett's phone and in the articles online I looked up when I first found out that Emmett was hockey royalty.

"Are you Jonah Brooks?" West asks.

I'm trying not to be intimidated, but it's not because they're two NHL legends. It's because these guys are Emmett's brothers.

"I am. And you're Westly and Asher Dalton." I pocket my keys.

Asher screws up his face and turns to West. "Does he have to say it like that, where it sounds like we're husbands instead of brothers?"

Talking as if I'm not even here? That makes this easier. "As much as I'd love to stay and chat to you about how your brothers screwed me over, I have a class to get to."

They're not the Daltons I wanted to see today. Then again, I don't really want to see Emmett either. Mainly because I know if I look into his eye, I won't be able to remain strong.

Asher steps in front of me like a bouncer at a club who's refusing entry.

"Please hear us out," West says softly.

"What is this? A bad cop, good cop routine?" I snark.

Asher gazes over his shoulder at West. "He really has been hanging out with the twins." Then his green eyes pierce through me. "They say we play that game all the time, but I don't see it. I'm a kitten."

"A murder kitten," West mumbles.

"You know, I don't appreciate being cornered in my place of residence by the parents of my students, and I don't see how this is any different."

"Do we really need to spell it out for you?" Asher asks. "I thought professors were supposed to be smart?"

"Just because I slept with Emmett, that doesn't change what he and Ben did."

West steps closer. "We know. We have no excuses for them, and we're not here to ask you to look the other way. We want to explain their situation and hope that, one, you can let us deal with informing the school, and two, that you ask your professor friend to do the same."

"If the school found out that I knew cheating was going on in one of my classes and I didn't do anything about it, I'd lose my job and the chance to teach anywhere else in this country."

"The boys are going to tell the school today, with us by their side. We'll also say that you just found out and said if they don't come forward, you were going to. They know what they did was wrong, and they're going to fix it as best they can."

"How do you propose they fix something like this? No college will touch Ben."

When West runs his hand through his hair and looks away, it becomes clear.

"You're going to use your position at CU to get Ben a spot," I say.

"Ben will lose all his math-related credits, and he'll redo them in Vermont."

Redo? Like it will be that easy? "You do know he has dyscalculia, don't you? Do you know what that means?"

"That it'll be difficult, sure, but my husband is the head of the math department, so if anyone can teach him, it's him."

I try not to be offended because I could've taught Ben had he been honest.

Beside me, Asher snorts. "I still can't believe Jasper never picked up on it."

"He's going to hate himself." West sounds genuinely upset.

I find myself now wanting to reassure him. What is it with these two? They make me annoyed while simultaneously wanting to join their side. "In your husband's defense, the twins said they've been switching places since middle school."

"We know," West says. "They told us. And while it's one thing for their teachers or classmates not to notice, it's very different to living with them for years and not realizing something is up."

Asher groans. "Ugh. I hate to be the nice one here, but the only two people to blame for this are Ben and Em. They made a mistake and dug themselves a hole that was impossible to climb out of, and instead of asking for help, they thought they could dig through it. It might be too late to ask for forgiveness, but it's not too late for them to turn it around."

I smile at seeing Asher's soft side, something Emmett says only happens when it comes to his partner or his younger siblings, and it's obvious that while he's absolutely pissed at the twins, he also loves them.

"I won't go to the dean until you have."

West lets out a loud breath. "Thank you. You have no idea how much we appreciate it." Then, he pauses. "And you'll—"

"I'll also tell Dr. Sinclair to do the same, but I can't promise he hasn't already done it. I was on my way to do it now, and my class starts late. Speaking of which, my classroom is filling up."

"Thank you. Uh, again," West says. "We're going to go get the boys to come up with a written statement to give the dean this afternoon. We promise they'll be out of your hair by tomorrow."

I give them a curt nod and head for my lecture hall at a quick pace, making it just in time. And as I go to turn the lock to keep anyone who is late out, I take a breath and think about who I am and what I'm doing with my life. Not for the first time, I think about the asshole professors I had who also locked late students out of the room so the lecture is not interrupted. They were all pompous sticklers for the rules, and I've just proven that's not me.

My teaching technique of getting students to go through the work and come to me with any questions because that's how I liked to learn is an inefficient one. If they're someone like Benny, who has trouble with the material but is embarrassed to say so, they're not going to come to me.

Maybe I don't like my job as a professor because I'm forcing this strict persona that's not me. Maybe if I can be myself in the classes I teach, I'll enjoy it more.

So instead of locking the doors, and instead of going over to my desk while I make the class go through the coursework I set for them, I dump my bag and move to the center of the room.

"I'm going to do things differently today. Please raise your hand if you've worked through all the formulas I've set out each lecture."

Everyone raises their hand.

I grin but try to hide it by casually rubbing my chin. "Now, how many of you, really? You will not be deducted grades or anything like that. I promise."

More than half put their hand down.

Yep. Thought so.

"How many of you here are still struggling to understand the formulas?"

A lot of hands go back up, while most of the people who have worked through them already drop their hands.

"All right, here's what I'm going to do. I'm assuming the ones who haven't completed the formulas got to a certain point and then stopped altogether, so I'm going to go through each formula, from the bottom of the list to the top. Those of you who have a firm grasp on the concept, I'll ..." I walk over to my desk, where there's an old-as-fuck printer, and turn it on for it to warm up and calculate what it's supposed to do in life. "I'll print off the next set of formulas for you, and then you can get ahead. For everyone else, I'll explain everything as I'm going through it all, but if at any time you get stuck, raise your hand, and I'll go over that part again."

I get everything going while my students all glance around the room like they've walked into an alternate universe, but I'm already feeling better about the small improvements I've made to my teaching style.

When the class ends, it's the first time since I became a professor that I feel like I've actually helped students understand statistics better, which puts me in a good mood. No, a great mood. Until I realize there's only one person I want to share this moment with, and I can't. West and Asher said Ben and Emmett will be out of my hair by tomorrow, and reality is just setting in now.

If Ben is going to CU, then Emmett is moving home to

Vermont too. Where one twin goes, the other follows. It's as easy as that.

And if I don't want to say goodbye to Emmett, I have to do something about it.

I have to stop them.

emmett

BENNY LOOKS like he's about to pass out.

We both knew this day would come eventually, but Benny was hoping for it to be after he had completed all his other subjects. Now, he's looking at an actual transfer back home where he can do the next year and a bit full-time at CU instead of only redoing any math components. He might need longer than another year to get it all done, but at least he'll be in a supportive environment to do it.

Benny and I came to California to escape Vermont. To stand on our own two feet. Well, four feet if we're being technical. Yet, we didn't consider what leaving our family, our support, would do to us.

We wanted to get away from being the Dalton Duo, somewhere where we could continue to dupe our teachers and earn easy degrees and where life would be "easy."

I think this goes to show that it's not the learning disorders holding us back; it's our stupidity.

Just like Asher keeps telling us.

"Moron one, you're up." He grips Ben's shoulder and pushes him toward the doors of the administration building.

"I really wish there was another way," I say to West, who's standing with me as we watch Ben walk to his doom.

"Have you thought about getting tested for dyslexia yet?"

"Do I really need to if I'm going to play hockey?"

"I guess not." He shakes his head. "I'm so disappointed that you didn't come to Jasper and me. Like I said, I understand why you didn't, but fuck ..."

"I know you're disappointed in us—"

"Not in you. I'm pissed as hell at you, but I'm disappointed in myself. And Jasper. Not that I'd ever tell him that because he's going to feel as guilty as I already do, and I won't do that to him. If only we could've had our heads out of our asses long enough to have seen the signs."

I turn to him. "I don't know of any teenagers who'd be happy to tell their parents they think there's something different with them. That they're not like everyone else in their family. You and Asher with your NHL careers, Zoe with her artistic talent, Rhys, the literal math prodigy, Hazel with her hockey skills that have taken her all the way to the PWHL. We had impossible standards to live up to, and the pressure became too much. That's why we wanted to pave our own futures any way we could."

"I don't think you and Benny understand that you both had more hockey talent than Asher and me combined."

"That might be true, but the potential of not living up to that talent was paralyzingly terrifying. And that wasn't any of your faults. It just means that in a family full of overachievers, it was doubly hard to come forward. I know this isn't going to help ease the guilt, but it needs to be said, and I'll say it every day if I have to: this is not your or Jasper's fault. If you need me to call him later and say that, I will."

"I think it'll take more than that for either of us to accept that to be true."

I need to prove to him how it would've been impossible for

either of them to know any different. "West, Benny and I are masterminds when it comes to switching personalities and mannerisms." I put on my Benny smirk and add his infliction to my words.

West studies my face and my body and then slowly narrows his eyes. "Are you ... Show me your hand."

I laugh and show him my scar. "See? If we can still fool you, of course we're going to be able to get away with it with everyone else. Honestly, if Benny hadn't met Harrison, we would've continued to do it. He would get his degree on time, start working for a news outlet or online magazine, and we would've kept it a secret forever."

"Do you really think you could've done that?"

In reality? Probably not. I was reaching my end point. I wanted everything to stop being so complicated. Only now, I'm thinking we've made it even worse. We're on the right side of morals this time though.

We're growing.

"No. Come to think of it, I was about ready to snap. I don't think I could've done another year pretending to be Ben."

Asher and Ben have only disappeared through the doors for about a second when Jonah rounds the side of the building, running like he's being chased by a demon.

West and I stare at each other wide-eyed, having a silent "What the fuck?" moment.

Then, as if simultaneously agreeing we can't let Jonah in there until Ben has explained himself to the dean, we take off running toward the doors too.

It's an all-out race to see who can get there first, but as Jonah reaches the steps leading to the entrance, he sees me.

He stops running. "You haven't gone in yet?" He pulls back. "Wait. You're not Ben." To be sure, he looks down at my arm, where my tattoo is peeking out of the bottom of my shirtsleeve.

"Why are you here, Jonah?" I ask. "We told you we were going to come clean."

For a moment, I'm hurt he doesn't believe that, but then West says, "To be fair, your word isn't the most trustworthy to him, rightfully so."

I'll give him that.

"Where's Ben?" Jonah asks with panic in his tone.

I point to the doors. "Doing the right thing."

"Fuck." He takes off running again.

We watch him disappear behind the doors. "Any idea what that's about?" West asks.

"Nope, but we need to find out." We chase after him.

Only a few steps inside the administration building, we find them. Both Jonah and Benny are hunched over, breathing heavily.

"What happened?" I ask. "Who hit who?"

Asher, who's leaning against the wall and rubbing Benny's back, covers a laugh. "Your professor boyfriend can't catch his breath from running, and this guy is having a panic attack."

There wasn't a fight? That's good, but Benny's anxiety claws at my throat, threatening to make me follow him over the edge from panic to full-blown meltdown. I don't let it.

I sink to my knees in front of my brother. "Benny, look at me."

His eyes are glassy as his gaze meets mine.

"We've got this." I hate seeing him this way, and I hate that my first thought is to go in there as him and do it for him. That's what got us into this in the first place—our fierce need to protect one another. "I can't go in there for you, but if you need me to, I'll go in there *with* you."

Ben takes a deep breath.

When we both stand upright again, Jonah's there, watching us, seeming to have caught his breath now.

"You don't have to do this," he says.

"Don't have to do what?" I ask, because if he's saying I don't have to go in with Benny, then he's still not understanding us at all.

"You don't have to go through with this. I had an idea."

Benny's still coming down from his panic attack, but it's like he stops breathing completely at the glimmer of hope Jonah's giving us.

"Hear me out."

I tell myself not to get ahead of myself, but I think I'm already there.

ALL FIVE OF us walk to the nearby Bean Necessities cafe— the actual sit-down establishment that provides the campus with the coffee carts—and I order coffee for everyone except Benny, for who I order a kid's hot cocoa with extra marshmallows in a passive-aggressive way of calling him a child. Still mad? Me? Little bit.

In my defense, I would have ordered him coffee, but he doesn't drink it.

It's possible I'm bribing the other Dalton men and buttering them up so they like me.

I can't let Emmett walk out of my life that easily, and if I have to swallow my pride, some of my morals, and forget about the school's policy on cheating, then I'll do it.

Before I can tap my card to pay, a tall presence appears behind me.

"I've got this," West says, beating me to the machine with his card. When I turn to him, he shrugs. "If you really have come up with a way to save my brothers' asses, it's the least I can do."

"That's if they'll even go for it. For all I know, they hate me for being quick to judge."

We move to the side to wait for my name to be called.

"If anyone has the right to hate anyone here, it's you. You should hate the twins. Hell, I hate them a little bit." He gasps like he wasn't supposed to say that and glances back to where the others found a table to sit at. "Don't tell them I said that."

One side of my mouth hitches into a small smile. "I think it's pretty universal for parents to hate their kids at some stage of their lives, but I don't hate them. I'm angry and disappointed, but there's no hate there."

"How is that even possible?" West asks.

I lick my lips to delay the vulnerability that's about to come out of my mouth. "I won't pretend I know what it's like to be a twin, but I am close with my sister, and I will do anything to protect her. Okay, maybe I wouldn't do her homework for her, but I understand that need." When she got pregnant with Cullen, I defended her to our parents. When Cullen's dad left her, I was ready to kill him.

Our order is called, and West helps me carry the cups over to the table. When I hand Benny his cocoa with a side of a million little marshmallows, my passive-aggressive message is lost on him.

Should've known better than to try being snarky by giving candy.

When I turn to Emmett next and hand him his, his fingers brush against mine, and I want to intertwine our hands and never let go.

Asher breaks the spell. "So what's this plan, and how is it supposed to help Benny?"

Straight to the point.

I take a sip of my coffee, which is scalding hot, but I refuse to do the open-mouth panting thing in front of people I want respect from. So instead, I force my mouth to remain closed and then start coughing like I smoked ten cigarettes at once.

All four Daltons are staring at me, so I pound on my chest even though the pain is in my mouth and croak, "Wrong pipe."

"You don't really have a plan, do you?" Asher accuses. "Is this just a distraction so your professor friend can get to the dean before Benny, and then he'll have no recourse for what's next?"

I cough some more. "I have a plan. I promise." It will risk everything I have—my position at Franklin, my entire future as a professor—but I'm starting to think losing all of that would be worth it if I got to be with Emmett. I just hope I'm right about him. About us.

That what we have is something really special. Something to fight for.

And when I see the same hope reflected in Emmett's eyes, I know I have to fight for the chance to find out if I'm right.

"I want to tutor Ben," I say.

"I'm a bit past tutoring, aren't I? You heard me when I said even basic math is hard because I've never had to do it? I have trouble telling time on an analog clock."

"Wasn't this going to be your plan when you went home?" I counter. "To get West's husband to teach you? If I can do that, you can stay at Franklin."

"You're going to get me through your statistics class?" Ben asks. "Wouldn't that be similar to cheating?"

"Nope. Because I'm actually going to show you how to work it out in a way that makes sense to you. And also, if you think I'm only talking about statistics, you're wrong. I'm talking about going all the way back and starting simple. You may never be able to memorize multiplication or tell time, but I'm at least going to show you how to do it using tools at your disposal. It will be difficult, you're going to hate me for a lot of it, and if you get frustrated and want to quit, I'm only going to work you harder."

"Why would I agree to that?" Benny asks.

"Because it will give you the chance to graduate on time. At Franklin. And no one would have to know how you've gotten this far when you can't do middle-grade math."

Out of the corner of my eye, I see Emmett's mouth drop.

"You would cover it up?" he asks with a sexy rasp in his voice. "For us?"

"For you. All for you."

Everyone at the table goes silent for a beat, and the fear that I'm about to be embarrassed in front of half of Emmett's family has my heart racing, preparing for rejection.

But what comes out of his mouth is anything but embarrassing. "I think I just fell in love with you."

Whether he's joking, being serious, or means it in the light-hearted hyperbole way, I also don't care. Him saying anything in that realm is everything I want to hear. No, need to hear. Especially if I'm going to do this.

"We really should've gotten the twins therapy when they were younger," West says.

"We all need therapy," Asher replies. "Even this guy." He grips my shoulder.

That's probably true. Here I am, putting everything I've worked for on the line for a man I've barely started seeing. Granted, I haven't been sure that the path I've chosen to become a professor was the right one, but that doesn't diminish how much of a risk I'm taking.

We all now turn our attention to Benny, who's staring at his marshmallows.

"You don't have to take my offer," I say. "But it's this or going to the dean."

"I don't think there's much of a choice there," Benny says

dryly and then winces. "Did you kick me under the table?" he asks Emmett.

"Why are you taking so long to say yes?" Emmett scolds.

"Because ..." His gaze flicks between me and Emmett. "What if you fuck up dating him, and then it will all be for shit anyway, and I'll have to go to the dean and get kicked out even closer to graduation."

"You think I wouldn't be fair if Emmett and I didn't work out?" I genuinely ask.

"Well, you're only giving me this chance because you're fucking him."

West covers his ears. "I'm not listening to this. La la la la la la la."

Asher laughs. He's probably the most confusing Dalton. He laughs at the wrong times, finds the serious stuff ridiculous, but might actually be the most levelheaded one of them all. Somehow. I wonder what it would be like to be his partner. Not in an I'm interested kind of way, but more from an anthropological kind of way. His partner either has to be completely fucked-up or so put together that he can handle the chaos that is Asher Dalton.

"You're wrong," I say to Benny. "I'm not doing this on the proviso your brother and I stay together or fall in love or whatever. I'm doing it because I want to see where Emmett and I can go. It's still relatively new, but if you get kicked out of school, I won't even have the chance to find out if there's more. You'll move home to Vermont, and where you go, he goes. I understand that, so I'm offering a way for both of you to stay."

"I so wish we could get out of here," Emmett murmurs to me.

"Jesus." West's hands fly to his ears again. "Still not listening."

Asher, out of nowhere, bursts out laughing. I don't mean

the snarky snorts or the derisive grunts he has been giving. This is full-on belly laughter.

"What's so funny?" I ask.

"I just realized something," he says, sounding like he's on the verge of tears.

"What?" West asks him.

"Well, at Christmas when we met Harrison, I kept noticing how he deals with Benny. How he supports him but is laid-back yet kind of bossy. No, bossy isn't the right word. Basically, I noticed similarities between him and the way Kole treats me. And Jonah ..." He laughs some more. "He's so ... he's so ..."

I'm hot under the collar, like he's about to make fun of me, but then he says the last thing I expect.

"Benny fell for Kole, and Emmett's falling for Jasper."

I'm so confused.

The twins are horrified.

And then West bursts into laughter too.

emmett

BENNY and I may look the same, even share similar tastes when it comes to music, movies, and all of that, but we are two completely different people. Because while I sit here, mortified at the thought of being attracted to Jonah because he somehow resembles my pseudo-father figure, Jasper, Benny doesn't seem to give a shit about the comparison made between Harrison and Kole.

Either that, or he's trying to get revenge on Asher for even suggesting it because as Benny stands, he turns to him and says, "On that note, I'm going to go home and fuck my Kole. Might even call out Kole's name. Picture him. Think of all the things I could do—"

Asher stands too now, so fast that his chair almost topples backward. "Do that and I'll—"

Benny runs away, using the small side entrance instead of the main one out the front and calling out, "Shouldn't have made the comparison."

Asher sits back down. "I'm sorry to be the one to have to tell you this, Emmett, but after today, you will no longer have a twin."

"He only did it to get a rise out of you," I say. "He has to be as disgusted as I am."

"Hey, what's wrong with falling for a Jasper?" West asks.

"How would you like it if I pointed out you practically married Dad?" Oh, dear God, Jonah is like my dad. And Jasper.

West screws up his face.

"See?" I point out. "How is it we both have daddy issues?"

Jonah reaches for my hand on top of the table. "I would assume becoming an orphan probably had something to do with it."

I pull my hand out from beneath his. "Yeah, I'm going to need you to not touch me for a while."

Jonah has the balls to chuckle at me. "Over before we even got a real chance."

"Oh, we are so not over, but yeah, I'm never having sex again. Hope you're okay with that."

"I'm okay with that," West says. "Then I don't have to picture you in all kinds of compromising positions when you're like my damn child. Just no. No."

All it takes is for West to acknowledge me as his child for me to let everything go. The thing is, Jonah and Jasper do have a lot of similarities, but that's not a bad thing. Jasper is an amazing husband to West. When West gets flustered or overwhelmed, Jasper is there to fix whatever problem he's having. If it's not a fixable problem, then Jasper is still by his side, being supportive.

Yeah, there are worse things that could happen than having my ... boyfriend-type person being compared to an amazing husband. It will just be difficult to push past imagining Jasper whenever Jonah touches me now.

I hate Asher.

"Are you two going to fly home now?" I ask West and Asher.

They look at each other.

"Part of me wishes one of us could stay so we could make

sure you and Benny are back on track, but I thought you were going to come home and try to get back into hockey and training with me? Has that changed now because of ...” West glances at Jonah.

That was my plan, and it should still be my plan. But as I take in Jonah, his nerdy-ish appearance, and the acknowledgment that he is willing to tutor Benny on the DL so I don’t have to leave, I can’t up and abandon him now.

Jonah cuts in. “I’d like to clarify that I offered to tutor Ben so you had the chance to stay, but you don’t have to take it. You can still choose to leave, and I’ll still tutor Benny.”

The thing is, if Benny’s not moving home, then I don’t want to either, and I also want to stay so I can see where this thing can go with Jonah. Eventually, I will want to move because I know this isn’t the place for me. This isn’t home. But Jonah could be. “I’ll get Fletcher to do some training with me at the rink. At least enough to get me physically ready for all the technical reconditioning you’ll have me do back in Vermont. Eventually.”

“Eventually,” Asher mumbles. “I’m not saying you’re making a mistake, but you know how fast the hockey industry moves. You and Benny were hot commodities three years ago. There’s only a small window of opportunity before hockey forgets you completely.”

No fucking pressure. “I know. But ...” I reach for Jonah’s hand this time and don’t get the heebie-jeebies over the Jasper comparison. “I had a choice three years ago between Benny and hockey, and I chose Benny. Here I am, with the same decision but with Jonah, and I’m realizing I do love hockey. I want to be a part of hockey. But that doesn’t mean it has to be in the NHL. Or AHL. Or even playing. I will work my ass off to try to get back to where I was, but I don’t need to make it in professional hockey. When it comes to priorities, it’s Benny”—I lift my hand above my head to show where Benny sits on the important list—

"hockey"—I move it down now—"Jonah"—a bit lower—"NHL."

Am I worried Jonah won't like being third on my list? Yes, but if he knows me at all—

"Really? I'm third?"

I hold my breath because I can't decipher his tone.

Then, he smiles. "That's awesome."

"It is?" all three of us reply at the same time.

"From the moment I found out that you and Benny were two different people, and watching you and him defend each other so forcefully, I knew that I would always come second to your brother. As for hockey, you're still figuring out what you want with life, and that's okay. Hockey should be your priority. I'm excited that I'm a factor at all. You're choosing what we have over pushing yourself to have a chance at the NHL. You're prioritizing me over being a famous hockey player." His eyes are soft. "No one ever has shown that kind of loyalty to me before. It really makes me accept that what I'm doing here, what I've offered ... I made the right choice too."

I can't hold back anymore, and I don't even care that we're in public, in front of my older brothers, or that I still can't get the Jasper comparison out of my head. I lean over and kiss the man I'm easily falling for.

The man I probably just fell completely and totally in love with.

"Eww, get a room," Asher says.

"Real mature," West replies.

When Jonah and I pull apart, we can't take our eyes off each other.

"On that note," West says. "We'll leave you two to it. I'll let you know when we both get flights home so you can at least pull yourself away from your boyfriend for enough time to say goodbye. Same goes for Benny."

I tense at the boyfriend label out loud, but only because I'm scared Jonah will freak out. He doesn't. Of course he doesn't.

"I need to find a flight to Dallas so I can catch up with the team on the road," Asher says.

West huffs. "Did you see that article this morning, speculating over why you were a scratch when you've been playing your ass off this season and are probably the only reason Buffalo is playoff-bound?"

"Do I want to know?" Asher asks.

"They think you told your coach to eat shit and die and so you got put in the time-out corner." West snickers.

"Pfft," Asher scoffs. "I haven't told anyone to eat shit and die in years, thank you very much. I'm a grown-up now."

"So, I won't pull up the viral video of you mouthing it at one of the refs only a few months ago?"

"Mouthing it isn't saying it."

They keep bickering as they walk out of the coffee shop, leaving Jonah and me alone. Finally.

"I can't believe you're doing this for me," I say.

"What's so unbelievable? You're worth giving the world to."

"Okay, we need to go back to your house. Right now." I don't even feel guilty about abandoning my full coffee, and as Jonah throws his out on the way outside, he doesn't seem to either.

No sooner do we get back to Jonah's apartment, we're naked and I'm on my knees.

Jonah's cock is warm and hard on my tongue, his velvety skin pulled tight around his shaft. He tastes like the best decision I've ever made.

Not that it would be difficult to be that, considering every decision up to this point has been questionable, but being with him feels like the right choice.

I keep my eyes on him while I bob my head and suck his cock. His perfect, amazing cock.

But when Jonah throws his head back and I can no longer see his face, the comparison to Jasper fills my mind again, and I have to pull off him.

I shake the thought free, but not before telling Jonah to watch me while I give him pleasure. I need his brown eyes on mine. I need that eye contact. That connection.

My own cock aches, and as much as I want to reach between my legs and jerk myself off until I come all over the floor, I don't want to come until I'm on his dick. I want him to fuck me. Face-to-face. With him on top or me, I don't care.

I'm so desperate for it that instead of pulling off him again to wet my fingers with saliva, I let myself drool all over his dick while I suck and then stroke him, covering my fingers with as much spit as I can.

Jonah groans as I reach behind me and start prepping my hole. "I want to do that."

I shake my head as subtly as I can with a mouth full of cock. I'm not finished tasting him, driving him so close to the edge without letting him dive right off it.

Jonah grips me under my arm and hauls me to my feet despite my whine. He turns us so he can drop back on the bed and move up so his head is on his pillow. "Climb on top of me and face that way." He points toward his feet.

"No, I need to be looking at you."

"Is this the whole comparison thing to West's husband?"

I hesitate. "Maybe?"

"What if I keep talking to you? Please let me do something. I'm itching to touch you."

"Fine. But you need to keep talking." I do as he says and

throw my leg over his waist, shuffling backward until I'm sitting on his chest facing his feet.

Jonah runs his hands down my back and then shoves me forward by the middle of my shoulder blades.

I bend over, exposing my hole to him while my face lands right in front of his cock again. I lick the tip of his dick and hear the snap of a lube bottle opening behind me.

When his slippery fingers push inside my hole, I engulf his cock all the way to the base.

"That feels so good." Jonah's hips lift up.

Good, he remembered to keep talking.

Because the idea of him being … I shudder, nope. Not going to think about that. Not while I'm doing this. And not while his fingers are pressing against my prostate and driving me wild.

I have to release his cock so I can take a deep enough breath. "Keep … talking," I rasp and then take him in my mouth again.

"Your hole is so tight. I can't wait to be inside it. I can't wait for the day we can go bareback and my cum will drip out of you."

I moan around his cock.

"I want to claim you." He adds to his fingers now. I have no idea how many he's up to, but I hope it's a billion, and I'll be ready for all of that to happen.

I want to be claimed. I want him to come inside me so I can feel all of him.

I want—

"Time to hop up, or I'm going to come in your mouth instead," Jonah says.

Thank fuck.

I sit up and look at him over my shoulder. "How do you want me?"

"You said face-to-face, didn't you?" He taps my leg to get me to climb off him, and when I do, he pulls himself into a seated position, using the headboard as a backrest. He looks so hot with his hair a spikey mess, his plump lips shiny, and his eyes hooded. His hard cock points up toward his abs, the head of his dick all red and needy.

He holds out his hand for me. "Come here."

I take his hand and throw my leg back over him so I'm facing him this time.

Our cocks line up between us, and while I'm eager to get him inside me, the way he's looking at me has me rooted in place.

"You're so amazing," Jonah says.

The fact he could still think that after everything Benny and I did ... it almost breaks me.

I want to say I'm not amazing. I don't make the right decisions, but Jonah having faith in me that everything I have done was for what I thought was the best for everyone involved ... It gives me faith that this decision? Choosing him over moving back to Vermont?

It's the first time in a long time where I've made the right choice.

CHAPTER THIRTY-THREE

"ARE you sure you want to do this bare?" I double-check. I'm still cupping his face with one hand while the other works us both over with lube. Our foreheads are resting against one another, and if I weren't so desperate to be inside him, to own his ass, I could stay like this until we both came. I'd mix our cum together and then lick it off his skin. I almost suggest that as an alternative, but he speaks first.

"I've never been more sure," he whispers. "Are you?"

"More than sure." I trust him, and I know I'm good to go, health-wise.

The moan he lets out rings in my ears, and it's the sexiest sound I've ever heard. It's so desperate. I love the noises he makes, and they only urge me to try to draw more out of him.

His mouth claims mine just as desperately, and he rises up on his knees so we can shift into position. I line my cock up with his hole, and when he slowly sinks down on me, I almost blow immediately. My hands fly to his hips to steady him.

I'm glad we're face-to-face now and I no longer have to talk because I have no words.

Emmett grabs hold of the back of my hair and pulls my

head back so I'm looking up at him. "I love how blissed-out you look already. I haven't even brought out any of my moves yet."

"Please don't." I breathe heavily. "Not yet anyway. I just need ..."

He rotates his hips.

"Oh, fuck," I moan.

He looks damn smug and proud of himself.

"You do know if you keep going, I'm not going to be able to stop myself, and then I won't be able to get you off the way I want to," I warn him.

"How do you want to make me come?"

"By pegging your prostate over and over until you come hands-free all over me."

"Mmm." Emmett licks his lips. "That does sound fun." He rotates his hips again, taking me deeper and unraveling one of the last few threads of control I have. "You know what else would be fun? If you came inside me and then got me off with your hand while you stay lodged in my ass until you're soft."

That sounds like a quick answer, one I would gladly take if I weren't so determined to get my way. My lips quirk. "Who do you think's going to win that race?"

"With the way you're basically trembling, I'm going to say I'll win, and it'll happen my way, but if we're talking in the big scheme of things, we'll both be winning when we unleash." He leans in close to my ear. "I want to feel you come inside me."

Now, I don't even care how it happens. All I care about is that he gets what he wants, any which way I can give it to him.

So when he lifts up and then rotates his hips as he sinks down on my cock again, I thrust upward at the same time and hit his prostate.

Now, he's the one trembling and letting out a string of curse words.

Our bodies come together over and over again as he bears down on my cock, and I push up into him. It takes no time for both of us to become frantic and find a rhythm. The only question that remains is who's going to beat who to the finish line.

"Come on," I say more to myself than him. I want to hold out. I want him to—

Emmett makes this guttural sound at the back of his throat, and every muscle in his body tenses, but he doesn't stop his rhythm. His cum splashes against my abs, and when he says, "Fuck, Jonah, I fucking love your fucking cock," I get what we both want—for me to unleash inside his ass and fill him up with my cum.

My orgasm seems to last forever, long after Emmett's done emptying onto my skin, but I continue to hold him close, each thrust upward getting further apart.

Just when I think I'm done, another ripple shoots through me, and I bury my head in his shoulder.

"All right, you win."

I lift my head and smile. "No, you were right. We both won."

Emmett's blueish-green eyes are soft as he stares at me.

"What are you thinking?" I ask.

"I'm thinking I can't wait to see where this can lead."

"Funny you should say that," I murmur. "I can't wait either."

I regret all my life choices, but I'm not going to let that show. I won't let Benny win.

He's already thrown his pencil across the room, given up on learning math about six times, and now he's pacing my living room and yelling at his workbook while I pretend not to care.

I do care. Not only because I want to see Benny succeed, but because I'm finding teaching much more rewarding when he finally gets it. The thing is, sometimes he does it right, and then he could do the exact same problem again, and he'll get it wrong. I don't think it's a matter of him understanding it and then not understanding it. It's more that he's not retaining the information.

He has his checklists with each step he needs to take to work through the given formulas, his calculator, his times table printed out in front of him. He doesn't have to know any of them off by heart. He can refer back to them as many times as he needs, but that still doesn't mean it's any easier for him.

"You're a stupid piece of shit, and who needs you anyway?" he keeps yelling.

"You do know that math doesn't care if you hate its guts?"

"Are you sure? Maybe I can bully it into submission. If it didn't fight so hard, it would be easier to solve."

Yes. It's all math's problem.

"Math doesn't change for anybody. Try it again, from the top of your checklist."

He throws himself back in his seat. "I have no idea what Emmett sees in you."

"Hey, now. Is there really any need to get personal? Your brother thinks I'm an eleven."

Benny glances over at me. "I was still talking to the math."

"Oh. Right. Carry on, then."

"I totally understand what Emmett sees in you. I mean, you're not my type, but I get it."

"Thank ... you?" I think? Not that I would want Benny to find me attractive, but nice backhanded compliment, dude.

"Hey, what did Professor Sinclair say when you told him you weren't ratting us out?"

The change of topic doesn't help his case.

"I didn't word it that way, but I did let him know I was going to see if you could pass your statistics class with some help. You know, legitimate help. Not Emmett help."

"And he was okay with that? From what I've heard of him,

he doesn't let any leeway when it comes to the rules. What if we're doing this all for nothing and he tells the dean anyway?"

I want to reassure him that Silas won't do that, but for all I know, he might. I trust him when he says it's my class and up to me how I handle cheating.

"Are you just trying to prolong having to start from the top and running through your checklist again?"

Ben throws up his hands. "Duh."

"You've got this."

But as he starts going over it again, it's clear that he doesn't have it. He bangs his head on the table. "What if I can't do this?"

"Then I'll have failed you, and you'll try again with someone else who has actual practice teaching those with learning disorders."

"Are you trying to guilt-trip me into learning? So you don't feel bad about yourself?"

"Is it working?"

He scowls. "Sadly, yes. I want Emmy to be happy, and apparently, you make him happy, so therefore, you need to be happy."

"So start again." I point to his checklist of steps.

He goes to get back into the work at the same time there's a knock at my door.

"I'll get it." Benny tries to jump up, but I push him back down.

"It's my apartment."

"But we both know it's going to be Emmett."

Truth. Emmett went to go skate at his work, which is step one of getting back in shape for hockey, and said he'd come back when he was done. We've already spoken about this summer and how he's going to go back to Vermont so both his older brothers can help recondition him. He made an offhanded comment about me going with him but then said it wouldn't be much fun for me because reconditioning for him will be so grueling we'd never see each other.

But I mean, I'd see him more if I did go with him instead of staying in California.

I answer my door, and it is Emmett. He greets me with a wide smile and a soft kiss.

"Get a room," Benny sings, but he hasn't actually taken his eyes off his work.

"You're not even watching," Emmett points out.

"I can hear the slurpy kissy faces, and I'm not allowed to go to Harrison's until I've finished this."

"Still going at it, huh?" Emmett gives me a sympathetic look. Or maybe it's a worried one. Because if I can't get Ben to pass my stats class, he has to redo it all again.

"How was skating?" It's my turn to change the subject.

"Umm, good." He doesn't sound too confident in that.

"Not great? Amazing?"

"It felt good, but I'm not sure yet if Fletcher really has the skills to get me to where I need to be. He's used to teaching kids and teenagers, not pro wannabes."

Ah.

Meaning, he might have to go back to Vermont sooner than summer.

"You do know if you had to go to where your brothers are to train, that I'd understand, right? I'd still be tutoring Benny whether you were with me or not."

"Why would me temporarily going back to Vermont mean we'd be over? You wouldn't even consider long distance?"

"Where did I say any of that? I just meant I'd support you if you had to leave. I want you to chase your dream."

"Yes, you fucker!" Benny yells out, making us both flinch.

"What you call me?" Emmett snarks.

"I did it." He holds up his paper.

"Did you check your work?" I ask.

He groans and goes back to it.

Emmett turns back to me. "I'm not saying I'm definitely moving back or going back right this second. Or next week. But there will eventually come a time where I'll need to, and—"

"And we'll cross that bridge when we come to it."

"You mean burn that bridge," Emmett says.

Benny snorts. "You're mixing analogies there, brother. Though with you, you could mean burning, literally."

Emmett flips him off while I ponder what he means. The fire at San Diego that Emmett swears wasn't his fault? Or a different kind of burning?

Emmett must see the sudden doubt on my face because he says, "He's making fun of me. The reason Benny took me at face value when I said I started the fire instead of my roommate is because when we were younger, we both … might have been slightly obsessed with lighting things on fire. Just two little pyro twins running around the place."

"We were so cute." Benny sighs wistfully.

"I promise it was a phase," Emmett says. "And I'm not lying about the San Diego fire."

I wish I could say I didn't need to hear that, but I did. Being blindsided by them once was enough for me to question my judgment when it comes to both of them. I don't want it to be that way, but that's the thing about trust. Once it's broken, it's incredibly difficult to get it back.

I want to trust Emmett again, but it's going to take some time.

"Motherfucker," Benny hisses. "I got a different answer this time."

"It's going to be a long night, isn't it?" Emmett asks.

Benny lets out another string of "Fucking, fuck fuck."

I mutter under my breath. "A long semester, honestly."

emmett

FLETCHER HUNCHES OVER, gloved hands on knees, trying to catch his breath.

I've barely started to sweat. I skate a circle around him. "Are you going to throw up?"

"How ..." He breathes deeply. "Do your ..." Another breath. "Brothers ..." He's gulping down air like someone gulps down a beer bong. "Think you're not in peak physical condition?"

"Hmm, maybe because you're in your thirties and anyone could kick your ass?"

He stands upright now. "I am your boss, and you're not allowed to hit me with the truth like that."

I laugh. "I mean, you're very fit and very awesome at all the things you do, but I am, uh, a superhuman?"

"That's better. Seriously, though, I don't know how much I can really help you other than making you do suicides in full gear for eight hours. I can get you physically in shape, but when it comes to skills, there's only so much I can do."

The thing is, I know he's right. There's no way I can stay here and train the way I need to be trained. With Asher's team making the playoffs and West still coaching until the Frozen

Four championship is over with, neither of them can come out here to force the rigorous training regime I'm going to need. Not to mention pulling them away from their lives and their partners.

I'm happy here, and I'm not ready to leave yet.

Okay, so I don't like the beach, the always warm weather, or that my friend group consists of people who thought I was Ben for so long, but Benny's here. Jonah's here. And Jonah and I have a real shot with no secrets between us.

I'm probably holding on too tightly, considering our start was rocky, and I can tell he still doesn't trust me completely, but there's something about him that has me rooted in place.

"Can I ask you something?" Fletcher says.

"I dunno, can you? You still look like you're going to pass out."

He gestures to head for the railing so he can hold on to something, but as he speaks, I wish he'd rather pass out. "Why are you still here?"

"I love you too, boss."

He smiles. "That's not what I mean. You're the best coach I have on staff, and I don't want to see you go, but I've had many guys come through this place who haven't had half as much talent as you do, and they've gone on to do big things. I don't want to hold you back. But that's exactly what I'm doing. Or, more specifically, you're holding yourself back by staying in California."

"I don't know what you're talking about. Everything is great, and I can focus on proper reconditioning over the summer. It's great. Really great. My plan is flawless and—"

"Let me guess. Great?"

"Yup. Great."

"Maybe say it one more time, and I'll believe you."

I slump and lean against the railing. "There's this guy."

Fletcher laughs. "Now it all makes sense. It's Cullen's uncle, isn't it?"

"Yeah."

"Remind me again, why did you stop playing hockey to begin with?"

"Because the media—"

"Nope. The real reason, because the way you are about this sport, your talent, your pedigree—"

"That's what I was about to say. The media had way too much attention on Benny and me, they put so much pressure on us that we couldn't handle it."

"And what makes you think they will be any less invasive with only you? You won't have your twin to take part of the brunt of it."

"Well, one, I'm not announcing that I'm going to try to get back into the game until I'm sure I could possibly make it, and two, they won't be less invasive, but I always had thicker skin when it came to that kind of thing. Benny wanted to quit, and I was nearing that point anyway, so—"

"So you gave up your opportunity to make it to the big show because your brother wanted you to."

"Nope." I don't blame Benny, and I wouldn't want anyone else to either. "I was willing to quit, but ... I think my motivations had more to do with me wanting to make a point to the media than actually wanting to say goodbye to the sport. The motivation to leave was there, but I guess Benny was that extra push."

"And now you're holding yourself back because you like a boy."

"You're holding yourself back because you like a boy!" It's not the smartest of comebacks, but it does lighten the mood.

"You don't want to become wasted potential. Otherwise, you'll find yourself as a thirty-something-year-old who can't catch his breath after some hotshot young dude shows you up on your own damn ice."

He's not saying anything I don't already know. But the thing is, I've been good at ignoring those thoughts up until now.

I don't want to leave California yet, but if I don't do it now, will I ever?

What happens if Jonah tells me he loves me? What happens if I admit to myself the reason I haven't already packed up and left is because I'm in love with him?

If I do move and I ask him to come with me, would he even consider it? He has Cullen here. Responsibilities. I can't ask him to give that up.

I can already hear Fletcher's reply if I were to say that out loud. "But you'd give up hockey for him?"

I hate that I have to think about this stuff. I'd much rather stick my head in the sand like I've been doing ever since I agreed with Benny to quit hockey.

"What's really holding you back?" Fletcher asks. "It can't only be about the guy."

That's the other thing I've been avoiding. I don't want to acknowledge that maybe I don't have what it takes anymore. "What if I'm already wasted potential? What if I try to make this great comeback and I can't even make the minor leagues?

"You're never going to find out unless you give it a proper try, and you're not doing that here."

Fuck. I'm going to have to leave.

Leave California.

Leave Jonah.

But worst of all, leave Benny.

For the first time in our lives, we won't be living a maximum of twenty minutes away.

For the first time in our lives, we won't have each other to fall back on.

No contingency plan.

We get to be our true selves.

It's everything I've wanted since leaving for college but

something I've never been able to achieve.

Fletcher's right. If I'm going to do this, I need to put everything else aside and only focus on hockey, on my future, and what I want.

I need to sort out my priorities, and I need to be at the top of that list.

Of course, prioritizing myself also includes stripping down naked as soon as I walk through Jonah's front door and leading him to his bed, but now that we're coming down from another amazing high and I have my head in the nook of his shoulder, prioritizing my future is back at the forefront of my mind.

I've never been able to put myself first before. Other than with the Jonah situation. That was putting my wants above anyone else's, including Jonah's. But that was selfish. This is ... this is my future, and it's the one thing I think I should be allowed to be selfish about. I've never known how to do that when it comes to Benny. Or Jonah, really. Not after everything he's done for me and Ben.

He's putting his whole career on the line for us, and now I'm contemplating turning around and moving across the country anyway? I'll be the biggest asshole on the planet if I did that.

Though, let's face it, I've been gunning for that position ever since I got kicked out of college and forced myself into Franklin U's own little world as someone else.

Jonah runs his fingertips over my arm, from my shoulder down to my elbow and back up again. It sends shivers down my spine and silences my mouth from saying what I need to say.

"What are you thinking about?" he asks.

"Brain cum dumb. I'm not thinking about anything."

"Well, that's a lie."

I pull back. "What?"

"You're here, but you're not really here, if you know what I mean."

Ugh. He's right.

I snuggle back into him. "Sorry."

"Don't be sorry. Talk to me about it."

"I can't," I say into his chest.

"Why not?"

"Because I don't want to."

It might be subtle, but I feel it. His whole body goes rigid, like he's pissed or ... fuck, thinks I'm being deceitful again.

"Wait." I shift back so I can see his face, but there's no way I'm letting go of him. "The only reason I don't want to is because I realized something about hockey today, and I worry it's going to come between us. The only thing that should come between us is our dicks. Literally. Now I'm rambling because I don't want to lose you, and—"

Jonah cups my face. "Hey, hey. Take a breath. Did something happen at practice today with Fletcher? What's going on?"

I take a deep breath. "Fletcher can't keep up with me. He was excited to help, but the more we get into it, the more we realize he's not at the level he should be at to coach those wanting to go pro. He's more kids and young teenager equipped. So unless I call West and ask him to pay for an extremely expensive private coach ..."

"You're going to have to move home to be closer to West."

"I can't push myself here like I would there."

The stiffness leaves Jonah's body, but it remains on his face. It looks like it physically hurts when he says, "Well, you have to leave, then. There's no question about that."

And now we're both filled with that same overthinking tension he called me out on, but there isn't anything I can say to make this better.

The worst part is I still have to tell Benny.

If I thought this with Jonah was difficult, I don't even want to go talk to my brother.

"When will you leave?"

"I haven't figured that out yet." I refrain from saying "As soon as possible," which it will be once I tell Benny and call West.

But for now, I'm going to stay in Jonah's arms a little longer.

We may be quiet, but neither of us falls asleep. I'm too worried about how Benny will react, and that worry is either so loud in the dead silence that Jonah's picking up on it, or maybe he's processing that I have to leave.

Either way, we continue to hold each other until it becomes uncomfortable, and then I roll onto my other side so he's spooning me. I love being the little spoon. Being wrapped in Jonah's arms, I never want to leave. And when he starts peppering my shoulder with soft kisses, I think this might be part of an evil plan to get me to stay. It's tempting to push back and rub my ass against his cock, even though I don't think I'll be able to get it up again, but when a shuddery breath hits my neck, I realize he's not trying for a sexy moment. He's trying not to show that he's upset.

"Jonah?" I look back at him over my shoulder, at his glassy eyes.

"Can I be the little spoon for a while?" he croaks.

My heart melts. "Anytime you want."

He winces at whatever thought enters his head in that moment and rolls over.

He doesn't need to tell me what that depressing thought was because I already know. He can't be the little spoon anytime he wants if I'm not going to be here.

Yeah, I'm not getting to sleep anytime soon. "We skipped dinner," I say.

"Not my fault someone came over and got immediately

undressed."

I smile into the back of his neck. "Some could argue it was your fault for being so damn sexy."

"Are you hungry? I can make you something." Jonah tries to escape my hold, but I stay firm.

"Let's order something so we can stay like this until food comes." The only time I pull away from him is so we can order food, and then we're right back to that same position, with me at his back, making him feel safe and reminding him that I'm still here. For now.

It's midnight by the time food comes, twelve thirty when we finish eating, and 2:00 a.m. when we've both come again.

He's making it really difficult to want to go talk to Benny. Before all of this happened, if I'd told my brother I planned to move across the country and he asked me to stay, I probably would. But things are different now, and I know that if I tell him I need to be at home to pursue this hockey thing seriously, Benny won't let me stay.

Once I tell him, it's real.

"I could stay," I say to Jonah as we climb back into bed. "I could push myself harder without Fletcher's help. I could focus on weight training instead of hockey and then focus on hockey come summer. I could—"

"You're leaving," he says firmly.

"What?"

"Like you said before, your brain is cum dumb right now, and you're doubting yourself, but you shouldn't. I don't want to be the reason you don't chase your dream."

"Ugh."

He laughs. "I give you what you want, and your response is 'Ugh'?"

"That ugh wasn't for you. It was for having to break the news to Benny."

"That's the real reason you roped me into round two, wasn't

it? You're putting off telling your brother."

I nod. "The only reason. It wasn't at all that I realize I want to spend what little time we have left naked and coming all over each other."

"You make it sound so romantic."

"The romantic-est."

"Are you going to be able to sleep, or do you need to go tell your brother?"

I've put it off long enough. "I need to go."

He shoves me. "In that case, off you go."

As soon as I'm out of bed and throwing on my clothes, Jonah starfishes in the middle of the bed.

I gasp. "You're only kicking me out so you can hog the whole bed."

"Duh." He sits up. "I'll see you tomorrow?"

"Every day until I leave. I promise."

Though, I don't think that will be many days at all. I have nothing tying me here other than people. I could use the excuse that I should give Fletcher two weeks' notice so he can find a replacement, but Scarlett can cover my classes until that happens, and Fletcher has already told me to leave, so he's not going to hold me here.

I kiss Jonah goodbye and make the walk to the DIK frat house. If he's not there, he'll be at my place with Harrison, and the DIK house is kind of on the way.

But as I reach Benny's window, I see the sleeping lump that is my brother. I try the window, but it's locked, so I tap on the glass.

He doesn't stir.

I know I'm allowed to use the door now, but there's something final about ending this the way it's been for the last three years. Whenever I've needed or wanted a place to crash, I would do this. When I got kicked out of school and moved in permanently, this window was my door in and out of the house.

This is us. Me and Benny.

I knock again and say, "Wake up, fuckface," and even that is us too.

He throws up his middle finger but covers his head with his pillow. I laugh because he can ignore me all he wants, but I'm not going to stop.

Tap, tap, tap, tap, tap, I continuously knock. This is new. Because it doesn't matter who sees me coming and going anymore—though they might get mad because I'm not supposed to sleep over here—I can be as loud as I want. And seeing as I'm going to be dragging Benny out anyway, I won't be sleeping over.

Finally, he gets up and unlatches the window, pushing it up but resting on it so I can't come in. "What the fuck is wrong with you? It's the middle of the night." He quickly snaps out of tired, grumpy mode and turns to overprotective brother with a snap. "Wait, did Jonah hurt you? Break up with you? Whatever he did, I'll kill him." He yawns. "But in the morning, okay?"

"Wanna go to that sketchy twenty-four-hour diner in between here and San Diego State so we can drink milkshakes and talk?"

We used to do that a lot in the beginning but haven't done it since freshman year. We were both so worried about being found out that in the dead of night we'd each sneak away to meet up so we could get our stories straight and update each other on things we needed to know around each other's campuses.

"Fuck." Benny's eyes soften now. "Did someone die?"

"No, but I'm worried someone might be about to. That someone being me."

His face falls. "You're moving back to Vermont, aren't you?"

"That was always the plan," I remind him.

"But ... you're leaving now instead of end of the school year."

Of course I didn't need to actually tell him. He can read me like no other and vice versa.

"I'm sorry," I whisper.

He forces a smile. "Don't be. You deserve all the happiness in the world."

"So do you." I avert my gaze. "It'll be the first time we've ever lived apart. Not just a town away, but with an entire country between us."

"I know." He hangs his head.

"We can do it though," I say, even though I don't believe it myself.

He can see right past that too. "We can, and we will. But not before we go and get shakes at Betty's diner."

"It's still not called that," I say. "No matter how many times you put it in their suggestion box."

"You're a suggestion box" is his smart retort. "I'm just saying, they should have a different name other than Diner, and the overnight waitress totally looks like a Betty."

"Because she's in her fifties but looks like she's in her eighties and sounds like she's smoked a pack of cigarettes every day of her life? On second thought, maybe we shouldn't go back there after you said that to her face last time."

Benny laughs his head off. "Is that why we stopped going?"

"No. We stopped going because we finally got our place-switching down to an art, and we didn't need to meet up that much anymore."

"Even though we didn't need to, I knew you'd always be there if I asked."

"Ditto. And I'm asking. We need to do it one last time."

Benny pauses before agreeing. "One last time."

And just like that, everything becomes cement.

My plans, my heart, my everything outside of hockey.

I'm doing this now.

CHAPTER THIRTY-FIVE

I PACE MY APARTMENT, getting more and more frustrated as the minutes tick by. Emmett went home to break the news to Benny and start packing. That quickly, it's all happening.

Part of me was hoping it was only a bad training session with Fletcher and that this morning he'd say he was going to give it another go, but nope. As soon as he left last night, the whole situation has been like a weight sitting on my chest. I don't even want to contemplate what it's going to be like when he leaves for good. But that's not what's frustrating me. What's frustrating me is that Benny is late for his session with me, and he should know that I hate tardiness. I mean, sure, he wasn't actually in my class, but I'm certain he knows of my reputation for locking students out if they're late.

I look at my phone again at the time. He's only ten minutes late. That's nothing, especially for someone who doesn't have a sense of time.

Ten minutes is the standard wait time for coffee. Though, Benny doesn't drink coffee. Maybe he's bringing me caffeine reinforcements after what I'm assuming was a hard conversation with Emmett this morning.

Oh shit, what if that conversation is still going?

I give the twins leeway because I know that's going to be difficult for both of them, but when it moves to fifteen minutes and then twenty, I can't stop myself from calling.

"Yeah?" His voice is rough, like he's been asleep.

"Are you forgetting something?" I ask.

"What?"

"Tutoring session. With me."

"Huh?"

Real eloquent, Benny.

"It's almost eleven. Are you only waking up now?"

"No, no, I'm awake. I've been awake since stupid o'clock when my stupid brother woke me up to break my heart."

"Hey, if anyone's heart is getting broken here, it's mine."

He huffs. "I'm not going to play this *Emmett loves me more* game with you."

"Well, duh. You'll always win that game."

I can hear his smile as he says, "Good. At least you know your place. But again, why are you calling about a tutoring session that's not even going to exist soon?"

It's my turn with the literary genius that is the word "Huh?"

"Well, Emmett's leaving. He's the only reason you offered me tutoring in the first place. Ergo, why should I get out of bed and stop wallowing when you're not going to follow through anyway? I'm surprised you're not already in Dean Kirwin's office starting the paperwork on getting me kicked out of school."

The frustration over him being late bubbles over to downright anger. "Did Emmett say I'd stop tutoring you when he left?" I told him I wouldn't do that. Numerous times. So why in the fuck—

"No, he was adamant you'd keep your word, but why would

you? We tricked you for almost an entire semester, lied to you, and now the only reason you're giving me a chance is leaving, so—"

Oh, it's not Emmett I need to be pissed at. It's Benny.

"First of all, I'm offended you think I'd go back on a promise I made you. Not your brother: you. Secondly, I didn't offer to tutor you just so Emmett would keep sleeping with me out of some fucked-up sense of guilt. And thirdly, how little do you think of me?"

"If it wasn't for Emmett, what was it for, then?"

"For you. Because you went through so much during your developmental years that you never got the chance to find a system to deal with your learning disorder. Because you're a victim of falling through the cracks."

"Even if I—"

"I mean, granted, had you not been a twin, it would probably have been picked up a lot sooner, but that's not the point. The point is you went so long without getting the help you really needed to succeed at school, and I would rather see you get the degree you've been working hard for than to see you kicked out and having to make up all your math subjects from middle school to college."

"You're ... doing this ... for me?"

He sounds so bewildered, but that pisses me off too. "Having Emmett stay was a side bonus. And okay, maybe when I first offered it, it was so Emmett would have a reason to stay, but after only one session with you, it all became about getting you that passing grade. You're so close, and it would be a waste to throw it all away now."

He yawns. "Okay, okay, I'm getting up and heading over."

"Good. I'll see you in ten minutes."

"I have to make a stop first to get my favorite tutor a coffee."

"Please be talking about me and not Harrison."

He laughs. "Oh, when it comes to Harrison, I'm more the

tutor, if you get what I mean." The innuendo in his voice is so thick even a child would pick up on it.

"Uh, yeah, don't need to know that."

"I'll be there soon."

Good. Because I need the distraction from having to say goodbye sometime soon. As soon as Emmett can pack and book a flight to Vermont.

Ugh. This sucks.

I hate this.

I hate that I can't pack up and go with him. If he asked, maybe I'd find a way. Quit my job, tell Dean Kirwin to find someone else for the remainder of the school year. It would only be for a couple of months.

But then I think about leaving Cullen, my promise to Benny, think of how it will only be a couple of months, and that Emmett has already said he's going to be too busy to eat, let alone spend time with me. He's already warned me about it being like that if I go see him over spring break or the summer.

We haven't exactly talked about doing long distance or whether we're hitting pause on us, and the thought of him dating and going out in Burlington makes my insides squirm uncomfortably, but I'm not going to think about that. Or bring it up.

Emmett is going after his dream, and I'm not going to stand in his way in any capacity.

Even if saying goodbye sucks.

I haven't even had a chance to get used to the idea yet. It's been a whirlwind of him deciding he's leaving, him telling Benny, and then the very next day, he called West, who booked his flight, and now here we are, a measly twenty-four hours later, and he's all packed up and ready to head to the airport.

I'm not going to be selfish here. I'm not. I'm going to be strong, tell him I'll call him, text him, internet stalk him, and the only distance between us will be physical. At least on my end.

Who knows, maybe he has an old high school flame he'll reconnect with, and he'll end things with me before even spring break rolls around.

I refuse to bring any of that up here though—at his place, with his brother and roommates watching on.

"All ready to go, then?" I ask.

I offered to drop him off because apparently, I like drawing this shit out, but then Benny and Harrison said they're coming too.

Because saying goodbye isn't going to be difficult enough, we need to have an audience. Actually, in reality, it will probably be Benny and Emmett who have the audience. This is about them even more than it's about Em and me.

"Will you judge me if I say I've changed my mind and I don't want to go anymore?" Emmett blinks up at me.

"No, but I will get my hopes up, so don't say it unless you mean it."

"I want to mean it. No, I do mean it in the sense that I don't want to go, but—"

"You have to. I know that."

Emmett steps closer to me and wraps his arms around my back, holding me to him.

"Ugh," Ben says behind us. "If this whole trip to the airport thing is going to be one big sob fest of goodbyes, I don't think I want to be there for that."

Emmett chuckles against my neck but then sniffs and pulls back, his eyes red and watery. "As if you're not going to be just as bad. You need me, Benny. Admit it."

"I need you like I need a hole in the head," Benny mumbles.

He's such a liar. Even I can see that.

"Ten bucks says he cries more than I do," Emmett says.

While I thought that Emmett putting Benny before me could possibly be a deal breaker or would be difficult for me, it's strangely not. The twins are codependent as fuck, and while I don't think it's all that healthy for them, it's not my place. My place is by Emmett's side, to be in his corner. I don't mind making him my number one, even if he could never do the same with me.

It makes sense for Emmett and Ben to be the way they are. Siblings bond through childhood trauma, and fuck knows the twins had enough of that dealing with the loss of their parents and their overachieving siblings.

Under other circumstances, if a partner put their family before me, it would be a problem, but with Emmett, I know Benny is part of the deal. I accept it, the same as Harrison does.

And that's not to say that Emmett will always be on Benny's side of things. He made his brother go to the dean to tell the truth about not sleeping with me because it was the right thing to do. Sure, he didn't tell the complete truth, and it might have taken me a moment to understand why they did what they did, but I know Emmett has my back.

I do wonder how I'll go being around Benny when Emmett will be so far away. Seeing someone identical to Emmett sitting across from me, it has the potential to have a calming effect or make the longing worse.

"Are we going or what?" Benny breaks into my internal ramble.

Not. We're not going. Never ever. Emmett is going to stay.

"I guess so," Emmett says.

"Would you be opposed to me kidnapping you and locking you in my apartment so you can't leave?" I ask.

"I really hope you're talking in relation to Vermont," Felix says from the couch. "Otherwise, that's called false imprisonment, and it is illegal. Ask me how I know."

"I don't think I want to know," Emmett says.

Exactly what I was thinking. "I meant in a cute, romantic way," I say.

"So did I," Felix says.

My gaze meets Emmett's. "On second thoughts, I'm glad you're moving away from possibly crazy stalker roommates."

"There's only one man I stalk now, thank you very much." Felix wraps his arm around Marshall.

"Let's goooooo," Benny says.

"Benny loves me so much he doesn't want me to leave either. All this *let's go* and *are we going* and all the other whining he's doing is to cover that he's dying on the inside. He can't live without me."

"I can live without you drawing this out," Benny says.

"Fine." Emmett turns to his roommates. "It's been quick, but you're the best roommates I've ever had."

"That makes me think we're the only roommates he's ever had," Marshall says.

"Not true. The dude who burned down our dorm was my other one."

"Woohoo. We're one step above arsonist." Felix fist pumps the air.

Watching him hug his roommates and say goodbye, I'm frozen. Because soon, that will be me saying goodbye to him.

It's ridiculous how much I'm getting torn up over someone who has lied to me, pretended to be someone else, and I've only dated for an extremely short time. It's possible Emmett is one huge walking red flag and that's why I'm so attracted to him, but there's something deeper telling me that if I was willing to risk my job for this man, if I chose Emmett over protecting myself, my heart, and my future ... that has to mean something, doesn't it?

I wouldn't have done it for anyone else.

So why is Emmett the outlier? What is the deep-seated meaning of us as individuals and as a couple?

It's not until we're halfway to the airport that I realize: I love this man. I'm *in love* with him. I'm so far in love with him that it's breaking my heart to see him leave.

I know he's not leaving *me*. He's chasing the future that he has always wanted. He put Ben's needs ahead of his dreams, and I won't let myself become another person who holds him back.

Ben didn't do it purposefully, but I know he feels as guilty as I would if I asked Emmett to stay.

So as I park the car in the airport parking lot, I decide to stop making jokes about kidnapping him and not letting him go, and be the supportive boyfriend-type person.

Emmett's doing the right thing. Staying would be easy. Being with me, coaching hockey—it would be an easy life for him. I'd make sure of it. But he wants hard. He wants a challenge. And he deserves to give it a try.

I wish him all the success in the world. And I mostly mean that. Like ninety-five percent of me wants him to succeed and become a hotshot NHL player who'll still be interested in me even with a million different people throwing themselves at him because he's semi-famous and hot and—

Okay, maybe it's more seventy-five percent wanting him to achieve that, and the other selfish twenty-five percent wants him to fail spectacularly so we have a shot at a future.

Not that we don't even if he gets all of that.

Ugh. I'm in my fucking head, and I fucking hate it. He hasn't even left yet, and I'm already picturing a future where he has too much temptation around him.

The next few months are going to be the test. If we can do long distance, or not ... if he's even planning to try long distance.

We've promised things to each other—like seeing each other over spring break and the summer—but a definite future isn't one of them.

He's already checked in online, so he just has to tag his bags and drop them off at the bag drop area, and it all happens way too quickly.

All that's left is to walk him to the security checkpoint, and he'll be gone.

Emmett interlaces his fingers with mine, and I hold on for dear life while trying to mask the doubt on my face.

"Hey," he says softly and pulls on my hand to get me to stop walking. Only, Ben and Harrison also stop, so Emmett waves them away. "Can we have a second?"

My heart thuds. I think I know what's coming, and I don't want to hear it. I force a half-smile. "Wow, ending it before we even reach security, huh?"

Emmett frowns. "Ending it?"

"Us."

"I-is that what you want?"

"Are you kidding? It's the last thing I want, but I don't want you to feel pressured to promise me anything. What if you go home and it's like one of those Hallmark movies. You run into your old girlfriend or boyfriend and sparks fly and—"

He smiles. "I don't have an ex-girlfriend or boyfriend at home. Sure, I went out with people in high school, but none of them were serious or anything."

"What if they've had a glow-up? All I'm saying is you shouldn't be focused on me, not while you're trying to make hockey work. I'll be here, not dating like I was when I met you, and I'll be thinking of you and wanting to be with you, but I refuse to be a weight trying to pull you down. If you meet someone else—"

He steps closer to me, pressing his chest against mine. "Jonah, what did I tell you the first time we hooked up?"

"That you couldn't give me more than one night?"

He sighs. "The fact you don't know you're a ten makes you an eleven. Why in the fuck would I walk away from an eleven?"

"Maybe you'll meet a twelve."

Emmett puts his finger against my lips. "I wish I could stay so we could see where this connection could go, but I'm not willing to give up on us yet. I want to put in the work if you do."

"I really fucking do. I ..." Don't say it. Now's not the time. Don't put pressure on him.

"I think I could be in love with you," Emmett says. "And if I am, and you possibly might feel the same one day, we'll figure it all out. Whether I end up becoming a full-time coach or I get a shot for the minors or—"

"Or if I don't sign the papers Kirwin sent me to extend my teaching contract with Franklin next year and move to where you are ..."

"Wait, is that an option?" Emmett pulls back, his eyes full of hope, and that's when I know he really does feel the same way about me that I do about him. "What about Cullen?"

I love my nephew and the rest of my family, but they don't need me the way I want Emmett to need me. "I'm pretty sure I'm already in love with you, and with you saying the same thing, we need to give this all we've got. I'd move now if I didn't have the school year to finish out and someone's brother to tutor so he can pass my class. I've thought about it though. About moving. I thought it was crazy soon and probably a mistake to bring it up, but I mean—"

"We're going to make it work. It's a lot of pressure on a new relationship, but I want to try." He's saying everything I wanted to hear, and as amazing as it is, I'm worried we're setting ourselves up for failure and heartache.

But I'm already in too deep, so it's either heartache now or later. I choose later. "I want to try too."

"If you don't sign your contract with Franklin, Jasper could get you a job at CU or—"

I rub the back of my neck. "I'm actually thinking of becoming a tutor for those who need extra learning tools to help them. I have to look into it more, but it might mean going back to studies, and I could do that anywhere. Vermont or whichever city you're playing hockey in. I'm not tied to being a professor. I don't think it's my dream like hockey is yours."

"We can make this work," Emmett says again, only this time, his gaze is determined."

"We'll make this work," I repeat. Now, if only I could believe it.

I'm going to give my all, I know that. I might have doubts, but I also know if I don't throw everything I have at being with Emmett and doing what I want with life, then I've already failed.

If we're determined, love can get us through anything.

Even hugging him goodbye and standing with his brother as we watch him enter the airport terminal and leave.

emmett

AS I LIE across the airport chairs inside the arrivals waiting area, I wish for death. From the minute I stepped foot in Vermont, West has been working me like crazy. It's practically torture, and I've been sore every day. It's only gotten worse since Buffalo was kicked out of the playoffs. Asher's on his summer break from the NHL and has joined in on the fun.

Their fun.

For me, it's fucking work. It's hard work. But even though I can't lift my arms or pull myself into a seated position because even moving an inch hurts, I know I'm where I belong. And I'm sure it will get easier. Eventually.

It's a long road, but it's still the path I want to take. I gave up on the sport way too soon, so I'm going to fight and claw my way back into it.

"You'd think he'd be excited about seeing his boyfriend, but all he's doing is lying there," West says to Asher behind me.

"Maybe he's practicing for later." Yup, Asher and Benny are so much alike.

"You did not make a sex joke about our little brother."

"He's an adult now."

"Still doesn't make it any less creepy."

I groan. "I can hear you two, you know? And if I could close my fist right now, I'd be giving you both the finger." I can't even lift my hand. "And if it helps at all, you're both creepy."

"Hmm," Asher says. "He's not truly exhausted enough if he can still run his mouth."

"Agreed. He needs to be so bone-tired he can't even talk."

I force myself up, even though every muscle in my body screams at me for doing so. "No. You two said I get three whole days off to spend with Jonah. My muscles need time to heal so they can grow. That's like, muscle-building 101."

They both laugh. They really are having way too much fun with this.

But even as I glower at them, I can't be mad. They're giving up their summer plans to train me.

Before I can snark at them, time slows down, there's a shift in the universe, and I watch as my boyfriend slow-mos it through the arrivals gate.

He's planning to stay the whole summer after only being able to give me a couple of days over spring break because he was taking time to restructure his whole teaching plan. Whenever I was at practice with West, Jonah would be working on that, and when I'd come home, we'd eat, fuck, sleep, repeat. I didn't get to show him around where I grew up.

That's going to change this trip.

With the adrenaline and arousal filling my veins, my body no longer protests when I move, though it's slow to do as I tell it.

Jonah reaches me as I get to my feet, and then I jump into his arms, quite literally. He almost falls over as I wrap my legs around his waist, but he drops his backpack and is then able to support me under my ass while I attack his face with my mouth.

"So much for being so sore he can't even move," Asher says.

"We definitely need to work him harder," West agrees.

"I hate you both," I exclaim and lower myself so my feet are back on the ground.

"I've missed you too," Jonah says.

Has long distance been easy? No. But it hasn't been as difficult as I was picturing. Mainly because I'm busy every day. If I'm not working out or on the ice, I'm watching video West took of me, analyzing my hip, stick, and feet placement, which way I lean when I shoot, my skating skills, my speed, everything.

I have a lot of things to distract me, and I guess so does Jonah, with the way he's been working to become a better professor.

"I've missed you more," I say and then hear a retching sound behind Jonah.

"Oh, yeah, I brought you something." Jonah steps aside, and there's Benny and Harrison behind him.

"Wait, what? You two weren't supposed to be here until the Fourth of July." I throw myself at them next and ignore yet another snipe about how I'm supposed to be sore.

I am motherfucking sore, but Jonah and Benny are worth being sore for. Okay, that sounds super sexual, and eww. Well, eww for the Benny part. I can't wait to feel sore from all the sex later.

I'm going to be walking like a cowboy on his first day riding a horse. Mmm, riding Jonah cowboy-style.

Later, Emmett. Focus. Benny's here.

"We had planned for July," Harrison says. "But then Benny decided he needed to see, in his words, the fuckery Florida could bring with Independence Day fireworks by seeing my family that week."

"Ooh." I turn to West and Asher.

"No, you can't have the Fourth of July off so you can go to Florida with them," Asher says.

Damn it.

"Also, I have some news," Benny says. "And I wanted to tell you in person."

"Ten bucks he's getting married," Asher says.

Doubt it. News like that, Benny would've told me immediately. Video chat or text. Something. He wouldn't be able to keep something that exciting to himself.

Benny looks at Jonah. "Do you want to tell him?"

"Nope. This is your thing."

I gasp. "You passed statistics?"

The proud look on Benny's face is answer enough, but he says, "I did all the assessments, all the work, put in long fucking hours, and Jonah was able to turn my incomplete from semester one into a pass. I'm all set to graduate. On time."

I throw my arms around my brother again. "I'm so fucking proud of you."

"It's all thanks to your boyfriend."

"Not true," Jonah says. "You fought it tooth and nail, but statistics finally became your bitch."

"Technically, I got a C-minus. That's hardly making it my bitch."

"Hey, Cs get degrees," Jonah cheers.

"Evidently," Benny mumbles.

Asher and West join in on my hug with Benny and congratulate him until Benny complains we're smothering him.

We pull apart from him, but I keep my arm around Benny's shoulders while my other hand reaches for Jonah's.

I'm fucking ready to make this summer last as long as possible. Because when next semester comes, Jonah and Benny will be back on the West Coast, and I'll be … I'm not getting my hopes up, but Asher thinks he can get me in with the Buffalo farm team. It wouldn't be a free pass. I'd have to earn my spot onto their starting lineup, and if I'm not good enough, they will send me down to the ECHL which is difficult—not impossible but very difficult—to climb up to the top. Most cases, anyone who lands in the ECHL will only reach AHL status.

But I can't think about any of that now. Not for the next three days, at least.

My focus needs to be on Jonah.

And then Benny.

Between them and hockey, I have my summer filled.

Like every afternoon after my brothers are done torturing me at the rink, I come home to my childhood house to a hard-at-work Jonah. Benny and Harrison are staying here too, while West and Jasper have their own place. We moved out of this house when we were around ten or eleven, not long after West and Jasper got together, but West couldn't bring himself to sell it. Asher and Kole lived here for a while before moving to Buffalo, and then Rhys and Zoe shared for a bit while they were in college. Now it's our turn to live in it, even if it's only for a summer.

Not going to lie, I love it. I love that Jonah's made this his own space, I love that Benny is here with us, and I'm really hopeful that when summer ends, there's a chance Jonah will stay.

Benny won't. He still has another year left at Franklin, and Harrison has who knows how long on his master's.

But Jonah ... it's a possibility. He didn't sign the contract with Franklin; he's not going to be a professor anymore, and as far as I know, he gave up his apartment in student housing, and all of his stuff is in storage.

He's been looking for a job, but whenever I ask him about it, he doesn't tell me where he's looking. He says, "All over."

Which in a weird way also gives me hope. Because maybe,

just maybe, if he doesn't know where I'll be next year, then he doesn't know where he'll be.

Training is going so well, and Asher has promised me big things, but it's the off-season right now, so everything in hockey has slowed down.

Jonah is extra focus-y today when I walk in the door, and it's not until I sit on the couch next to him that he takes his eyes off his laptop. "Oh, hey, when did you get home?"

"Like an hour ago. I've showered, done the laundry—"

"Liar."

"I literally just walked in." I lean over and kiss his cheek. "What are you working on?"

"Business plan."

"Business?"

"I'm thinking about creating a program for colleges around the country to give extra help to students like you and Benny. There was a chance Benny wasn't going to graduate because he couldn't get the right help. I'm sure there are others out there in the same situation—okay, not completely same—but you know what I mean.

I kiss the top of his head this time. "I do know what you mean, and I love that you want to pursue this."

"Why do I sense a 'but' coming on?"

"Where would you propose this? Franklin?"

Jonah shifts in his seat. "Actually, Colchester was my first thought. I know you're not planning on going back to college, even if it means you get to play D1 hockey, whatever that is, but I thought if you were going to be around here for a while, that—"

"I love you," I blurt.

"Is that a yes to me sticking around maybe longer than the summer?"

"Is this you promising to follow me wherever I go?"

"Not in a stalker way. In a cute way."

"Of course. That's totally what I mean."

Jonah presses his lips together before the tip of his pink tongue appears, wetting his top lip. "We made long distance work for the longest few months of my life. I'm sure we can find something that works for both of us. I'm willing to move wherever you are if it means I get to be with you. It just means I can't really execute any plan of mine until we know what your movements are going to be."

"Never fear, a solution is here!" Asher comes charging into the room.

"How ..." I glance at the front door and then the back. "How long have you been here?"

"Just got here. Came in through the back door." He points at me. "And no jokes about doing that often, even if it's true."

"Is Asher ever not inappropriate?" Jonah asks me.

"Never," Asher and I say in unison.

"I know where you'll be next year," Asher says and waggles his eyebrows.

"Y-you do?" I slump. "If you say CU, I might have a fit. That was a last resort, remember?"

"Nope. How would you like to be playing professional hockey?"

"Where?" is my immediate response.

"I emailed tape of you to Buffalo's affiliate team in Rochester, and they're interested. Whether it was the tape or your last name or even that you and Benny were set to be the next big things in hockey at one point, they want you. Offered a deal right then and there. I've already made a phone appointment with my agent at King Sports. They're going to look over the deal for you, maybe assign you a junior agent. Hey, Brady Talon is working there now, and he's a Franklin alum—"

"Ah, yes, the football royalty on campus. We knew of them." Stayed the fuck away from Brady and his brother Peyton because of the six degrees of separation with our families and sporting affiliations.

"The terms of the contract are good," Asher says.

I bite my lip. "You got them to agree to all of that without even meeting me?"

"I'm kind of a big deal. You should know that by now."

That's the thing though. I'm not being given this opportunity on merit. It's being given to me. "Won't people call me a nepo baby and say I only got it because of you?"

"Nope. You know why?"

"Why?"

Asher leans on the back of the couch where we're sitting and looks down at us. "Because you're going to prove yourself."

No matter how I got this opportunity, I have to take it, and like Asher said, I'm going to have to prove myself. That could take years. I might only play one season and get dropped.

Either way, I have to give it my all.

"What do you say?" I ask Jonah. "Want to move to Upstate New York with me?"

"It couldn't have been somewhere with a beach, could it?"

"Never again," I say, but I don't really mean it. If Jonah's willing to move anywhere for me, I need to be able to do the same.

"This offer isn't going to come by a second time," Asher says.

"Stop pressuring my boyfriend." I slap at him. "He has factors he needs to consider. Like Cullen. This is a decision he needs to make."

Jonah shakes his head. "There's no decision to make. I've already told Cullen that wherever I end up next year, he can come visit me during school breaks. Where you are, that's where I'll be because I love you too."

It's only then I realize he hadn't said it back until just now.

Not officially. We had the "I'm falling in love" convo back when I left California, but nothing else. Until right now.

"Rochester, here we come," I say.

"One question though: is Buffalo as cold as Colchester?"

I don't have the heart to tell him it's colder.

CHAPTER THIRTY-SEVEN

AS I FINISH up with my last student of the day, I rub my eyes and lean back in my office chair, picking up my phone to see if Emmett has messaged me. He's currently at an away game, but he usually sends me a "thinking of you" text whenever we're apart.

There isn't a text from him, but there is one from my sister.

LAUREN:

> Cullen has not shut up about hockey since getting back from summer break, and I blame you.

I laugh and reply:

> I blame Emmett. He's the one who spent most of the summer coaching him.

When we moved to Rochester, I promised my sister I'd still be there for Cullen in any way I could be. After Emmett left, Cullen wasn't as interested in hockey as before, and eventually, he gave it up like I'd hoped. Then ... then we offered to take Cullen for the summer. Now we're back at square one, where

Cullen's obsessed, and his mother and I are worried for his safety. But I am glad I can still be there for Cullen, even if I'm no longer in California.

Living in Upstate New York has been a whirlwind of surprises. Mainly of the freezing weather variety. This Cali boy still needs six layers to go outside in the dead of winter, while Emmett goes out in sweatpants and a T-shirt.

He's definitely not a beachy kind of guy.

When Emmett got a contract with Buffalo's AHL team in Rochester, I started pitching my services to local colleges. I managed to score a contract with State University of New York, which is an umbrella of colleges with about sixty-four different institutions around the state. Most of my work is on the Buffalo campuses, so driving out to Rochester to go home every day is getting tiresome, especially with the snow and black ice and all that other fun stuff I never experienced while growing up in southern California. But each day when I get home, provided he's not on the road with the team, Emmett is there. And he makes everything worth it.

Not that living here really is that much of a hardship. Aside from the cold, I love everything about this area. The greenery that turns to orange and red hues at fall, the lakes, the breath-taking scenery ... it's a nice place to live. I also love my job. I built a program from the ground up to help those with learning disorders, and I get to go from campus to campus to check in on my individual students, tutor them when they're struggling, and actually help these kids get degrees where they might have otherwise dropped out from it being too hard or failed out because they didn't have the right help.

I'm proud of what I've accomplished, of where I am, and of the man I've become. I might have been lost when I met Emmett, unsure if teaching was right for me, but he and Ben showed me I was heading in the right direction, just taking a detour.

I'm about to start packing up for the day when there's a knock at my door. I'm sure I don't have anyone scheduled unless I've forgotten someone.

"Come in."

Surprising me, when the door opens, Emmett's there, but that doesn't make sense because his team is in Rhode Island.

"Hey, shouldn't you be in Prov—" That's when I notice the subtle differences in his posture and the smirk on his face. Emmett's is usually sweet. Benny's, yeah, he could be hiding a dead body in the trunk of his car. "Oh, it's you."

"Is that any way to treat your favorite student of all time? Your brother-in-law to be?"

I cock my head. "You're marrying my sister?"

"Ha, you're funny. You're a funny, funny guy, but no, seriously. You and Emmett are going to get married, and then you get to have me as a brother! You're so lucky."

"What are you doing here?"

"Can't a guy show up unannounced to his brother's boyfriend's place of work and say hi?"

I narrow my gaze. "You really do have a dead body in your trunk, don't you?" I gasp. "It's not Emmett, is it?"

"What are you rambling about?"

"You live in Colchester, and you're currently in Buffalo for no explicable reason other than to say hi? You or Emmett have done something, and history tells me I probably don't want to know."

Benny and Harrison moved back to Vermont after graduation and Harrison's master's. Benny's working at getting his dream job of sportscaster but at the moment is working a research position for on-air talent and has a regular game recap article on Sportsnet. He and Emmett are both where they need to be to get what they want in life.

Benny rolls his eyes at my dramatics. "Relax, I'm here because we're all here. All billion Daltons. Asher called everyone to come to his game tonight. It's his thousandth NHL game, can you believe that? It's, like, a massive milestone, so we're all going to go out and celebrate afterward."

I won't dare breathe a word to any of the Daltons, but I only watch hockey for Emmett, and I know Emmett won't be there because he has his own game tonight in Providence. So I grit my teeth and say, "Can't wait."

It's not the first time I've been dragged to one of Asher's games. He's Buffalo royalty. He's spent his entire career with the one franchise and has two Stanley Cups to his name, but it's been a few years since the team has gotten anywhere close to a third. Before Asher, it had been ten years since the team even made the playoffs, so they treat him like the sun shines out his ass in this part of the country. Asher always gets "He's the Sidney Crosby of Buffalo," whatever that means. It's bad enough I know as much as I already do about Asher's career, I'm not going to go google someone else's.

The games aren't all bad though. Especially when the whole Dalton clan shows up. I get along really well with West's husband, Jasper, and Emmett's older brother, Rhys. We're three math nerds who drink and pretend we're paying attention to the score. A lot of the time, Asher's partner will join in on our fun and then get paged from the hospital for an emergency insert whatever long-ass medical term he uses here. I can't pronounce anything he says, but the three of us are certain he lies to get out of watching hockey.

Of course, when I go to Emmett's games, I make sure to pay more attention. I might dislike hockey with all the violence and the back-and-forth play that can get tedious and boring if no one is scoring, but when my man is out on that ice? I can't take my eyes away from him. I'm no expert, but he has so much talent, and watching him is awe-inspiring.

He's worked so hard to get where he is, and while he might never make it to Asher's level, I can tell he's doing what he was born to do. He loves it, and I love him, so I'm supportive. Even if I cringe every time he takes a hit out on the ice.

He's not as big as most of the guys he plays against, but he is quick.

He's been saying lately that he's worried about getting traded—or worse, being sent to the ECHL because the Rochester affiliate team is in Florida, which means moving back to the beach—and how it will screw up all the work I've done here to set up this new system for colleges. He's also worried he'll never be able to make the NHL and support me the way I do for him at the moment. I keep reminding him that money isn't everything and what we both make is more than enough to keep us fed with a roof over our heads. Of course, if he were to be traded to one of the bigger cities, we'd be screwed with paying rent, but for now, we're stable, and we're doing good.

Really good.

No matter where hockey takes him, I want to be by his side, and I'm willing to follow him anywhere. Now that I have one contract in place for the SUNY schools, I could set up similar programs at any college in the country.

"Are you coming or what?" Benny asks.

"Is what an option?"

"What?"

"Exactly."

It's obvious I've confused him with what was supposed to be a smartass remark, but hey, if Benny's right and I'm going to marry Emmett, I'm going to marry the rest of his family too, so I should be supportive. I don't know why they had to be a hockey family though. Why couldn't they be interested in chess or something that doesn't make me feel like I'm losing brain cells as I watch grown-ass men on skates beat the shit out of each other?

I'll admit, the fights are the best part. Just not when

Emmett's involved. He's on a good team who has his back though, so he rarely gets caught in the crossfire.

Unlike Asher, who is usually the one instigating fights on the ice. And off it. Apparently, he's done it since he first signed with Buffalo, but the fans love him for it, and the team gets headlines, so they're happy.

I know way too much about hockey for someone who doesn't enjoy it, but as Benny and I leave and meet up with all the other Daltons, I'm happy to be a part of it. Because Emmett is my world, which means hockey games, codependent twinly chaos, and Dalton family reunions are also my world now.

We're escorted to one of the corporate box things we get sometimes. Not often, but occasionally. Usually, it's Emmett and me in Asher's comped seats, but when there's a group, West usually scores a box.

The best part about the box is the free food and alcohol. They usually have celebration balloons for whatever milestone Asher's achieved, but today, it's empty of all the decorations.

Hazel, the other professional hockey player from the Dalton siblings, is here as well, even though she's in the middle of her own PWHL season. Zoe's here too, with her husband by her side and a round, pregnant belly.

It's been a long time since all the Daltons have been in the one room, and I guess I didn't realize how momentous one thousand games is until now. Though, that doesn't explain the lack of flair around the room.

"You'd think with it being Asher's thousandth game that they'd have streamers. They did for his nine hundredth, right? And that was only, what, late last season?"

My brain trips over the messy math. I know there are more games in Asher's season than Emmy's, but I don't know for sure how many there are in the NHL.

Benny approaches me with that trademark smirk. Before I

can ask him again if there's a body in his trunk, he points to the ice and says, "Notice anything different?"

Everyone in the room is staring at me, and I feel hot under the collar.

Then I turn my gaze out onto the ice where the team is warming up. There's Asher with Dalton on the back of his jersey, but then ...

"What the fuck?" I blurt, and everyone starts laughing at me. "What is happening?" My head swivels. "Why are there two Dalton jerseys out there?"

As I ask that, my man, the love of my life, turns toward us, searching, trying to see us.

I'm not sure if he can from where he is, but if he can't, then maybe he can hear me when I yell, "I love you and am so proud of you!"

He doesn't respond, so maybe he can't hear me after all.

My boyfriend is playing in his first NHL game ever, and it's going to be fucking amazing.

emmett

I'M in my first NHL game ever, and I'm choking.

I got the call-up this afternoon while skating at the arena in Providence, about to take on Boston's AHL team. Asher's teammate, Kappo, Asher's first-line winger, injured himself and is out for possibly the rest of the season.

I've been kicking ass and getting attention in Rochester, but even with doing that, when my coach came and told me to pack my shit, I thought I was being traded. Or sent down to Jacksonville to the ECHL. Then he said the most amazing words I've ever heard in my life. "They're calling you up to the big show."

This is my chance to shine, but the pressure is killing me.

Because of Kappo injuring himself, the lines have all been moved around to accommodate my appearance on the fourth line.

For years, the media and everyone tormented Asher over living in West's shadow, and then they were obsessed with Benny and me, whether or not we'd live up to Asher's and West's careers, whether there would be a time when two Daltons were on the NHL ice together, and now, here we are.

Asher's in his eleventh season, and I'm merely a fill-in tonight, but it's happening.

And that's why I'm positively choking. Because if I don't put on a good show, if I don't show up to play and impress, it's going to be a very short NHL career.

I don't know the team, we didn't even get a chance to practice, my linemates aren't willing to give me a shot on goal, and I get it. How many people get called up from the AHL and go on to score a goal in their first game? Actually, it's six hundred and thirty-one. I know because I looked that up on the plane.

I'd kill to become number six hundred and thirty-two, but I can't do that when I'm too busy freaking out about achieving it.

There's a slap at the back of my helmet as I take my seat after another terrible shift. We lost possession and spent most of the time in the defensive zone. I'm lucky my line is made up of some defensive forwards, and our goalie is on point tonight.

"Get your head out of your ass," Asher says.

"I'm trying." I wish I could be on his line. It would be dumb for the coaches to do that for obvious reasons, putting an unproven greenie on the line that sees the most ice time, but Asher trained me. He got me to where I am today, and we're in sync. I can read him like no other. Well, other than Benny, but he's not out here. It's me and Asher representing the Dalton name, and I need to prove myself.

I have this stupid image in my head of what I want my life to be like, and I find myself daydreaming about having the huge house in the suburbs, a professor husband at home who only works because he wants to and not because he has to, and maybe some kids or at least furry babies. In every single vision, I'm happy.

I mean, I'm happy now. I'm ecstatic. But I want to give Jonah everything, and this is my chance.

If, like Asher says, I can get my head out of my ass.

Buffalo pulls a lucky penalty out of Ottawa, and that puts us on the power play.

Us. I'm a Buffalo player, and this is fucking surreal.

Right. Head in game. Not in ass.

Asher turns to the head coach, the dude who has been Asher's coach for the last three years and is used to his shit, and says, "Put the kid in for extra offense."

"No," Coach says flatly.

"Trust me. One of us will put it in the net."

The coach side-eyes him.

"You don't need to," I say. It's a lot of pressure.

We're running out of time to change up the lines anyway.

"Okay, go." Coach taps my shoulder and pulls back Grimsby, one of the defensemen.

Asher skates up to the face-off, and this surreal night gets even more unbelievable when he looks at me and gives me an up-nod.

Oh God, oh fuck, I'm going to screw this up, and if Ottawa gets a shorthanded goal because of me, I will never live it down.

Asher's face-off percentage is one of the highest in the league, but for the first time ever, I hope he doesn't win this.

What was I thinking? That becoming an NHL star would be easy?

Oh shit, oh shit, oh shit.

Asher gets that puck right out of there, and it flies in my direction.

Fuck, fuck, fuck.

Thank God for reflex or muscle memory or whatever the hell it is that kicks in because I manage to pass it right back to Asher in perfect position for the tip of his blade.

Ottawa gets their men in position, all four on the ice protecting their goalie in a zigzag line in front of the goal.

Their penalty-kill game is abysmal, so we should have this in the bag, but as time winds down on the power play, where all we can manage is a few passes and some failed attempts on goal from everyone except me because I'm too scared to take the shot, that telepathy connection that I usually only have with Benny kicks in. I skate to the right of the crease. Asher skates near the face-off circle closest to me. Everyone has an eye on him, waiting to see which way he's going to pass. To Lewiston, our D-man, or to Houghton, the left-winger over the other side.

Everyone is expecting either of those. There's no way Asher would try to pass to me when I haven't taken a shot on goal all night. But none of these guys know Asher like I do, so when he finds his opening and lets that puck fly, I hold my breath and swing.

Ottawa's goalie dives, and it's like I watch it all happen in slow motion. He's moving toward the puck to intercept it, all his teammates join in, but my shot, as sloppy as it is, goes right in between all of them and over the goalie's shoulder.

I'm too in shock when the lamp lights up and that glorious home goal horn blasts. It's not until I'm almost knocked off my skates by my brother and my new teammates that it really sinks in.

I did it.

I fucking did it.

My NHL debut has blown all my dreams out of the damn water.

Asher lifts his glass and gets the whole bar's attention. "We may have lost the game, but my little brother got his first NHL goal and assist. Two fucking points on your first game. We're proud of you, Emmy."

For a second, I worry Asher's gone soft and lost his mind,

but when Houghton mocks, "Aww, Emmy. From now on, you'll only be known as Emmy. Or Emily. Or—"

Asher shoves him. "Shut it."

There's my big brother.

The rest of the game was a struggle, one we ended up walking away from with a loss, but after I got that first goal, my confidence soared. It was like I just needed to get the first one out of the way, and once I did, I was much more relaxed on the ice, which is how I ended up getting an assist in the third period with my fourth-line teammate, Roachie.

Would I have liked to have won? Of course, but if it came to a choice between scoring or winning, I'd choose that goal every time. At least for my debut.

Asher raises his glass into the air. "To the Daltons finally having two of us in the NHL at the same time."

This was our dad's dream. First with West and Asher and then with Benny and me. It's not how he would've wanted it, and with Asher pushing retirement, it's not going to be for a long time, but I know Dad is proud of us.

I glance over to where West is, standing with his husband, with a soft smile and shiny eyes. I turn to Jonah, who hasn't left my side since we left the arena. "I need to go thank West for everything that he's done for me."

West gave up this moment—the moment the media and the whole hockey world wanted from the beginning—to raise me and the others. My first NHL goal wasn't my achievement alone. It belongs to West. To Asher. And to Benny. Sure, Benny might have thrown a spanner into my hockey career in the beginning, but with our time apart, we've both been able to see how we held each other back in so many different ways.

We're still codependent as fuck. There have been many times where one of us have called and then driven three and a half hours in the middle of the night to meet at a seedy diner in Utica, roughly halfway between Colchester and Rochester. It's a bit further for Benny than me, but if the team found out I was taking a seven-hour roundtrip to have milkshakes with my brother when we have a game the next day, they'd kill me.

The diner is no Betty's, but it's our substitute place. Benny calls it Elaine's. There is no Elaine.

Benny and I will always have that need for each other that other siblings might not ever understand, but we've also grown in so many ways. We both have our own lives now, we're each going in the direction we want to go, and instead of holding each other back in fear of losing one another, we're supportive.

"You go thank your brother. I'll go get you another drink." Jonah kisses my cheek, and I'm really glad he didn't say he'll come with me because while I do need to thank West, I also need to check he remembered to get the thing I stashed at his house three years ago when I signed my contract with Rochester.

I bought it as a symbol. Or a goal, I guess. I knew, even back then, that I wanted a future with Jonah. But I wasn't going to use it until I got my first goal in the NHL.

Maybe that's the real reason I was freaking out there on the ice tonight. Because if I got that puck in that stupid, tiny, little net, I was sure my life would change.

Am I going to last long in the NHL? Probably not. Most likely, Kappo will heal and come back, and I'll be shuffled around, maybe traded, or sent back down to the AHL.

But getting that goal tonight ... it's almost as if the universe is telling me I'm ready for this next step.

I approach West and don't hesitate to throw my arms around him. When I pull back, he's still glassy-eyed, and if I have my way, he's about to be bawling like a baby. "I want you to have something." I reach into my suit pocket and pull out the puck from tonight. "You get my first NHL goal puck."

He backs up a few steps. "What? No, I can't take that."

"You can, and you will. If you refuse, I'll just give it to Jasper."

Jasper was understandably upset when he found out about Benny and me switching for so many years, but I think he's close to forgiving himself for not noticing we were struggling.

We've told him a million times to stop blaming himself. None of them, not Jasper, not West, not Asher, were responsible for what we did.

"After everything the twins have put you through, you deserve the puck," Jasper says. "Although, you'll probably get it lost with all the other pucks we have floating around the house for no reasonable reason."

"I'm a hockey coach," West says.

"You don't see me leaving math problems all over the house."

I butt in. "I remember one time you left college exams all over the dining table, but with you being in your sixties, you probably don't remember that."

Jasper gasps. "I am still forty-nine, you little shithead. *Forties*. That's this many." He holds up four fingers. "How ... I can't ..." He turns to West. "Our children are out of the will!"

"That's okay, I don't really want old math books when you die, but ... you called me your child." I touch my heart. "That means you love meeeee."

"I'd love you more if you stopped calling me old."

"Deal." I hold out my hand for him to shake, but he pulls me to him and wraps his arms around me in a hug.

"I am proud of you, you know. Both you and Benny. You made mistakes, mistakes I should've seen and hate myself for missing, but you fought your way back and for what you both want out of life. I know I came into your lives after your parents were already gone, but I do look at you like a son, and I do love you."

Fuck, now it's my turn to get all misty-eyed.

Jasper pulls away from me, and when he does, West is holding up a ring box to me.

"Is this still the plan?"

"Yup." I take it from him and put it in my pocket where the puck was.

"You chose good with that one," West says. "He reminds me of—"

"If you say your husband, I'm going to have to break your jaw so you can never say that ever again."

West laughs. "I was going to say he reminds me of Dad."

I groan. "I didn't need to know that either."

Jonah appears at my side with a new drink for me, and I jump a mile high, wondering how long he's been there or if he saw the ring box.

I pat my pants pocket and smile at Jonah. "Let's go for a walk."

The bar we've come to celebrate at is one we've been to many times before with Asher and the team. It's their celebration and commiseration place, but the rooftop view is amazing. They have a firepit that overlooks the city, and while Buffalo isn't exactly the prettiest or biggest place there is, it's where my heart is. I'm hoping it's where Jonah's could be too.

"It's fucking freezing," he hisses.

My poor Cali boy. I direct him closer to the fire. "Here, take my jacket." I slip out of my jacket and wrap it around his shoulders. You'd think he'd be used to the cold by now.

"How are you not freezing?" he asks.

"Too much adrenaline."

"From the game?"

I shake my head. "From what I'm about to do."

I suck in a shuddery breath, take out the ring box, and get to one knee.

Before I can tell him how much he means to me, how I love

him with all my heart and he was my end goal, my dream, my everything from the beginning, he beats me to it.

"Fuck, yes. I mean, just yes. We don't have to tell anyone I swore when you proposed, do we?"

I chuckle. "Well, technically, I haven't even proposed yet."

"Oh, shit. Right. Okay. Umm, go."

"This right here is why I love you. And why I want to spend the rest of my life with you. Will you marry—"

"Yes."

"—me?"

"Yes. Again. Yes. Yes, yes, yes, yes, yes."

I stand, and he grabs me around my waist and crushes me against him. We kiss to the sounds of hoots and hollers all around us, and when we pull apart, Asher's filming this on his phone. Well, shit, that's going to go viral, but I don't care if the whole world knows how much I love Jonah.

Whether I stay in the NHL or get sent back down, it doesn't matter. Hockey is important, but what's more important is making Jonah happy every single day for the rest of his life.

want more?

Meet all of the couples from FU2!

Perry and Theo
<u>The Hookup Mix-up</u>
Harrison and Benny
<u>A Stealthy Situation</u>
Blaise and Jordan
<u>Batting Style</u>
Jay and Ryan
<u>Level Up</u>
Silas and Everly
<u>Full Service</u>
Dex and Austin
<u>Tongue-Tied</u>
Chase and Amos
<u>Method Acting</u>
Emmett and Jonah
<u>Twincerely Yours</u>

thank you

Thanks so much for reading *Twincerely Yours*.

Emmy and Benny's older brothers have their own books in the CU Hockey Series, co-written by Eden Finley and Saxon James. Get their books here:
https://geni.us/EHaA
https://geni.us/5bqJ5

Also from this universe:
Football Royalty by Eden Finley is from the first season of Franklin U's shared world! Read it here: https://geni.us/royalty

MIKE BRAVO OPS

Iris

Rogue

Atlas

Zeus

BOOKS COWRITTEN WITH SAXON JAMES

Power Plays & Straight A's

Face Offs & Cheap Shots

Goal Lines & First Times

Line Mates & Study Dates

Puck Drills & Quick Thrills

Egotistical Puckboy

Irresponsible Puckboy

Shameless Puckboy

Foolish Puckboy

Clueless Puckboy

Bromantic Puckboy

Forbidden Puckboy

VINO & VERITAS *Sarina Bowen's True North Series*

Headstrong

STEELE BROTHERS

Unwritten Law

Unspoken Vow

ROYAL OBLIGATION

Unprincely (M/M/F)